Some Like It Rough

Some Like It Rough

KATE PEARCE
SUSAN LYONS
ANNE RAINEY

APHRODISIA

KENSINGTON PUBLISHING CORP.

www.kensingtonbooks.com

APHRODISIA BOOKS are published by

Kensington Publishing Corp.
119 West 40th Street
New York, NY 10018

All Kensington titles, imprints, and distributed lines are available at special quantity discounts for bulk purchases for sales promotions, premiums, fund-raising, and educational or institutional use.

Special book excerpts or customized printings can also be created to fit specific needs. For details, write or phone the office of the Kensington special sales manager: Kensington Publishing Corp., 119 West 40th Street, New York, NY 10018, attn: Special Sales Department, Phone: 1-800-221-2647.

Aphrodisia and the A logo Reg. U.S. Pat & TM Off

ISBN-13: 978-0-7582-9103-5
ISBN-10: 0-7582-9103-5

First Kensington Trade Paperback Printing: March 2010

10 9 8 7 6 5 4 3

Printed in the United States of America

Contents

Some Like It Rough

Kate Pearce

1

"**W**ell, hell."

Luke Warner leaned back and squinted up at the hole in the ceiling, certain he could see the blue sky beyond. He sure had his work cut out for him, but that was what he'd wanted, right? Something to do with his hands, something to connect him to his past. He grimaced as his gaze swept the broken countertops and shelves, the holes in the floor, the leaking pipes.

The old Warner family drugstore on the corner of Keystone and Main in Gulch Town, California had definitely seen better days. For some reason, he'd decided it was his job to put it right. It smelled of dirt and mildew now, but once, the store had its own distinct odor of popcorn, coffee, and candy. Luke remembered sitting on a high stool watching his grandpa weigh a handful of pills on the old scales, the way he'd wrapped them in brown paper and the clunking ring of the manual cash register.

His father hadn't wanted to run the shop, and it had been left to rot until Luke had shown up and demanded the key from his perplexed Aunt Josie. With a sigh, he picked up his sleeping bag and rucksack and walked to the back of the store.

There was one room with a door that still locked and an outside toilet with running water and a sink. That would have to do until he got himself fixed up.

He laid out his sleeping bag, stretched out on it, and kicked off his dusty boots. It was a small town. It wouldn't take long for folks to hear he was back. He smiled into the gathering shadows. What would Paul and Julia do then?

Paul let himself in through the back door of Julia's small condo and found her in the kitchen stirring something on the stove that smelled like chicken. He came up behind her and planted a kiss on the back of her neck. She squeaked, and he wrapped his arms around her hips and nuzzled her throat. Strands of her silky brown hair tickled his face. She dropped the spoon into the pan and swung around to face him.

"Don't you ever knock?"

He touched the brim of his Stetson. "No, ma'am, I was brought up in a barn, remember?"

She leaned back against the countertop, her gray eyes serious, her normally laughing mouth a worried line. "That joke is getting old."

"Yeah, I reckon I've been making that one since kindergarten." He raised his eyebrows at her. "So, what's up? You seemed kind of jittery when you called."

"I just spoke to Roxanne. She says Luke is back in town."

Paul blinked at her. "Our Luke?"

"Well, he's scarcely 'ours' anymore, is he? We haven't seen or heard from him in ten years. But Luke Warner is definitely here."

Paul studied Julia's flushed face. "And?"

"And what?"

"What do you want to do about it?"

"About Luke?" She shrugged, and one of the thin straps of

her blue camisole fell down from her shoulder. He noticed she had no bra underneath. "I don't know."

Paul stepped closer until his large body was only inches away from Julia's. Her nipples tightened through the thin cotton of her cami, and her breathing hitched. He put his hands on her waist and set her on the tiled countertop, reaching over to turn off whatever was cooking on the stove.

"You want to see him, don't you?"

She looked up at him, and he bent his head and licked a slow, lascivious line along the seam of her lips.

"He'll be hard to miss in a town as small as this."

"That's not an answer." Paul slid a hand under her camisole and cupped her right breast, used his finger and thumb to twist her nipple to a hard, needy point. She sighed and shoved her hand into his hair, wiggled closer to the edge of the counter, until her sex rode the thick ridge of his cock in his jeans.

"You want to see him up close and personal, right?" he murmured between kisses and nips. He went still when she caged his face in her hands.

"Don't you want to know why he left?"

"Of course I do, but . . ."

She smiled at him and unbuckled his belt and straining fly. "But, you're worried I'll run off with him?" She wrapped her hand around his cock and squeezed hard, just the way he liked.

"Yeah," he admitted, as she pulled down her shorts with one hand and let them fall to the floor. "You always liked him best."

His fingers plucked at her clit and then slid into the thick wetness of her pussy. He took her hand away from his cock and shoved himself deep into her slick heat, held still as she shuddered around him. Sometimes he liked it like this, hard and fast, Julia having to catch up, giving him every orgasm right around his thrusting shaft rather than against his fingers or mouth.

Tonight he wanted to fuck her hard, as if he could somehow

slow down time and make her realize she didn't want to go anywhere near Luke Warner, that she wanted only him. She cried out and her pussy clenched around his cock. Paul kept slamming into her and only climaxed when she came again, squeezing every last drop of cum out of his balls.

She stroked the back of his neck, her fingers soft. "I don't like him best. I like you. You stayed, remember?"

He lifted his head to stare at her. "I had no choice. I couldn't go off and leave the ranch, now, could I?"

"My hero."

She smiled at him, and he had to smile back. "I don't mind if you see Luke, honey. I'd like to see him myself."

"You would?" Julia studied him and then her gray eyes narrowed. "Not if you're going to beat him up, Paul."

"I wouldn't do that." He pulled out of her and handed her his handkerchief to clean up. "I'd sure appreciate an explanation though. He was my best friend, too. We did everything together, had our first smoke, our first beer, our first mutual jerk off . . ."

"Your first fuck."

Paul kissed her nose. "I prefer to think we were making love to you. It was so fucking sweet. *You* were so fucking sweet to let us."

Julia slipped down from the countertop and pulled her shorts back on. Her slow, dreamy smile indicated that she was as caught up in the past as he was. "If it was so sweet, why did Luke skip town right after?"

Paul tucked his cock back into his boxers and zipped up his jeans. "I don't know. That's one of the reasons I want to talk to him."

Julia washed her hands and turned back to the stove. "I hear he's staying at the old drugstore on Main."

"That wreck? Why the hell isn't he bunking with his aunt? Maybe he's out of money and came back because he had no

choice." Paul sat down at the table and stared at the stove ex-
pectantly. It was a five mile drive back to his ranch, and he already knew he had nothing but beer and beef in his refrigerator.
After Julia's call, he'd had no choice but to turn around and
come see her. If he was staying over, he loved getting fed as well
as fucked.

"I have no idea, but perhaps we should drop by tomorrow
and see how he's doing."

Paul grinned at her. "Yeah, perhaps we should."

"Paul?"

"Yeah, honey?" Paul croaked and opened his eyes to find
Julia propped up on her elbows looking down at him, her
breasts grazing his chest, her long legs straddling his hips. He
had no idea what time it was, only that he was in her bed and
that it was still dark. Despite the fact that they'd already made
love twice, his cock stirred against her wet, warm sex.

"That question you asked me. The one I didn't want to answer?" Julia kissed his forehead. "You're right. I would like to
get up close to Luke again."

Paul carefully lifted her off him and rolled onto his side. He
tried to sound casual, even though he knew she wouldn't buy
it. "So, do you want me to stay out of the way at the ranch
while you fuck him?"

"Why would you do that?"

He shrugged and tried to smile. "Because I'm trying to be
the better person here. I'm trying to give you choices."

"That's not like you at all."

"I know." Hell, it was the hardest thing he'd ever contemplated, giving Julia up, especially to Luke Warner.

She reached out and touched his chest, stroked her fingers
over his nipple. "I kind of thought you'd like to be there, too."

He studied her carefully in the dim light. "When you say
'there' do you mean like, physically there?"

"Yes."

His cock reacted quicker than his brain, showed its appreciation of the idea by filling out hard and fast. In the beginning it had always been the three of them and they'd learned about sex together. Somehow, it had felt right and he couldn't shake the notion that it would always feel right. "Like, both of us?"

"That depends on Luke, doesn't it?" Julia's tentative smile cut through the darkness. "I always think of us as a threesome, don't you? Or does that make me some kind of voracious slut?"

"Not in my book, honey." He rolled on top of her and drove his cock deep, felt her curl her arms and legs around him and hold him tight. "I'm happy to do whatever you want as long as I'm part of it."

She lifted her hips into his thrusts and he kept on pumping, slid his hand between them to finger her clit and bring her off with him. He couldn't contemplate sharing Julia with any other man but Luke, and, to be fair, she'd never expressed an interest in fucking anyone else. And, as far as anyone knew, they'd been a couple since high school. The least he could do was give them all a chance to explore every aspect of their old relationship. That was only fair. He groaned as his cum exploded into Julia. Sex with Julia was always excellent; with Luke involved, it might be awesome.

Julia sipped her second cup of coffee and squinted into the sunlight filtering through the blinds of her small kitchen. Paul had gotten up early and gone home to his ranch. Since his parents had decided to retire to Florida, he never had the luxury of walking away from it completely. Despite having some staff to help out, something always required attention, even if it was as dull as repairing fence line or doing the accounts.

When it got really busy out there, during cattle drives, birthing, or branding, Julia often went out and stayed with him.

She half smiled. Otherwise she would never see him. And she liked seeing him. Liked the way he used his big, strong, body too . . .

With a sigh, she got off the stool and picked up her briefcase. Time to get to work and face another day of exciting fiscal challenges at the one and only bank in Gulch Town. Not that much ever happened. The most exciting thing this year was when Mr. Murphy's crazy sheepdog had gotten loose and chewed up a load of paperwork and a couple of chairs.

She'd been beyond excited to become assistant manager because it meant she could stay in her hometown, but it also meant she had to deal with Mr. Glynn, the complete asshole who ran the bank and who was slowly driving her nuts. Unfortunately he had at least four years before he was due to retire, so unless she wanted to change jobs, or be sent to prison for murder, she was stuck with him. And she'd never wanted to leave, had she? With an ever-changing cast of stepfather's, her only security had come from Paul, Luke, and Gulch Town.

As she walked to her car, she wondered how Luke was doing. How on earth was he going to survive in that wrecked old store his family had abandoned years ago? She knew that several offers had been made to the family to buy up the prime retail space, but they'd all been refused. Had Luke intended to come back all along? Had he been the one behind the family decision not to sell?

On that tantalizing thought, Julia got into her car and drove the five minutes to work. If Luke was moving back, surely he'd need funds? And, as Mr. Glynn preferred golf to sitting behind his desk, she was nominally in charge of the only bank in town. It looked like she might be seeing Luke even sooner than she had anticipated.

2

"**I**s anyone home?"

"Yeah, in here." Luke leaned the broom up against the counter and turned around slowly. He knew that voice almost as well as his own. Standing in the doorway that opened out onto the street was Paul, his onetime best friend, and one of the reasons why Luke had left Gulch Town in such a hurry.

Paul touched the brim of his white Stetson and smiled. "What's up?"

Luke found himself smiling back. "Nothing much." He waited as Paul shut the door behind him and came closer. His buddy had sure filled out in the last ten years. At six-three, he had always been tall, but now he was all lean, hard, muscle, his blond hair cut close to his head, the skin around his blue eyes crinkled as if he laughed a lot or constantly stared into the sun.

Luke wiped his hand on his jeans and held it out. "It's good to see you, Paul."

Paul returned the handshake, his palm calloused from hard work. Luke wished he had some of those calluses; his hands were already blistered and bruised from just cleaning up the place.

"It's good to see you, too, Luke." Paul's gaze swept the dilapidated store. "Not sure what you're doing here, though. Did you lose a family contest or something, or are you just down on your luck and need a roof over your head?"

"I've wanted to fix this place up for ages and it just seemed like a good time to start."

"You're sure about that? It looks like a fucking mess to me."

Luke's smile deepened. God, it was good to hear Paul's leisurely self-deprecating drawl and dry wit again. Some folks thought he was slow on the uptake because he didn't shoot his mouth off. Luke had learned long ago to listen when Paul did speak, because he generally had something useful to say.

"I'm going to restore it and open it as an old-fashioned soda shop and ice cream parlor. You know, kind of like it used to be in my granddad's day after he stopped doing the pharmacy part of it."

"Yeah?" Paul looked around again. "And you're going to do all the work yourself?"

Luke shrugged. "Most of it."

"Good for you." Something beeped in Paul's pocket and he pulled out his cell phone. "Excuse me." He read something and texted back, his big fingers surprisingly nimble on the tiny keypad. He looked up at Luke, his blue eyes considering. "Julia's going to be here in a moment. She's looking forward to seeing you."

Needing something to do with his hands, Luke picked up the broom and continued to sweep the floor. "She is?"

Paul put his cell phone away and studied his brown scuffed cowboy boots. "Yeah. Although, being a female, she'll probably want a few answers out of you."

Luke stopped sweeping. "And you don't? I walked away from you too, buddy. Didn't it bother you?"

"What do you fucking think?" Paul met Luke's challenging stare with one of his own and then looked away again, but not before Luke had seen the pain in his eyes. "I'll go see whether Julia's here yet. She works just up the street."

Luke stayed where he was, still clutching the broom like a talisman. Paul had as much right to be angry with him as Julia did, but he'd always been good at hiding his feelings, far better than Luke and Julia anyway. Inwardly, Luke groaned. Why had he needled Paul? He suspected it was because Paul seemed so accepting of the situation, so disinterested in rehashing the past. Luke needed to face what he'd done, and would almost have preferred it if Paul had walked in and punched him in the face. At least then, it would all be out in the open.

He stiffened as he heard voices in the street and deliberately turned his back on the door and carried on with his chore. Paul had looked even better than Luke had imagined him—would Julia be the same?

"Hey."

Luke turned slowly around and almost swallowed his tongue. Julia was dressed in a dark blue business skirt and white blouse. He'd unconsciously been expecting her to be wearing jeans and a T-shirt. She'd definitely grown up. The coltish legs, elongated by killer heels, and her face . . . God, she was so fucking beautiful he wanted to kiss all her lipstick off.

"Hey." He nodded at her as if he'd never left and had just popped out to get a soda or something. God, he even felt like his eighteen-year-old self—stupid, inarticulate, and horny as hell. "How are you doing?"

She inclined her head a slow inch and a curl of her upswept brown hair touched her cheek. "I'm doing okay." She held up a basket. "Paul and I reckoned we'd bring you some dinner. Is that all right?"

He looked around the empty space. "Sure, but there's nowhere to eat in here yet."

"That's okay," Paul said. "I've got some camping supplies in the back of my truck. I'll go get them."

SOME LIKE IT ROUGH / 13

Luke watched Paul leave and reluctantly turned back to Julia, who was putting the picnic basket and cooler on the least damaged section of the countertop. He cleared his throat and she looked up at him, her gray eyes slightly wary.

He gestured at the basket. "Thanks for doing this. I sure as hell don't deserve it."

"That's true."

He'd always liked that about Julia, her no bullshit attitude to life. The way she'd nagged him and Paul to say what they thought, rather than relying on her to translate their pathetic man-speak.

"Your aunt Josie said you were back for good. Is that right?"

Luke shoved a hand through his hair. "It kind of depends on how things go here."

"Whether you can put this place back together again, you mean?" She frowned. "There's one of those new, pharmaceutical mega stores less than five miles away now. I doubt this place could survive or compete with their prices."

"I'm not thinking of reopening it as a proper drugstore. I was thinking more of a coffee and ice cream shop. I notice the town doesn't have anywhere for people to sit and relax anymore." Luke patted the countertop. "The bones are good, all I need to do is restore the parts that can function in the new design and get rid of the rest."

Julia looked up at the stained ceiling, her hands on her hips, her teeth biting into her bottom lip. As he watched her, Luke shifted his stance, wanted to sink *his* teeth into her lip and bite down hard until she begged him to fuck her.

She lowered her gaze and met his, and heat flowed between them. Julia was the first to look away, her cheeks flushed, her hands twitching at the hem of her skirt. Had she seen the lustful gleam in his eyes? Was she surprised by it? He'd never stopped wanting her, never stopped wanting to come back . . .

"Why did you come back, Luke?"

As if she could read his thoughts, the question he'd been expecting arrived. He shrugged. "It's complicated."

She raised her chin. "It doesn't seem too complicated to me. You walked out on us and didn't bother to contact us for ten years. That's not complicated, Luke. That's criminal."

He frowned. "I wrote to you."

She folded her arms across her chest. "Well, I never received anything."

"Are you sure about that? I wrote to you about six months after I left, to let you know I was working in San Jose."

"I never got that letter."

"And that's *my* fault?"

She opened her eyes wide at him. "I didn't say it was. Just because you're feeling guilty, don't try and take it out on me." She sighed. "Look, right after you left, my mom got married again. When her new husband decided to move back to the coast, I decided not to go with them." Her smile was wry. "Not that I was invited anyway. So I stayed here, rented an apartment and worked two jobs to see myself through college and pay the bills."

"So you probably weren't at the old address then." Luke shrugged. "I kind of figured you were too mad at me to want to write back, so I just kept on working and hoping."

"Hoping for what?"

He smiled at her. "To make enough money to come back home."

Julia opened her mouth and then closed it again when the door opened and Paul reappeared, his arms full of stuff. By the time she faced Luke again, she was totally composed; all her smiles were for Paul as he set up a makeshift table and camping chairs.

Ten minutes later, Luke found himself sitting down with his two oldest friends and wanted to pinch himself. He hadn't expected them to come to him. He'd assumed he would have to do a whole lot of begging and pleading to get them to even talk to him. But here they were, balancing paper plates on their knees and sharing barbecue chicken wings and pork ribs with a salad on the side.

"Does anyone want another beer?" Paul asked as he reached inside the cooler behind him and grabbed a couple more cans. He handed one to Luke and one to Julia. Luke concentrated on eating his chicken. God, he hadn't realized how hungry he was.

Julia glanced at Paul, who winked as if daring her to proceed. Did he think she was just going to start screaming at Luke or simply wrestle him to the ground and have her way with him? Luke looked so confused it almost made her want to laugh. Perhaps he'd expected to be screamed at as well.

He also looked amazingly hot, his black hair longer than Paul's, his long, lean body as familiar as ever, his fingers elegant as he devoured his food. His hazel eyes looked green in the subdued lighting and matched his tight-fitting T-shirt.

She took another swig of her beer and kicked off her shoes, watched as both men stared at her legs and the hint of stocking top her rucked-up skirt showed. "So you're going to make this into a coffee bar and ice cream parlor, right?"

Luke looked up at her. "Yeah, that's the plan."

"And how do you plan to finance that?" The words came out of her mouth before she'd even realized it. God, was she turning into a typical bank employee with nothing better to talk about than her job?

"I'm good, thanks." Luke nodded at her and then returned his attention to his food. Julia frowned at Paul who was grinning at her. Why wasn't he helping out? Did he expect her to bring the whole sordid mess out into the open? Of course, he did, he was a man.

"I know you said it's complicated, Luke, but that's not a real answer. Why did you come back?"

Luke sighed and put down his beer. "I always intended to come back. It just took me longer than I'd anticipated."

"Is that all?"

"Of course not. I had to grow up and realize that running away from things wasn't the solution to my problems." He met her gaze, his hazel eyes serious. "I had to understand that facing the people I'd hurt was an essential part of liking and forgiving myself."

"So it's really all about you, then."

He smiled. "God, when you put it like that, it sounds totally selfish, but that's not what I meant." He took a deep breath. "I hurt you both. I ran away from the two most important people in my world."

"Yes, you did. And I still don't understand why."

For the first time, Luke's gaze slid away from her and came to rest on Paul. "I figured two's company, three's a crowd. I knew Paul was a way better prospect than I would ever be. He had the ranch. He had all the stability you and I were lacking."

"So, you decided to make things easier for us by running away?"

"Basically, yeah, that's what I told myself."

Julia stared at him hard. She knew him far too well to believe him completely. And there was definitely something he wasn't telling them.

Luke chuckled. "The thing I can't figure out is why you guys aren't married with four kids by now."

Paul glanced at her. "You'll have to ask Julia about that. I'd marry her in a heartbeat."

Julia shifted in her seat. "I've never been comfortable with the idea of marrying anyone. My mom's four trips down the aisle kind of cured me of that." She tried to steer the conversation back to Luke. "So, why haven't you gotten married? Too busy playing the field?"

He sat back and considered her, his long legs, encased in

worn denim, stretched out in front of him. "I've certainly had time to work out what I like and what I don't like."

Julia sighed. Luke had obviously become as closemouthed as Paul. Were all men this difficult to talk to, or was she just lucky? She had no idea how to get around to what she wanted to say. Even for her, suddenly suggesting Luke jump into bed with her and Paul seemed a bit of a conversational leap.

As if he sensed her dilemma, Paul rose to his feet and came over to crouch beside her, his arm around her shoulders. "We might not be married, but we still have a hell of a sex life, don't we, honey?"

Julia sat still as Paul slid his fingers lower and cupped her breast, his thumb unerringly searching out her nipple beneath her blouse and bra. Luke swallowed hard, his throat working, his gaze fixed on Paul's moving fingers. Julia leaned into Paul's touch and arched her back.

Paul kissed her jaw. "Yeah, Julia always was something special. Do you remember that, Luke? How much she loved to fuck?"

"Hard to forget."

"Yeah, hard is a good word for what Julia does to a man." Paul took her hand and placed it over the zipper of his jeans. Julia couldn't help but look at Luke's groin, see the thick outline of his cock already pushing at his fly. "She makes me so hard I could hammer nails."

"I could do with an extra hammer for this place." Abruptly, Luke stood up. "And perhaps you two should get a room."

Julia met his gaze. "Why are you leaving? It's not as if you haven't seen it all before."

His smile was crooked and didn't quite match the blaze of interest in his narrowed eyes. "Thanks for the food." He turned and headed for the back room, leaving Julia gaping after him.

"Paul . . ." She swung around to face him and realized he was smiling. "Did he just walk out on us?"

"He didn't go far, honey." He leaned in to kiss her, his mouth so hot and voracious that she was immediately wet. He picked her up so that her legs straddled his. "If he can't see us, he'll still hear us."

Julia opened her mouth to argue, but Paul kissed her again and whether it was the thought of having Paul in such a public place or that Luke might watch, she didn't stop him from pushing up her skirt and settling her over his big cock. She gasped as he thrust deep and held her down over him, his hands clamped on her hips.

"I bet he's watching Julia, I bet he sees you sitting on my cock, my mouth on your tits, my fingers on your clit."

Paul kissed her again and finally let her move on him, his mouth and hands as busy as he'd said, his cock a thick, hot presence inside her. She felt cold air on her ass, realized he'd gathered her skirt up to her waist to expose her buttocks, to let Luke see his big cock filling her. The mere thought of it made her come, and she gasped out Paul's name. He groaned and began to move faster, taking control of the motion, lifting her and slamming her down over his shaft with a speed and strength that made her climax again, this time while biting his shoulder.

He wrapped his arms around her and came in great shuddering waves, held on to her for at least five minutes before he finally looked at her. His smile was full of lust. "Hey, thanks for dessert."

"You're welcome." She couldn't help smiling back at him. He lifted her off him and groaned as he examined his cock. She threw him a couple of napkins and pulled down her now-crumpled skirt. There was still no sign of Luke, so she concentrated on getting her breath back and finishing her beer.

Paul zipped up his jeans and tossed the used napkins into the trash sack. "Do you need to clean up, honey? I think there's a bathroom of sorts out back."

She smiled at him and stood up, saw his eyes widen as some of his cum trickled down her inner thigh. "I kind of thought you'd like it if you drove me home like this." She brushed the top of her stocking with a fingertip. "So you could touch me and play with me." She blinked slowly and then licked her wet finger. "Only if you'd like to, of course."

Paul crawled toward her and ran his tongue along the edge of her lace stocking. "Damn, honey, I'm hard again. I'm not sure if we'll make it home. Maybe we could stop somewhere along the way and I could tip you back in your seat and lick you all clean."

Julia shivered as he licked at her and she stroked his thick blond hair. The quality of the silence behind her had changed, she was almost certain that Luke was not only listening to them, but watching as well. The thought of it made her so hot she wanted to shove Paul's face into her pussy and make him make her come with his tongue and fingers until she screamed or until Luke couldn't stand it anymore and came to join them.

Paul slowly got to his feet, his expression as hard and sexy as she expected hers was. "Yeah, in the truck, right now. Go."

She blew him a kiss as he sauntered toward the partially closed door Luke had disappeared behind and said, "Night, Luke. I'll come see you tomorrow. You can keep the camping gear as long as you like."

There was no sign that Luke had heard him, but Julia knew Luke well enough to guess he was fully aware of everything that had just happened and understood that they weren't just going to leave him be. She smiled. It might not have been the welcome home he expected, but it was much more fun than shouting. Paul winked at her and walked out. She took a moment to straighten the kicked-over chairs and trash the beer cans. She paused at Luke's door and tapped on it.

"I know you're still there, Luke, and I know you watched. Did you like what you saw? Did it make you hard?" There was no answer, but she hadn't really expected one. She kissed the scarred wooden panel. "We're not going away, Luke, this is our town. You'll either have to deal or leave. Good night."

Luke held his breath until Julia slammed the back door behind her, and then waited for the roar of Paul's truck to fade down the street. With a stifled groan he managed to unzip his jeans without damaging his over-excited cock. He wrapped his hand around his throbbing shaft and lay back on the makeshift bed, images of Paul and Julia flooding his head.

God, of course, he'd fucking looked. How could he not? He'd been starved not seeing them together and not being with them. He pictured Julia sitting in the truck beside Paul, his big hand between her legs as he fingered her soaking wet pussy and clit. Luke had wanted to get back out there and lick her clean, to lick them both clean whether they wanted his help or not.

He tightened his grip of his cock and deliberately pumped hard, let his nails dig into his swollen flesh, imagined Paul and Julia watching him as he fucked himself. He climaxed and kept his grip tight, felt every agonizing pulse of his cum force its way out and cover his fingers.

He shuddered with the force of it and looked down at his shaft, which was already filling out again. There was no way back. He had to face up to his needs. If Julia and Paul wanted to play it this way, he was definitely up for it.

3

"Yes, Mr. Glynn, I'll take care of it." Julia nodded again at her boss and held the door open as he swept past her, still talking, still repeating the same old crap he said every single day so that he could get out of the office and play golf with his buddies. "It's not a problem; I'll make sure Mr. Brown knows how to get hold of you if he needs you."

Mr. Glynn stopped walking and stared at her, well more accurately, he stared at her breasts, which were at his eye level. "Don't tell him exactly where I am, Miss Lowell. That wouldn't be wise at all, would it?"

She forced herself not to snarl, smiled sweetly instead and remembered to talk to him like he was a five-year-old. "I'll just give him your cell phone number. Unless you're using a video phone, he won't know exactly where you are, will he?"

He stared at her grudgingly for a few moments. "I suppose not."

"Then I'll see you later, okay?"

"Good morning, Miss Lowell."

Finally, Mr. Glynn walked out of her office and toward the

back door of the bank. Julia let out her breath and leaned against the doorframe. The man was a disgrace. She kept hoping that some of the regional guys would make a surprise visit and find him gone. Hell, she'd even thought of putting an anonymous call in herself, to help things along. But despite his lack of abilities, Mr. Glynn had something she didn't have—a penis—and that meant he got to be in with all the good ol' boys on the golf course and in his clubs, and she didn't.

"Has he gone then?"

"Yes. Did you want to speak to him?" Julia smiled as Dave Askew, one of the young bank clerks, appeared at her door.

"Yeah, right. As if Mr. G. knows anything."

Julia lifted an eyebrow at Dave's dismissive tone and went back to sit behind her desk. "Whatever you think about Mr. Glynn, he's still the boss."

"I know, more's the pity. We all know that you run this place."

She opened her mouth to repeat her previous statement, but he was already laughing.

"It's okay. I'll shut up now. I came to tell you that a guy just walked in and wants to open an account with us."

Julia sat back. "Are we so desperate for customers that you have to tell me every time we get a new one? What am I supposed to do, sing him a happy song and give him a balloon?"

"Well there is that, but this guy only has one form of ID on him." Dave rolled his eyes. "And you know how strict the old guy is about proper identification. I decided to cover my ass and let you check him out. He *says* his family has lived her for years, so I figured you might know him."

"Is his name Luke Warner?"

Dave's smile was full of admiration. "Wow, you're *good*."

Julia shrugged off the compliment. "It's a small town and news travels fast. I went to school with Luke's cousin Roxanne, and his Aunt Josie taught me at school. They both called me to tell me he was back in town. Ask him to come in."

While Dave went to fetch Luke, Julia concentrated on taking deep, slow breaths and making sure that her hair was tidy and away from her face. She wanted to make a good impression on him when he entered her domain. She wanted him to see how far she'd come.

"Hey, Miss Assistant Manager." Luke's soft greeting and the absence of Dave surprised her for a moment. She stood up and held out her hand.

"Good morning, Luke." He took her hand and shook it and then sat in the chair she indicated. He had a faded blue T-shirt on today, but the same pair of ripped and paint-splattered jeans.

"You've done good, girl." His slow smile warmed her heart. "Hell, you've done double good."

She knew he'd appreciate her success. Unlike Paul, who'd always had the ranch and loving parents to rely on, she and Luke had been raised by families that were often absent or uncaring. Parents who hadn't noticed whether they'd skipped school, and who definitely didn't believe in the value of an education.

"Thanks. It got a lot easier after Mom left town with husband number four. I got to make my own decisions without her telling me I'd never make anything of myself."

"Hardly easy." He crossed one long leg over the other and settled deeper into the chair. "I bet you had to work your ass off to pay your bills and attend college."

"It was what I wanted to do, though." She shrugged. "It never seemed like a chore to me."

His smile was warm. "I know how that feels. When I first got to San Jose, except for that one stint at the local burger take-out place here, I had no skills at all. I had to get three jobs just to afford a place to sleep at night, but I did it."

She met his gaze, felt that tug of attraction again, of like finding like, of mutual appreciation. "So, what exactly did you end up doing over there that helped you come home and take on the old drugstore?"

He glanced down at his hands and spread his fingers wide on his thighs. "I started working in a smoothie and fresh juice bar, right in the heart of San Jose's Silicon Valley and ended up taking over and managing it myself."

"Managing it or owning it? They're quite different things."

He smiled. "I don't own it anymore. I sold it awhile back."

"And did what?"

"Nothing much. I just kind of dabbled in stuff." He sat forward and grinned. "What is this—an interrogation?" He dug a wad of bills from his back pocket and tossed them onto the desk. "I just want to open a bank account, not buy the whole town."

Julia felt herself blushing. "Sorry. It's just professional curiosity. When you go back out front, just tell Dave that everything is okay, and he'll get you started on the paperwork for your new account." She tried a smile. "I'm always interested in how people get their money and what they plan to do with it in the future."

"It's okay. I was just kidding. Can't you tell anymore?"

"Obviously not."

And there she was, staring into his eyes again, and feeling that spark. She bit her lip, saw he was watching her, and did it again. He contemplated her for a long moment.

"Now I'm wondering if I got the vibe right last night, whether you and Paul were just fooling around with me, or if you really meant what you said."

"About what?"

"About joining in the fun." He stood up and walked over to her desk, put his hands flat on the glass and leaned toward her. "The thing is, my tastes have changed and developed over the past ten years."

"In what way?" God, it was hard to breathe, let alone construct a coherent sentence. He was so close she could see all the greens, browns, and golds that made up the color of his eyes.

He reached out and brushed his thumb along her bottom lip. "Put it this way, I bet Paul still loves to fuck as much as he can—hell, if the guy could walk around with you permanently attached to his cock, he would, right?"

Julia found herself nodding, was rewarded by another sweep of his thumb across her lower lip.

"Paul probably shows up here whenever he's in town, and takes you out for lunch and fucks you, doesn't he?"

"Yes, so what?"

"So, nothing. There's no need to defend him. Paul knows what he likes and he's totally into you." His smile was sweet. "I'd just play it a bit differently, that's all."

"Like how differently?" She had to ask, didn't she? Paul would be proud of her and, if they truly wanted to explore all the sexual possibilities of Luke's return, she had to be bold. Luke's fingers trailed down her chin to the neck of her blouse and he undid the first button. She slapped her hands over his and he went still. "Luke, I'm at work."

"I know. Don't worry, I'm not going to fuck you here. Now, let go of my hands."

She looked up at him, tried to gauge the sincerity of his answer from his face and realized she'd either have to trust him or tell him to leave.

"What's it going to be, Julia?" he asked quietly. "Are you going to let me show you what I want from you, or not?"

She let go of his hands and placed her own on the desk in front of her. He undid the second button of her blouse and then the third. She shivered as his fingers spread the thin cotton, slid under the silk of her bra and cupped her breasts.

"See, this is what I'd want." He used his fingers and thumbs to bring her nipples to hard, aching points. "Your nipples tight and your pussy already creaming for me." He glanced up at her. "You're wet, right?"

She gasped as he increased the tug on her nipples until she was biting her lip and squirming in her seat. He let go of her breasts and straightened up.

"Get up, Julia." He came around the side of her desk and stood over her, his gaze taking in her shortness of breath, the way her taut nipples now pressed against the lace of her bra. He slowly opened the button of her pants and slid down the zipper to cup her mound.

"Nice little lace panties. I bet Paul likes them, too—easy to push to one side so he can get inside you fast." Luke demonstrated what he meant, one long finger sliding through the thick wetness and swollen flesh of her arousal. He rubbed her clit. "You're wet, Julia. You're so wet I could fuck you right now without any foreplay whatsoever."

He slid his thumb into the tight space between her panties and her sex and squeezed her clit hard. "But that's for Paul, right? Because sometimes I bet he's on you so fast you don't have a chance." He groaned. "Yeah, that's it; you're always ready to take him, aren't you?"

As Luke talked, Julia tried to keep a wary eye on the door, but it was impossible to concentrate as he focused his considerable skills on her clit, making it as hard and needy as her nipples. She went on up on tiptoes, tried to grind her mound against the palm of his hand.

He stopped moving his fingers. "Don't think about coming, Julia. That's not going to happen."

She managed to look at him. "You think you can stop me?"

"Hell, yeah." He stepped back and sucked his fingers into his mouth, licking off her taste. "That's where I'm different than Paul." He strolled around to the other side of her desk and sat back down in the chair. "I want you like this, all day, aroused, stimulated and ready for me. I want you thinking about me touching you. I want you touching yourself, so that when I see you tonight, you'll look just like you do now, ready to be fucked hard."

Julia managed to sit down and rebutton her blouse and pants even though her hands were shaking. "You think I can look like this all day and no one would notice?"

He shrugged. "So, they notice. The guys will wish it was them going to get lucky, and the ladies will just be envying you."

"I hardly think so." Despite the depth of her awareness of him, she was damned if she was going to let him see it. "What's to stop me bringing myself off the minute you leave?"

"Because that's not the point, is it? The point is that you have to wait to be satisfied. You have to wait until I let you come, or I fuck you."

God, why did his words make her sex throb in response as if all he had to do was snap his fingers and she'd do whatever he said? She licked her suddenly dry lips. "I'm not sure if I'd be any good at doing what I'm told."

His smile invited her to travel down the dark sexual paths he was creating, to experience emotions she'd never felt before. "I know that, Julia, but I also know that deep down, you've always wondered what it would be like to give yourself to a guy like that, haven't you?"

She thought about following him home that night, of kneeling before him in the dilapidated building, of doing whatever he told her to, simply to get fucked. It should have frightened her, but it was Luke who was asking. Although there was one thing she needed to clear up.

"Do you think you're going to stay in Gulch Town, then?"

He sighed. "I don't know. Are you saying you'll only go along with me if I'm leaving? That you'll try me on for size for a while because you'll get some kind of sexual revenge for what I did, or another way to kink up your sex life?"

"I hadn't thought that far ahead. I was more worried about how Paul and I will feel if we do this and you walk out on us again."

"But don't you see that 'doing this' and seeing if we can all get along together is crucial to whether I stay or not?"

Julia studied his face. "What do you think Paul's going to do while you're telling me whether I can come or not?"

As she changed the subject, some of the tension disappeared from Luke's face. "Paul will do whatever he wants, although I suspect he needs some discipline himself." Luke got up and readjusted the huge bulge in his jeans. He picked up one of her business cards and slid it into his pocket.

"Paul?" Julia laughed. "I'd like to see you tell him that."

Luke's smile was full of anticipation. "So would I." He walked toward the door, put his hand on the panel. "You'll come over tonight? Try it my way?"

Julia fiddled with the pens on her desk. "I'll have to talk to Paul."

"Sure."

The thought of Paul gave her courage. "If he can't make it, I won't be coming."

"Yeah, I get that. Paul's definitely part of the deal." He nodded at her and left. She got up and ran to the door, peeked through the crack to see that Luke was busy with Dave, and then locked the door. She slid a hand between her legs and cupped herself. God, she wanted to come so bad, her clit was throbbing with it. If she just pressed a bit harder she'd climax, she knew it. But Luke was right. Where was the challenge in that?

She slowly withdrew her hand and glanced at the clock on the wall. In less than seven hours, she would be walking out of here and she knew exactly where she'd be headed next.

Luke let himself back into the dilapidated store and dumped the three bags of stuff from the hardware shop on the countertop. Despite his best efforts to think about hardware rather than hard sex, his cock was still trying to drill a hole out of his jeans. He groaned as he studied the mess around him. All he wanted to do was shove his hand in his pants and jack off, not get on with the repairs.

A knock on the door brought his attention away from his cock and back to the present. He walked behind the counter and started to unpack the bags, called out a "Come in" as he worked.

Paul appeared, accompanied by a shorter, darker skinned man with a slight stoop. "Hey, Luke."

Luke nodded at the two guys. "Hey. What can I do for you?"

Paul patted the older guy on the shoulder. "I wanted to introduce you to Ramon. His son works for me out on the ranch, and Ramon does most of the handyman stuff that needs doing around the place. I thought you might like to borrow his skills for a couple of days a week until you're set. He can fix almost anything."

Luke grinned at Ramon, who smiled politely back. "It's nice to meet you, Ramon. That would be great. What's your hourly rate?"

Before Ramon could speak, Paul said, "It's okay. I pay him anyway."

Luke's smile died. "Then he'll get paid double. I'm not a pauper, Paul."

"Sure, whatever works for you." Paul shrugged off Luke's pointed comment with all the ease of a man who'd never had to worry about earning a dime. It used to bug Luke, but now he realized that Paul's workload at the ranch was way more intimidating a load than he would ever take on and that he deserved every cent he made.

"When can you start, Ramon?"

"Tomorrow, Mr. Warner?" Ramon looked at his employer, who nodded. "Today I finish up a job for Mr. Paul. Then I'm visiting my daughter in town, so I will be here first thing in the morning."

"Cool." Luke shook the old man's hand. "I'll see you tomorrow, then."

Paul didn't follow Ramon out; he remained leaning against the wall, hands in his pockets, brown cowboy boots crossed at the ankle. Luke finished emptying out the contents of the bags and looked right into Paul's blue eyes. "Is there something else?"

Paul stirred. "Julia said you visited her in the bank."

At the thought of Julia, Luke's cock started to fill out again. "Yeah, I needed to open a bank account."

"So I heard. I also heard that you want Julia to come over here tonight."

"And you."

Paul nodded. "Yeah, I got that message." He strolled across to the counter and looked at the supplies Luke had bought at the store. He smelled of fresh hay, sunshine, and leather. "I don't see anything edible here, so I reckon we'll need more food."

Luke managed a laugh. "Aunt Josie came by earlier. She's bringing me an old refrigerator she has in her garage. I was too grateful to argue with her."

"Good, let's hope she fills it with food as well."

"Knowing her, she probably will, but you might want to bring some takeout just in case."

"What time do you want us over tonight, then?"

Luke consulted his watch and realized it was already way past lunchtime. "Whenever Julia gets off work." He almost groaned at his choice of words. The thought of Julia getting off in front of him wasn't helping his constant hard-on. He walked back toward his makeshift bedroom and hoped Paul would get the hint that it was time to leave. He needed a little quiet time before he had to face them both again.

Keeping his back to Paul, he cupped his aching cock and

balls and promised them release as soon as he could get rid of his visitor.

"What's up, Luke?"

"Nothing." He tensed as Paul walked past him into his makeshift bedroom and studied him closely.

"Doesn't look like nothing to me. Looks like you're about to burst out of those jeans."

Luke stared at Paul. "So?"

"So, why not get on with it? It's not as if it's the first time I've seen you jack off."

Luke licked his lips. "You want to watch me?"

"Why not? I might even join in. The thought of Julia doing what you tell her has me so fired up I can barely walk straight, let alone concentrate."

Luke leaned up against the wall and slowly and deliberately undid the snap of his jeans and eased down the zipper. He sighed as the pressure on his cock diminished and shoved down his boxers and jeans. Without taking his gaze away from Paul, he wrapped one hand around the base of his already swollen and wet shaft and squeezed hard.

"Ah . . ." He groaned as pre-cum dripped down from his crown and covered his fingers. He was even more aroused to see that Paul's eyes didn't move away from the sight of his cock. "That's better." He pumped slightly, let the thick shaft slide between his fingers, thumbed the crown on every up-stroke. "I got hard when I was with Julia in the bank, pinching her nipples and her clit, did she tell you I did that?"

"Yeah," Paul said hoarsely, his hand settling over his groin, the bulge of his cock evident. "I bet she loved it."

Luke tightened his grip on his cock. "I told her she'd have to wait to come, to wait until I let her come."

Paul shoved down his zipper and grabbed at his cock which was already pushing out of his boxers. "I wish I'd been there. Seen you touching her."

"You'll see me touch her later, buddy, and she'll be touching you, too." Luke said. "Think about it, Julia on her knees, begging for it, begging us to let her come." Paul groaned, his fingers moving in unison to Luke's, both of them gripping their cocks as hard as they could. "Begging us to fuck her."

Luke dragged his gaze up from Paul's shaft to his face. "Do you want some help with that?"

Paul went still. "With my cock?"

"Yeah. If you come over here we can double the fun." Luke held his breath as Paul considered him. Had he moved too fast? Would Paul agree, or walk out on him? Keeping his hand wrapped firmly around his cock, Paul walked over to stand beside Luke.

Without saying anything, Luke curved his left hand around the thickness of Paul's shaft and started moving his fingers. Paul groaned and leaned up against the wall, head lowered to watch Luke manipulate both his cock and his own.

Luke nipped at Paul's ear, made him shudder, and made his breathing catch. "Do you like this? Do you like the thought of me having your cock in my hands?"

"Hell, yeah, but I'd like this even more."

It was Luke's turn to groan, as Paul returned the favor and touched his cock, so that all four of their hands were working together.

"That's fucking good—that's . . ." Luke gasped out the last words as his cum exploded through his fingers, heard Paul groan alongside him, and saw the thick stream of cum emerge from Paul's cock. He closed his eyes and leaned back against the wall, tried to catch his breath. Watching Paul come had made him instantly hard again.

He blinked slowly and stared at the other man. Paul took a handkerchief out of his pocket and cleaned himself up then buttoned up his jeans. He handed Luke the cloth, his smile slow and full of satisfaction. "Now don't you feel better for that? I know I do."

"God, yeah." Luke slid down the wall to sit on the floor. Paul set his Stetson back straight on his head and nodded.

"I'll see you later, then. I've got to go and find Ramon." He dropped his cell phone in Luke's lap. "Don't forget to call Julia and make sure she's okay with everything."

Luke could only watch him leave, amazed at the other man's ability to appear so unaffected by such a salacious encounter. His smile died. But maybe Paul wasn't as bothered by it as he was. Maybe Luke had it wrong after all and Paul was only humoring him for Julia's sake.

4

After he dropped Ramon off at his daughter's, Paul checked the time and headed back into the center of town. He had to talk to Julia and work out what they were going to take to eat at Luke's. Paul shifted in his seat as his cock swelled. He'd barely managed to get out of the old store with his dignity intact.

If Luke had bothered to keep looking at Paul's cock, he would have noticed that he was ready for more immediately after he'd come the first time. Paul stared down at his groin and pictured Luke's long fingers bringing him to a climax, his cum covering those fingers as he climaxed so hard he'd wanted to bite down on Luke's neck and mark his skin.

"Shit."

He just remembered to stop at a red light. The problem was, he'd never been able to get enough sex to satisfy himself. Julia kept him real busy, but he really liked sex about four times a day and that was just unnatural. As a teenager, he'd like to think of himself as a kind of stallion with a whole bunch of mares just waiting for him to fuck them. But unlike most teenagers, he'd never seemed to get out of the constantly hard horny phase.

He eased the truck forward and flicked on his right-turn signal. When Julia told him that Luke wanted to dominate her, his own reaction had been so intense, he'd wondered what the hell was wrong with him. He sighed as the old lady in the white Buick in front of him dithered over which lane she wanted and drove down the middle of the lane divider.

When Luke had jacked Paul off, all he could think about was both him and Julia on their knees in front of Luke . . . both of them doing whatever Luke told them to. Hell, if Luke had told him to go down on his knees earlier, he probably would've done it. And that was the real problem—it wasn't the first time he and Luke had given each other a hand, so to speak, but he'd never taken another man's cock in his mouth, never wanted to until he'd seen Luke again.

Paul sighed and found a parking spot between the bank and the corner of Keystone and Main. What would Julia think if he told her what he'd imagined doing with Luke, and more to the point, what would Luke think?

With a soft curse, Paul readjusted the fit of his jeans, opened the truck door and climbed down. Luke probably hadn't even noticed his confusion, and perhaps that was for the best until Paul made up his mind what the fuck he was doing. Jeez, Luke might be disgusted by the very idea of Paul doing anything to him. He eyed the façade of the bank and checked his watch. Ten minutes until Julia finished up, so he might as well go and order up some take-out food. Even though he couldn't focus on anything much right now except the upcoming evening with Luke and Julia, a man still needed to keep his strength up.

Julia stared at her reflection in the employee's bathroom and applied some fresh lipstick. Her color was high, her nipples hard, and her body wanted sex. Her cell buzzed in the pocket of her pants and she took it out and flipped it open.

"Paul?"

"Julia."

She went still as she recognized Luke's voice. "Isn't this Paul's cell?"

"Yeah, it is. He loaned it to me so I could call you. Where are you? You sound all echoey."

She smiled even though she knew he couldn't see her. "I'm putting on lipstick in the bathroom."

"Yeah?" He paused for so long that she could hear her heart racing. "I like the idea of your lipstick around my cock."

"You do?" God, she sounded like some lame teenager. "It's called True Red."

"Even better." He paused again and she found herself gripping the phone. "Are you all by yourself in there?"

"At the moment, yes."

"Good, then you won't mind sliding your fingers into your pussy and making sure it's all nice and ready for me, will you?"

Julia stared at her reflection, saw the lust in her eyes and closed them. Clutching the phone tightly to her ear with her left hand, she used her right to unbutton her pants and slide her fingers inside her panties.

"Are you wet, Julia?"

"Yes. I'm very wet."

"How many fingers can you get inside?"

She slid her fingers lower, moaned as they met no resistance, only a slick, wet welcome. "Three. God . . ."

"Thumb your clit, make sure it's primed and ready to come for me."

Julia did as he told her to, her harried breathing echoing in the small space.

"That's good, Julia. I'll see you in a while."

Luke cut the connection so abruptly she almost jumped. She

heard voices in the hallway and quickly did up her pants and washed her hands again. Thank God it was the end of the day. She didn't think she could stand the sexual anticipation for another second.

She emerged from the bathroom and went back to her office. Dave was putting a new file on her desk and he glanced up at her.

"This is the paperwork for Mr. Warner. He said his family owns the old drugstore on the corner of Main and that he's doing it up. Is that right?"

"Apparently." Julia gave Dave her most professional smile and dumped the new file in her inbox, ready to send it on to Mr. Glynn for the ultimate approval.

Dave grinned. "Well, seeing as he only deposited five thousand bucks into his current account, he's not going to get very far. He'll be tapping us for a loan next."

"And if he does, we'll be totally willing to help him out to the best of our professional ability, won't we?"

Dave walked out of the door. "Yeah, yeah, that's us, your friendly neighborhood bank, I get it."

Julia sighed as he disappeared whistling some piece of tune less drivel. Sometimes working with eighteen-year-olds made her feel ancient. Had she ever been that confident and cocky? Probably not, she'd been too busy trying to get her life together. Now, Paul had always been like that, still was sometimes, to tell the truth.

As if she'd ordered him up from her brain like a lunchtime special, Paul appeared at her door.

"You ready to quit, Julia?"

"The job? No. The day? Definitely. Let's go." She smiled at him, picked up the jacket of her pantsuit, and draped it around her shoulders. Paul followed her out to the parking lot behind the bank. She looked down to find her car keys in her purse and he almost bumped into her. He kissed the side of her neck.

"Did you know I can see your nipples through your blouse?"

Julia looked at her blouse and realized he was right. "Sorry about that."

His soft chuckle warmed her skin. "Not a problem, honey, just makes me want to suck them into my mouth, right here and now."

She turned around and put her hand on his shoulder, pretended to frown. "Don't say things like that here. I have to work with these people, remember?"

"Yeah, I remember, otherwise I'd be fucking you right now up against that ATM and to hell with who saw us." He kissed her nose. "Maybe we should leave both our cars here and walk down to Luke's. It'll only take a few minutes."

"Why don't you want to go in your truck?"

His smile was pure lust. "Because the moment I got you up in that cab I'd be inside you and I wouldn't care who caught me."

She touched his cheek, felt the burn of his unshaven beard. He moved his face so that her fingers brushed against his lips. "You seem pretty fired up tonight. It is because we're going to see Luke?"

His pupils dilated until there was hardly any blue left. "I saw him earlier."

"You did?" Julia kept on staring into his eyes. Something was troubling him, something important.

"Yeah, we . . ." He swallowed hard. "We jacked off together."

"And . . . ?" Even though she knew he'd take his own sweet time to tell her, Julia tried to encourage his reply. "Did you think I'd mind?"

He smiled then and she relaxed a little. "Not when we were both fantasizing about you. But . . ." He took her hand and marched her firmly toward his truck. "Are you okay with all this? It's happening so fast, but I kind of like that—"

She put her hand over his mouth. "Yes, it's fast, but maybe that's for the best? If it all goes wrong, we'll be able to move on, get over him quicker, and know that we were finally done with him."

He drew her hand away from his mouth and kissed her palm. "And if he doesn't go? If he wants to stay?"

She stood on tiptoe to kiss him. "Then we'll work it out somehow."

He kissed her back, crowding her against the side of his big truck, shielding her from the windows of the bank. God, he tasted so fine, a hint of beer, warm saddle leather, and laughter. Sometimes she just wanted to crawl inside him and stay there forever.

"I'm not sure if I'm going to be able to stand there and watch Luke play you."

She stroked his hair. "If you don't want me to do it, I won't. You know that?"

"I know, and honey, it's not that I'm jealous or anything, it's just that I kind of want to be more involved."

"I'm sure you do." Julia thought about them both having her, realized with a sensual thrill that she'd love it. "I wouldn't mind sharing."

His expression gentled. "You never did, honey. You made us both feel like kings. But we don't know exactly what Luke wants now, do we?"

"Well, there's only one way to find out." Julia nodded in the direction of Main Street. "Shall we?"

Paul smiled. "I ordered Chinese takeout—we can pick it up on our way."

Julia slipped her hand through his arm and hugged him hard. "I love Chinese."

* * *

She was still smiling when they arrived at the back door of the old drugstore. She opened the door for Paul and waited until he moved past her before continuing into the room. She wasn't quite sure what to expect, Luke dressed in leather with a long whip had crossed her mind, but she couldn't imagine it really happening.

By the time she entered the main shop, Luke and Paul were engaged in a discussion about the old shelving that covered the walls behind the main counter. Luke was insisting they could be saved, whereas Paul wasn't so sure.

Julia sighed and decided to check on the food. A battered old refrigerator now occupied a prime position behind the counter. She peeked inside, saw a completely iced-in freezer box, twelve bottles of beer, and six of water.

"Do you guys want beer with your food?" She looked back at them, eyebrows raised.

"Yes, please," Luke said.

She grabbed two frosted bottles of beer and one of water and put them on the counter beside the Chinese. The guys had returned to their discussion about the shelves. Julia cleared her throat. "Are we going to eat or not?"

Paul winked at Luke. "God, I love it when she gets all bossy, don't you?"

"Yeah."

Luke's slow smile stirred things in her body that made her forget her hunger and think only of pure sex. She swallowed hard, aware of his gaze on her breasts. Paul shifted beside her, his gaze flicking between the two of them.

"How about a little appetizer before we eat?" Luke asked softly. "How about Julia takes off her pants and shows us just how wet she is?"

Julia found herself nodding and then Paul lifted her to sit on the countertop. Her fingers trembled as she undid her pants and slid them down over her ass.

"Yeah, just like that." Luke sighed. "Push those little panties down too, Julia, so we can really see you."

She complied, felt the coldness of the recently refinished wood against the warm skin of her ass and waited for Luke's next instruction.

"Open your legs, honey," Paul urged as he took up a position to the left of her, leaving Luke to the right. "I want to see you so bad."

She slowly opened her legs wide and fought a sudden impulse to close her eyes. At least the shop had shutters so she wasn't displaying herself to the whole of Main Street.

Luke groaned. "God, she's so wet and open, I could stuff four fingers inside her, right now. Touch yourself, Julia, make yourself come."

Paul stepped so close the front of his jeans brushed her outstretched knee. He opened her blouse to reveal the opaque lace of her bra and the tight tips of her nipples.

She slid her fingers down and toyed with her clit, hoped they could see how stiff and swollen it already was. With a soft moan, she slid two fingers into her pussy and worked them back and forth, aware that both men watched her intently, that her pleasure was mirrored on their faces.

"God, Julia . . ." Luke kissed her knee, continued to kiss his way up her thigh. "Suck her breasts, Paul. I've got to taste her again."

Julia gasped as Paul's mouth descended over her breast, his lips sucked hard at her nipple. At the same time, Luke's tongue flicked over her clit and embedded fingers, making her shudder. She worked her fingers faster, found a rhythm that encompassed both the drag of Paul's mouth on her nipple and the stabbing of Luke's tongue over her clit. She climaxed hard, screamed out her pleasure as both men groaned against her flesh.

When she opened her eyes, Luke was still licking her pussy clean and Paul was watching him, one hand absently playing with her breast. When Luke finally straightened, he smiled at them both.

"Shall we eat, now?"

Paul helped her down and held her steady while she stepped out of her pants and retrieved her lace panties. She could clearly see the outline of his cock in his worn jeans, the damp spot where he was already wet for her. She didn't bother to do up her blouse and just straightened her bra. She had a funny feeling that she'd soon be naked anyway.

Luke divided up the food and they sat down to eat, Julia in Paul's lap, Luke close by. He studied Julia's flushed face, saw the traces of her climax in her eyes and in her languid motions. He'd soon wind her up tight again; have her screaming his name this time when she came. He finished his food and then his beer and sat back to let them digest.

He noticed Paul couldn't keep his hands off Julia. Even while he ate, he kept stroking her bare skin. Not that she seemed to mind. She'd always been very amenable to being touched by them both. Luke's cock twitched and he focused on his plans for after dinner. If all went well, his cock would soon be as satisfied as his stomach.

He cleaned up the remains of the food and sat back in his chair. Paul was smiling down at Julia as she wiped a stray grain of rice from his cheek. Luke patted the seat next to him.

"Paul, come and sit down. I reckon it's time Julia gave us something back for that orgasm we just gave her."

"If she's okay with that." Paul took the seat, his hands relaxed on his knees, his blue eyes narrowed and intent on Julia. "Are you, honey?"

"She knows what I wanted her to do and she's already agreed. Didn't you see how wet she was when she came in here?"

Paul turned to stare at him. "Yeah, but—"

"But how about you let me deal with this?" Luke tensed as Paul's expression darkened and he watched the struggle unfold in his eyes. "And while Julia is sucking our cocks you're not to touch her. You're going to keep your hands behind your back."

"Says who?"

Luke refused to look away. "Me. And if you want to argue about it, I'll fucking tie your hands behind your back."

Amused interest flashed over Paul's face and he didn't move an inch. Luke held his breath as the silence lengthened and then Paul let out his breath.

"Okay."

"You'll keep your hands to yourself?"

"Yeah."

"Good." Luke turned to Julia who was standing between them, her hands twisted in front of her. "You want to do it, right?"

She nodded and dropped to her knees in front of them both.

"Start by undoing our jeans." He sucked in his breath as her fingers went to work on his zipper where his cock was taking up all the space it could. She slid her hand between his hot wet shaft and the teeth of the zipper, both protecting and arousing him more. The air felt cold as she pushed his jeans down to expose his balls as well.

"Now do Paul." He watched as she turned her attention to Paul, heard his stifled curse as she revealed the thick purple crown of his cock and the long length of his shaft. "Start with him, I want to see you take all that into your mouth, I want to see you take him deep."

As Julia's red lips closed around Paul's shaft, he groaned and bucked his hips off the seat. Julia grabbed his thigh and kept swallowing him down. Luke's cock throbbed with anticipation, making pre-cum drip down the sides. Paul's fingers clutched the edge of his seat, white with tension as if not touching Julia was almost impossible for him to bear.

"Stop and do me. Do me slow."

Julia sat up, her color high, her breathing short, her nipples so tight he wanted to bite them hard. She angled her body toward him, and reached in to cup his balls before she slowly licked the slit at the top of his crown. When she bent forward, her blouse rode up at the back to display the soft curves of her ass.

"Yeah, just like that, Julia." Briefly, Luke closed his eyes as she sucked him slowly into her hot, warm mouth. Somehow, it felt like he was coming home. "Look at her, Paul. Look how I'm fucking her mouth."

He tried to relax into the amazing sensation, the feel of her mouth, her hand on his thigh, the light brush of her breasts against his jeans as she sucked him. He half opened his eyes and saw Paul's big cock straining and kicking against his stomach. He wanted to lean over and pump it hard, make Paul as desperate to come as he was.

"Stop, Julia." He waited until the pressure on his cock disappeared, hated losing it almost as much as he wanted to share it. "You want to get real close, Paul? You want her to take us both, make us come together?"

"Hell, yeah," Paul said hoarsely and he stumbled to his feet and moved as close to Luke and Julia as he could. "It reminds me of the old days." He stroked Julia's hair. "You okay with this, honey?"

Julia kissed first Luke's cock and then Paul's. "Don't I look like I'm enjoying myself?"

"Yeah, you do. I was just making sure before my cock took over my brain."

She laughed and licked the crown of Paul's cock. "I'll try and be fair, okay?"

"No worries," Luke assured her as she grasped his cock around the base. "We're not keeping count." He gasped as she took him deep again, worked Paul's cock with her hand, and then did the reverse. He stopped thinking when she grabbed both of their cocks and licked them, drawing groans from both of them. Luke felt his cock press against Paul's, the motion of Julia's tongue, the fucking fantastic nature of all of it, and started to come. Paul came too and Julia kept licking and sucking at them until Luke's knees gave way and he pitched forward out of his chair, bringing Paul and Julia with him.

He rolled off Julia, and buried his face in her pussy, found Paul's mouth and fingers already there, widening her, pumping into her. Luke nuzzled her clit, sucked it into his mouth, and felt Paul's fingers graze his cheek as they both worked her. God, she tasted so sweet, so slippery and wet, that he added his fingers to Paul's, his mouth sliding over both their hands, his tongue tangling with Paul's as they both tried to bring Julia to orgasm. And fuck, Paul's tongue was in his mouth and he was kissing him even as he finger-fucked Julia, even as Julia bucked and screamed and came against their interlocked, embedded fingers.

Luke rolled over onto his back and stared up at the ceiling, aware of Paul cradling Julia in his arms as she shuddered out the rest of her climax. He licked his lips, tasted Paul and Julia and wanted to start all over again. Had Paul kissed him deliberately or had it just been one of those things that happen in a frenzied moment?

He didn't know the answer and he wasn't sure he even wanted to ask the question. Paul lifted Julia into his lap and sat up. "Next time, guys, how about we try a bed? I'm getting a little too old for fucking on the floor."

Julia kissed his cheek, her eyes were shining and her hair was disheveled but, to Luke, she looked beautiful. "If you like, you can both come over to my place for dinner on Friday. I have a bed and I'm quite willing to share it."

Luke looked at Paul, who didn't seem to be either avoiding his stare or actively seeking it. He'd always been good at keeping his emotions to himself. And how the hell was Luke supposed to know how the man felt when he wasn't even sure how he felt himself?

5

Julia frowned at the file on her desk and walked out into the main office to find Dave. She waited while he served a customer and checked the rest of her staff as she pondered the night ahead.

"What's up boss lady?"

Dave's cheery greeting made her smile. She held out the file. "Do you know why Mr. Glynn turned down Luke Warner's account application?"

Dave blinked at her. "He did?"

"Don't you look at the files he asks you to sort out?"

"Not really. I'm usually too busy getting away from his boring lectures to care."

Julia frowned down at the file. "There's no reason why this application was denied. Mr. Warner even put cash into his account straight away." She glanced up at Dave. "If Mr. Warner comes in, just treat him like any other customer, and give him his money. I'll sort this out with Mr. Glynn myself."

"If he's ever here." Dave smiled and strolled back toward the counter where another customer awaited him.

"He'll be here on Monday. It's the last day of the month. He has to be here."

Julia nodded at Dave and at the customer, and headed back to her office, Luke's file in her hands. She really had no idea why Mr. Glynn had denied the application. It was most unlike him to bother with such a minor detail as an account. She put the file back in her inbox and concentrated on finishing her tasks for the end of the week.

Fridays were always busy at the bank because of people depositing their paychecks. She was always surprised by the number of people who still didn't trust the automatic check deposit system on the ATM outside and insisted on joining the long line inside the bank and handing the check to a teller. She wiggled her toes in her high-heeled sandals. She'd probably have to help out if things got busy and suddenly regretted her choice of shoes.

She'd seen nothing of Luke or Paul since their last sexual encounter in the old store. Julia licked her lips as she remembered how it had felt to have them both bringing her to a climax, to have both their cocks to suck, to simply have them both. She sighed and tried to concentrate on the stream of financial data on her screen.

Tonight she was seeing them again and she couldn't wait. What would Luke be like in bed now that he'd matured? Paul had certainly proved to be extraordinary, but part of her was dying to find out about Luke. Despite the fact that she considered herself a kick-ass kind of woman, it had been strangely liberating to kneel before the two guys and let them tell her what to do, to let go of having to be the adult, responsible one, to just *enjoy*.

She'd struggled so hard to succeed in the workplace that sometimes she felt like she needed Paul to dominate her in bed just to feel like a real woman. She smiled to herself. God help her if her more militant female friends heard her admit that.

Maybe she'd be kicked out of the girls club, but that was how she was made. She liked the power of being the woman who turned two such beautiful guys on. She liked it a lot.

Before she left for the weekend, she remembered to type an e-mail to Mr. Glynn asking about Luke's checking account application and that she'd discuss it with him on Monday. She shut down her laptop and grinned like a silly kid. That was, if she managed to crawl into work on Monday, after what she hoped would be the most spectacular weekend of her life.

Paul parked his truck behind Julia's beat-up Honda, got out and sniffed the air appreciatively. She was cooking something good. He could smell it from here. The evening promised to be interesting in many ways, not only would he get to see Julia naked, but Luke as well. Paul settled his Stetson on his head and strolled up to the back gate.

"Hey."

The soft scrunch of bicycle tires behind him made him pause. He looked round and saw Luke dismounting from a bicycle that looked as if it had seen better days. He raised his eyebrows.

"That's your idea of a hot ride?"

Luke grinned at him, his hazel eyes glinting as he faced Paul and the setting sun. "Yeah, the ladies love me. I'm so environmentally friendly."

"And *so* not getting any." Paul gestured at his truck. "What you want is a Ford 450. You can fit a king-size bed in the back and still have room for a couch."

"I'm sure you can." Luke propped the bike up against the back fence. "But you're still a gas guzzler."

Paul shrugged and opened the back gate. "But at least I'll go to hell with a big, satisfied smile on my face." Luke brushed past him and Paul closed the gate. "How did it go with Ramon today?"

"Jeez, that guy is awesome. He got the ceiling fixed, the shelves sanded back down and usable. On Monday we're going to check out the lighting and the plumbing. I'm hoping to create an apartment out of the old stockrooms in the back, but Ramon thinks I'll need a contractor for that."

"You probably will, but I know a couple of guys who would do a good job at a reasonable price."

Luke glanced sideways at him. "That doesn't mean you get to pay half the bill, though. You'll tell me the truth about what it's going to cost."

"Sure." Paul wasn't going to lie to Luke's face. He'd get the bids and then decide how much he could get away with by editing the truth.

"Didn't Julia tell you I owned a business in San Jose?"

"Yeah, she also told me you sold it." Paul opened the back door to Julia's condo. "I'm not interested in your money situation, Luke, that's your business, but if I can help out a friend, I'm going to do it regardless." He faced Luke. "You had a shitty start in life and I didn't. You're a good man, Luke."

Luke stared at him and his smile died. Paul couldn't look away. He had the strangest sensation that Luke was going to kiss him. He remembered the way their mouths had tangled over Julia's pussy; how it felt to slide his tongue over Luke's and feel his response. Paul cleared his throat. "Yeah, well."

"Is that you, guys?" Julia's voice broke the spell and Luke turned away.

"Yeah, it's us." Paul recovered his voice first, although he sounded a bit hoarse. What the hell was going on between him and Luke? Was he attracted to the guy? He'd never felt the slightest urge to kiss anyone apart from Julia, but when Luke looked at him like that . . . Christ.

Paul followed Luke into the kitchen and waited while he kissed Julia and then got his kiss as well. The succulent smell of garlic and red wine permeated the small space and the table was already set for three.

"This is nice, Julia." Luke was looking around with great interest. After the basic comforts of the old drugstore, Paul reckoned Julia's place must look like a palace.

"Thanks. Paul helped me fix it up and find some furniture."

Luke met Paul's gaze. "He likes helping out, doesn't he?"

"Yes, he does."

Paul shrugged and wondered why he suddenly felt like the odd guy out. "Why wouldn't I? I had it easy compared to you two."

Julia came across and squeezed his arm. "I'm not complaining, Paul." Her warm smile and the way she was petting his arm made his uncharacteristic flare of irritation die. "Do you want wine now, or with dinner?"

"I'll have some now. How about you two?" Paul showed the bottle to Luke and Julia and ended up pouring three glasses of the jewel-colored brew. Luke took his glass and wandered through to the main living space, commenting as he went. Julia stirred something on the stove and shouted back answers to his questions.

"Can I help you with anything, honey?"

Julia shook her head. "Not really." Luke's voice faded as he moved on down the hall. "Only you might tell me what's going on between you and Luke."

Paul almost choked on his wine. "What do you mean?"

"You're circling each other like two big cats."

"I don't know what you're talking about."

Julia stalked over to him, the wooden spoon still in her hand. "Bullshit. Now, what's up?"

He sighed and lowered his voice. "I'm not sure, I keep thinking about him."

"Thinking about him what?"

Paul licked his lips. "Touching me . . ." He raised his head and stared into Julia's startled gray eyes. "Yeah, I know, kill me now."

She touched his cheek. "Well, something weird is going on. Why don't you just sit down and talk to him about it?"

"Christ, we're not girls." Paul glanced around Julia and saw Luke was coming back. "We don't discuss personal stuff like that, and we both know he came back for you."

"We don't know anything of the kind."

A timer went off, and Julia huffed and turned back to the stove, leaving Paul to finish his wine and contemplate her lack of horror over what he'd just told her. He studied Luke, who had taken the chair opposite him. Maybe he was nuts and there was nothing going on after all. And maybe one of his cows really might jump over the moon.

Luke stretched out his legs and contemplated his empty plate and his full cup of coffee. Hell, he was just happy to be sitting in a real chair in a real apartment rather than roughing it in the drugstore. He and Ramon had accomplished a lot over the past two days, but it would be awhile before it was how he wanted it. Still, he felt a great deal of personal satisfaction at getting his hands dirty again and of waking up still aching from all the physical labor.

Okay, so his last job had some merits, but it had detached him both emotionally and physically from his roots. He'd been brain-fried, dead, done for. Coming back to Gulch Town had made him realize that even more clearly. He glanced at Paul and Julia, who were loading the dishwasher. Finding his two best buddies again was working out even better than he'd expected. Julia seemed totally happy to share herself with him and Paul.

But Paul was uneasy. Was he worried now that Julia had rediscovered Luke she'd no longer want him? Did he think that Luke was going to make it a "have me or have him" kind of choice? It wasn't as simple as that. Perhaps it was time to show Paul that there was more than one way to have a happy ending.

He bided his time, waited for Julia to sit down on the couch, for Paul to relax and share another glass of wine. Holding Julia's gaze, he slowly unbuttoned his only decent shirt and pulled it free of his jeans. He slid off the chair and crawled across to kneel in front of Julia and Paul.

"I think it's my turn to touch you." He kissed Julia's knee. "If that's okay."

Julia put down her coffee cup and looked down at him. "It's okay with me—Paul?"

"Sure."

Luke smiled as he slid his hands up the sides of Julia's legs until her reached the tops of her thighs and flipped up her short black skirt. She was naked underneath, and he could already smell her arousal.

"That's nice, Julia. Open your legs so that I can see you better."

He nuzzled her clit with his nose and breathed her in. So fucking fine, so ready for his mouth and fingers. Beside her, Paul stirred, and placed his big hand on Julia's naked inner thigh. It didn't worry Luke if Paul joined in; he'd be involved enough sooner or later.

Luke angled his body so that Paul could see everything he was doing to Julia, deliberately made it slow so that his buddy wouldn't miss a single excruciating detail. Paul's cock was already straining against his jeans.

Luke added another finger to Julia's tight pussy and took a long, salacious lick from her clit to her ass, watched Paul's hand tighten on her thigh.

"Undo your jeans, Paul. You look like you're in pain."

One-handed, Paul did was he was told and groaned with relief. Without asking permission, Luke shifted across and took as much of Paul's cock into his mouth as he could. He kept his fingers buried in Julia's pussy and worked them both to the same rhythm.

He kept expecting Paul to grab him by the hair and throw him against the wall, but nothing happened, except that Paul started to move with him, thrusting his hips forward, stuffing as much of his cock into Luke's mouth as Luke allowed him to. And God, Luke was happy to take it, to feel that thick, wet shaft at the back of his throat, to suck on him so hard Paul started to grunt with every thrust.

Luke closed his eyes and concentrated on the moment, tried to bring them both to orgasm, tried to forget the agony of his own cock trapped inside his jeans. But he couldn't quite do that. He slowly released Paul's cock and looked up. Paul's blue eyes glittered with lust.

"We can make this even better."

Paul swallowed hard. "How?"

"We get down on the rug and we finger-fuck Julia, and we suck each other's cocks." Luke held Paul's gaze. "Do you want to do that?"

"God . . ." Paul said, his gaze flicking between Luke and Julia. "I've never . . ."

Julia touched his cheek. "I don't mind, if that's what's bothering you." Her smile was hot. "And I'd quite like to watch."

Luke held his breath as Paul considered. The taste of the other man's pre-cum still on his lips, the scent of him, the pure essence of him, burned deep into Luke's very soul.

"Okay, yeah . . ."

Luke helped Julia onto the thick suede-fringed rug and Paul followed her down. "Let me and Paul get into position first and then you can kneel over us." Luke tried to sound businesslike, which was crazy when his heart was pounding so hard he could barely speak.

He curved his body around, until his head was opposite Paul's already straining cock and saw Paul replicate his movements in reverse. "Now, Paul." It was the last thing he was able to say before he opened his mouth and took Paul's cock deep, shuddered as he felt Paul do the same to him. God, the rough, inexperienced pull of Paul's mouth over his shaft made him so overexcited he hummed his approval against Paul's cock and sucked him hard and fast.

Despite the pleasure, he remembered to walk his fingers up Julia's leg and find her pussy, stuff his fingers inside her to the same rhythm he sucked Paul's cock. Paul's fingers joined him, both of them soon meshed together with the thick cream pouring from Julia's pussy as they finger-fucked her.

Paul came at the same time as Julia, his muffled shout and her scream sent Luke over the edge. It gave him the ultimate satisfaction of feeling Paul's cum pump down his throat and know that Paul was swallowing his, too. When Paul released his cock, Luke rolled onto his back, panting. Julia leaned against him, her whole body trembling.

"Can we go to bed, now? And can one of you make love to me? I'm so ready for you both, I'm almost ashamed of myself."

Luke touched her knee. "As soon as I can get off this floor and get hard again, I'm all yours." He hesitated and dared to look at Paul. "How about you, man?"

Paul looked dazed and he constantly licked his lips as if savoring the taste of Luke's cum. Luke's cock immediately jerked to attention. "Yeah, I'm all yours, honey."

Luke helped Julia up and Paul led the way to the bedroom at the back of the condo. The cream blinds and drapes were already drawn, and soft lamplight illuminated the king-size bed. Paul stripped off his shirt and pushed down his jeans and Luke just had to stare at him. There wasn't an inch of fat on Paul's big, hard body. He had the six-pack abs and toned physique of a guy who worked out in the gym all week.

Paul glanced at him as he helped Julia unhook her bra. "Aren't you getting naked, Luke?"

"Yeah . . . sorry." Luke stripped, aware that both Julia and Paul were watching him intently. His cock stiffened and straightened. By the time he climbed on the bed, he was ready to fuck again.

Julia couldn't help but stare at the long, elegant lines of Luke's body as they emerged from his clothing. He wasn't as buff as Paul, but he had a beauty all his own. She glanced at Paul and realized he was equally fascinated by Luke's nakedness. She lay back on the pillows and simply looked at the men who were waiting for her to choose which one she would fuck first. What a lovely, wickedly sexy choice.

She beckoned to Luke. "You first, I think, seeing as it's been awhile."

Luke crawled toward her, one hand wrapped around his cock. He looked around distractedly. "I had some condoms in my jeans pocket . . . I'll—"

Julia touched his knee. "I've got some in the bedside cabinet. Can you get one, Paul?"

Paul reached across her and found the condom box, shook one out, and handed it to Luke. Luke opened the foil and worked the condom down over his long cock.

"Thanks." He smoothed his fingers over the latex, "I'm totally clean by the way, and I've always been careful."

"And I'm on the pill, so we should be fine." Julia held out her arms to Luke. "Come here, please?"

He lunged for her, his cock pressed against her belly as he drew her into a deep kiss. He rocked his hips and she rose to meet him, brought her feet up closer to her ass to get the angle just right for him to slip inside her.

"God." He gasped as she managed to get the first couple of inches in. "That's . . ." Now she was the one crying out as he pushed himself deeper and deeper with each urgent thrust. She wrapped her arms around his neck, her legs around his pumping ass and held on tight. He felt so fine, she climaxed fast, but it didn't stop him, he just kept on thrusting into her.

She managed to turn her head to the side, saw Paul watching them and reached out one hand for his cock. He was so slippery and wet she had to grip him hard to keep hold of him. He moved closer, his knee bumping up against her shoulder. Luke looked up and held himself still over her.

"Do you like watching me fuck her, Paul? I can't wait to see you fuck her again. Maybe she'll let us both inside her before we're done." Luke groaned. "Imagine that, buddy, both of us in her pussy and her ass."

Luke grabbed Paul's hand and placed it on his back. "Touch me while I fuck her, Paul. Touch us both." He started to move again, grinding himself against Julia until she kept coming and couldn't stop writhing and moaning beneath him. Paul's hand squeezed her breast, her ass, her knee, his rough fondling only adding to her excitement, to the pleasure of having both men in her bed again.

Luke's movements became jerky, his breathing shallow as he froze over her. "God . . ." His cock jerked inside her and she felt his release, held him close while he shuddered and then went heavy on top of her. She lay still, aware of Paul beside her, of Luke's hand tangled in her hair. Was it wrong to feel so complete with both of them? Was it possible to want two men at the same time, to need two men to satisfy all her desires? All she knew was that, with these two men, it had always been like that for her. She'd always wanted them both.

A little while later, Paul's fingers trailed down to Julia's pussy and he stroked her clit. "You ready for more yet, honey? Cuz I'm more than willing to help out."

Julia's chuckle warmed him, made him feel obliged to slide his fingers farther down to push into her thick wetness and her channel. "You want my cock?"

She pulled his face down over hers for a kiss. "Always."

He was ready for her. He always was. He moved between her legs and sat back on his knees, spread her legs wide, exposing her to his and Luke's gaze. He heard the sudden intake of Luke's breath, the feel of Luke's hand on his ankle and drew Julia's ankles up over his shoulders.

He slowly entered her, held her hips right where he wanted them, and allowed her no room to do anything but take his cock just the way he wanted her to. He grimaced as he leaned over her and let some of his weight press onto her mound.

"Ah . . . that's so deep." Julia tried to angle away from him, but there was nowhere for her to go, trapped as she was between his hands and his cock buried deep inside her. He slowly withdrew until only a half inch of cock was inside her and then drove back in hard. Was Luke watching him? God, he hoped so. He was aware at some level that he was performing for Luke, too, showing the other man exactly what he could do with his big cock.

He slowly pulled out again and bent his head to lick Julia's clit. She moaned and writhed against him as he rubbed his chin against her most sensitive skin, felt the tremors of a climax shiver through her. Luke's hand slid up his leg and caressed his butt cheek, adding to the build-up of tension, of need, of desire to show them both how he felt about them.

He slid his cock home again, shuddered as Julia came around him, held still and deep even as he felt Luke's fingers probe between his ass cheeks. Julia's brown hair was loose and tangled on the pillows, her gray eyes were wide, her skin flushed.

Luke leaned into him. "May I?"

Paul didn't answer him, he couldn't. He wasn't quite sure what Luke intended, but he'd already decided he wasn't going to stop him. The faint scent of lube filled his nostrils, the lube he and Julia kept by the bed for the times when he fucked her ass. She loved him doing it, but he was big and the lube certainly made it easier for him to get inside her.

Paul held still as Luke's slick finger circled his ass and slid inside him. He closed his eyes at the unfamiliar sensation and started to fuck Julia, knew that if he even thought about what Luke was doing to him, he'd probably come. The fucking took all his concentration. At this angle he was coming right down on her, each stoke carrying his weight and pounding into Julia's clit.

She gripped his arms, her head thrown back as she writhed against the sheets. And, hell, there it was, the other amazing sensation of a finger in his ass, the sense that Luke had stroked something inside him that had just been waiting to be found and fucked.

Paul stopped thinking and just focused on the pleasure, forgot to be careful of Julia and just fucked her for all he was worth as new sensations engulfed him and brought him to a sexual climax he had never reached before. His cum flooded out of him, took forever, drowned Julia's pussy and still kept coming.

When he raised his head he was shaking so hard he could barely get off Julia. Without saying a thing, he climbed off the bed, picked up his clothes and headed for the kitchen, his cock and ass still throbbing with excitement, his brain flooded with conflicting emotions.

"Paul?"

Julia called his name but it didn't stop him pulling on his boots and jeans and walking out. He took a deep shuddering breath as he settled himself into his truck. What the hell was going on with him? He'd been worried that Luke had come back for Julia, and now he was more concerned as to what exactly Luke wanted from him. He started the truck and slowly drove down the street.

And, hell, that wasn't right either. He had no way of knowing exactly what Luke wanted. Paul stared bleakly into the peaceful night sky. What he *did* know was what *he* wanted, and the whole notion of that scared him to death.

When she heard the kitchen door open, Julia scrambled to the side of the bed and called Paul's name again. There was no answer except the slamming of the door and the start up of the truck engine. Julia stared down at Luke who was watching her with great care.

"What the hell happened?"

"I reckon he scared himself."

"What exactly is that supposed to mean?"

"He's a big, tough cowboy with a high sex drive." Luke shrugged. "You work it out."

Julia narrowed her eyes at Luke. "What did you do to him?"

"I finger-fucked his ass while he was fucking you."

"What else?"

"Nothing else."

"But he seemed to like it, didn't he?"

Luke's slow smile was like warm taffy. "Yeah, I think he did."

"And that's the problem, isn't it?"

"I reckon so."

Julia shivered and pulled back the bedcovers. Settled herself and Luke underneath them. "What are we going to do?"

Luke put his arm around her shoulders and held her close. "Wait for him to come back?"

"You think he'll do that?"

"Not tonight." Luke kissed the top of her head. "But when I worked out what I wanted, I came back. Now how about we get some sleep here?"

Julia tried to close her eyes, but images of Paul and Luke filled her head. Perhaps she'd gotten it wrong all along. Perhaps Luke hadn't come back for her after all, but for Paul.

6

Julia frowned at the sight of Mr. Glynn's golf bag propped up against his half-open door. It was the end of the month and they had a load of work to get through to balance things up. Surely Mr. Glynn wasn't contemplating taking off early? She knocked on his door and went in, waited for him to finish his phone conversation.

"Good morning, Miss Lowell. What can I do for you?"

"Good morning, Mr. Glynn." Julia held out Luke's file. "I wanted to ask you why you've declined Mr. Warner's account."

Mr. Glynn drummed his short, stubby fingertips on the desk. "You know why, you've lived here all your life. His family is scum."

"I beg your pardon?"

"Well, not all of them, I suppose his Aunt Josie is a respectable enough citizen, but Luke Warner's father and mother were drunks and layabouts."

Julia struggled to keep her temper. "Whatever your opinion of Mr. Warner's parents, they're dead now. You can't judge him by their actions."

"Yeah, I can." He gestured at the file and she handed it to him. "This guy turns up with five thousand bucks in cash, and you believe he came by it honestly?" He tossed the file down on the desk. "I can't prove anything, but I can at least keep him out of my bank, make him travel down to the next town to get his filthy money out."

"Sir, I'm certain that's against the bank's policies."

Mr. Glynn's cheeks flushed dark red. "And what are you going to do about it, missy? File a complaint?"

Julia held his gaze. "Yes, if I have to." So much for being promoted, so much for her dreams. Sometimes a gal just had to take a stand for her friends.

Mr. Glynn's smile disappeared. "I think you've been getting a bit above yourself lately, Miss Lowell, acting as if you run the bank and not me."

"For all intents and purposes, I do run the bank, sir." Julia manufactured a smile and reclaimed the file. "I'll have the monthly summaries on your desk in an hour." She turned smartly on her heel and walked out before she overcame her desire to leap over the desk and throttle the little shit.

She sat down at her desk and contemplated her next move. Luke had as much right as anyone to open an account at the fucking bank. She knew what it was like to grow up in a small town where the sins of your parents were regularly brought out and attributed to you. There was no way in hell that she would allow Mr. Glynn to do that to anyone, let alone Luke. So what that Luke only had five thousand bucks to his name? That was nobody's business but his.

Julia sighed. If she stood up for Luke, there would be consequences and because of Mr. Glynn's contacts, she might be the one who ended up without a job. She typed in a secure bank e-mail address, filled out the form, clicked SEND, and sat back. Whatever happened, she had done what she needed to do and to hell with her career. There were always other banks in other towns.

Luke waved at Ramon, who was heading for the ranch offices and walked down to the barn. He'd borrowed Julia's car to drop Ramon off at home. It also gave him a great excuse to drop in and see what Paul was up to. As he hesitated in the shadows of the barn, he heard Paul's voice out back in the corrals and changed direction.

It took him only a moment to locate his best friend. Paul was riding a young horse around the circular arena. From the look of it, the horse had just been broken in. Luke leaned up against the railings to appreciate the sight of Paul talking to the horse, the gentleness of his commands, the subtle way he used his voice and his body to soothe the frightened animal into accepting a man on his back. He rode like he'd been born on horseback, something Luke had never managed despite all Paul's early coaching. Paul's body swayed with the motion of the horse, his hips perfectly aligned with every skittering jump the horse took.

Luke didn't say anything. He knew that Paul would come over to him when he was done with the horse. He would never leave a job unfinished, just as he would never leave a friend.

Eventually, Paul patted the horse's neck and slowly dismounted. Luke opened the gate and Paul and the horse moved by.

"Thanks." Paul nodded, his blue eyes hidden beneath the low brim of his Stetson.

"You're welcome." Luke followed him into the barn, waited while Paul took his time removing the tack from the horse and brushing him down. "I'd forgotten how awesome you are at breaking a horse."

Paul looked at him for the first time, his gaze guarded. "I don't break them. I just try and convince them that having a human on their backs isn't so bad after all."

Luke shrugged as Paul shut the stable door and walked down toward the feed and tack rooms. "Whatever you want to call it, it's awesome."

"Why are you here, Luke?" Paul leaned against one of the neatly stacked hay bales, his arms crossed over his chest.

"I brought Ramon back. He finished up the wiring early so I offered to bring him home. It was the least I could do."

"Thanks," Paul said. "Do you want to walk over to the ranch office and get some coffee before you leave?"

"I'm not leaving yet." Luke shut the door into the feed room behind him and locked it, blocking the only exit. "Not until we've straightened out a few things."

Paul sighed. "Hell, I knew you wouldn't let this go."

"Let what go?"

Paul swallowed hard and then locked gazes with Luke. "The fact that I'm attracted to you."

"To me?" For a second Luke could only blink at him. He'd been expecting Paul to say many things, but not that.

"Yeah." Paul grimaced. "Yeah, go ahead and laugh. I know why you came back to town, Luke. You came for Julia, not to hear some pathetic crap from me."

Luke straightened and walked across to Paul until they were nose to nose and, more importantly, cock to cock. He shoved his hand between their two bodies and cupped Paul's cock and balls through his jeans.

"So tell me, what do you want from me that's so pathetic?"

Paul's cock filled out beneath Luke's fingers, and he squeezed him hard. Paul closed his eyes and tilted his head back against the wall, didn't even protest as Luke ripped open his jeans and thrust his hand inside. "What do you want, Paul?"

"This," Paul groaned. "You, touching me, my cock in your mouth, my mouth around yours . . . Christ."

Luke kept working Paul's shaft as he unzipped his own jeans

then closed his fist around both of them and made Paul do the same so that they pumped each others shafts together. Luke bit down on Paul's ear.

"Do you want it all, Paul? My cock in your ass, your cock in mine?"

Paul groaned. "Fuck it, yes."

"Do you want to do me right now?" Luke used his free hand to shove down his jeans. "I want you to."

In answer, Paul grabbed him and pushed him face down over the bale of hay. Luke's cock made contact with the rough hay and he almost came before Paul's big hand covered him. Luke shuddered as Paul's wet cock brushed against the crease of his ass.

"I don't suppose you have any lube on you?" Paul asked hoarsely. "Because I want to be in you, like, right now."

"No lube, just spit on it. I don't care, just *do* it. Do me." Luke deliberately urged Paul on, wanted this first time to be hard and fast and crude, wanted to remember it forever, this taking, this harsh possession.

Paul swore and Luke let out his breath as he felt Paul shove one wet finger inside him and then another and another. "Just do it, Paul. Fuck me." Luke gasped as Paul's big cock pushed inside him, groaned as Paul's fingers gripped his shaft and played him to the same rhythm as the fast, frantic thrusts of his cock.

Paul went still when his balls hit Luke's ass, and Luke savored the sense of being filled, the heat throbbing from Paul's shaft and the beginnings of pleasure. "Yeah, that's good, Paul, fuck me hard now."

Paul took him at his word, his rough movements strong enough to make Luke have to brace himself against each forward thrust, to revel in Paul's strength and luxuriate in being thoroughly fucked and played by the one man he'd always dreamed about.

When Paul climaxed he lowered all his weight on Luke, almost flattening him into the straw. Luke came too, his cum spilling over Paul's still-working fingers.

"Fuck," Paul muttered. "Just . . . fuck."

Luke waited for Paul to roll off him and then turned to face him. "If you haven't worked it out yet, I'm not averse to being your fuck buddy as well as your best friend."

Paul smiled as him. "I guess not." He busied himself tucking his cock back into his jeans. "But how does this work with Julia? I kind of assumed you came back for her."

Luke tucked in his shirt and zipped up his jeans. "I did."

Paul grimaced. "I can't hurt her. If she wants you, I'm not going to stand in her way."

Luke nodded and unlocked the door. "I hear you. Let's see if she'll meet us for dinner at her place tonight so that we can sort it out." He checked the entrance to the barn, saw no one about, and gestured to Paul to follow him into the warm sunlight. "I have to go into the bank today anyway. Paying Ramon and buying the supplies wiped out my cash supply."

"You're welcome to borrow a few bucks whenever you want." Paul shoved his hands in his pockets and studied the dusty ground. "You know that, right?"

"I don't need your money, Paul." Luke started off along the path leading to the main house.

"That's right, you *choose* to live in a building that's falling down, and own three T-shirts, a pairs of jeans and one pair of cowboy boots with holes in them."

Luke couldn't help but smile. "Yeah, that's right. I like my life just the way it is."

"Bullshit."

"Money doesn't change a man, Paul. It just makes everything more complicated."

"You think I don't know that?" Paul spread his arms wide. "I love this place like I would a child, but sometimes I just wish

I could walk away from all the responsibility and simply do what I want."

Luke stopped walking. "If I'd asked you to come with me after graduation, would you've come?"

"I thought about coming after you, about leaving it all." Paul's smile was full of regret. "But my mom was sick and there was the ranch, and then there was Julia who couldn't believe you'd really left her." He sighed. "And yet, I still wanted to follow you."

"I don't know what I would've done if you had, Paul. I didn't really know what I wanted then."

"Yeah, I get that. And you didn't ask me, did you? You asked Julia." Paul ran a hand through his hair. "How about you go see her and I'll see you both this evening."

Luke nodded. "Sounds like a plan. I'll get Julia to call you if it doesn't work out."

"Hell, you don't have a phone, do you?"

"Nope, or a laptop or an Internet connection. I am truly a free man."

Paul held his gaze, his blue eyes serious. "Not that free, Luke. After all, you came back home."

Luke drove back to town, his thoughts in turmoil. Paul had fucked him, really fucked him. And now he had to talk to Julia. He avoided a pothole on the bumpy ranch drive and then straightened the wheel. He liked seeing her in the bank, her air of authority, the confidence she'd always longed for so apparent in everything she did.

He remembered to park around the back of the bank in the employee spaces and separated Julia's car keys from the tangle of his. The bank was cool inside, the neutral wood floor and beige furnishings making it feel more like someone's house than a place to do business. He walked up to the counter and recognized the young guy who'd first helped him.

"Hey, Dave, isn't it? Is Ms. Lowell available?"

"Wow, you got here quick. She only just put down the phone."

Luke grinned. "Well she couldn't have been calling me. I don't have a phone, cell or land." The expression on Dave's face was priceless, as if he couldn't imagine a world where you weren't connected 24/7 to everything.

"I'll take you in to her." Dave headed for Julia's office and Luke followed along behind. Julia sat behind her desk, her head bent, her attention on a sheet of graph paper covered in figures.

"Ms. Lowell? It's Mr. Warner."

Julia's head shot up. "Are you psychic or something? I was just about to come around and see you."

Luke smiled at her, "Yeah. That's it. It's totally a mind thing." He took the chair in front of her. "What's up?"

She sighed. "My boss, Mr. Glynn had denied your application for an account."

"Denied me?" Luke fought an unbearable desire to laugh. "What the hell for?"

"Because apparently he had issues with your parents." Julia rubbed her forehead. "And, yes, that's total shit, and I'm already onto Regional about it."

"He won't like you going over his head."

"No, he won't, but I'm sick of covering for his incompetence." She smiled slightly. "If he won't let me do my job properly, I'd rather get another one."

Luke sat forward, his hands clasped loosely between his knees. He knew Julia far too well to believe that. Security was way too important to her.

"You wouldn't really leave Gulch Town because of a disagreement over me, would you?"

"If I had to." Her gray eyes met his unflinchingly. "I've realized that my desire to stay here has cost me a lot in my life."

"Like me?"

She nodded. "I should've come with you when you asked me to."

"No, you shouldn't have, and I was a fool to ask." Luke studied her beautiful face. "I was so fucking mixed up, I would've ruined everything in six months."

"You reckon?"

"I *know*." He got up and leaned across the desk to give her a kiss on the nose. "Perhaps we all needed to grow up a bit, right?"

"I suppose we did." She gazed at him thoughtfully. "Did you speak to Paul?"

"Yeah, I did. He wants to meet up with us both at your place for dinner—is that okay?"

"Sure, and don't worry about your bank account. I promise you I'll get that all sorted out."

Luke snapped his fingers. "Oh, right. Can you lend me your cell? I need to make a call."

She handed him her cell just as the phone on her desk rang. "I have to take this. Bring the phone back with you, tonight, okay?"

Luke blew her a kiss and sauntered out into the parking lot. He flipped open the phone and entered a number he knew by heart, smiled when a familiar voice answered.

"Mike? Yeah, I know it's been a while, but there's something you can do for me. It's about my bank account."

7

Julia slammed the oven door shut on the chicken casserole she'd hastily constructed for dinner and turned on the timer. Paul and Luke were due at any moment and she wanted her hands free and all sharp cooking implements put safely away before she saw them. She heard them talking and laughing as they walked up to her condo and folded her arms over her chest.

Paul's smile was warm as he came across to hug her, Luke's just as bright. Julia held up her hand.

"No hugs, yet. I need to ask Luke something."

Paul's smile faded. "Is this about what happened in the barn this morning? I told Luke I'd sort it out with you, there's nothing to worry about."

Julia opened her mouth to continue and then stopped to refocus on Paul. "What happened in the barn?"

"Paul fucked me," Luke said. "And now he's worried you won't approve."

"Why would I mind? It's not as if it's a complete surprise."

Julia let out her breath. "And I'm also totally okay with the idea that you two are meant to be together—without me."

Paul straightened. "Hold on a minute, it's the other way round, isn't it? Luke came back for you, Julia, not me. Me having the hots for Luke is neither here nor there."

Julia glared at Luke. "You have a lot of explaining to do, buddy. Perhaps you'd like to start by telling me what you did to get Mr. Glynn fired."

"Me?" Luke raised his eyebrows and sat down on one of the kitchen chairs, legs crossed. "What the hell did I do?"

"Don't lie. This afternoon I got a call from a Mr. Mike Pritchard. He said he managed your business accounts."

"Oh, hell," Luke groaned. "I told him not to call you directly."

"Well I'm glad he did. Apparently he's on good terms with one of the guys on the bank's board, and 'apparently' Mr. Glynn denying the application of a multimillionaire client of his pissed him off."

Luke shrugged. "Well, it would, wouldn't it?"

Julia pointed her finger at him. "You said you sold your juice bar and just dabbled in stuff."

"That's true, I did."

"I thought you meant you'd lost all your money."

"I never said that."

"Hold on a minute," Paul said. "Luke's a millionaire? So, how did you make all this money?"

"I owned a juice bar in the heart of Silicon Valley. Over the years, I met all kinds of geeks and computer geniuses, even invested in some of their companies, you know, like eBay, those Google guys, that kind of stuff."

"You made enough to sell the shop and just focus on managing your portfolio?"

"Yeah, I did, and then last year I realized I was tired of just doing that and looked around for something else to do." Luke looked at them both. "And I realized I wanted to come home."

"And pretend you had nothing," Julia said.

"I didn't do that, Julia." His hazel eyes were steady. "You and Paul just assumed that as I'd left with nothing, I'd returned with nothing. I tried to tell you that wasn't the case, but you were both too busy offering me advice and loans to actually pay attention."

He got to his feet. "I know you don't want to believe me, but I'd gotten to a point in my life when I realized that all the money in the world couldn't compensate for the things that really mattered—having a home, a family, someone to love. I came back here to see if any of that still existed for me."

Julia glanced at Paul who was watching her intently. "I suppose Luke's got a point." Her lips twitched. "And you should've seen Mr. Glynn's face when the bank director called him. It was priceless."

Luke grinned. "I'm glad the narrow-minded bastard lost his job. He sure didn't deserve it."

"I hate to sound vindictive, but I agree with you." Julia smiled at both the men. "And I won't be after you about getting a loan out on the drugstore, okay?"

"Okay." Luke's smile died. "And now I might as well answer the rest of your questions, the important ones." He shoved his hands in his pockets and studied the tiled floor. "I ran away that night because I realized I wanted you both, and at eighteen, that idea scared the shit out of me. I certainly wasn't old enough to know how to deal with it, and I reckoned if I took myself out of the equation, you two would work it out just fine."

"Except we didn't," Julia whispered. "We always felt like there was something missing." She reached for Paul's hand. "And I just want to say that if you came back for Paul, I'm okay with that. I'd like at least two of us to be happy."

Luke moved closer took her hand and Paul's. "But it's not that simple, is it? I still want you both, and I'm the one who will be bowing out if that doesn't work for all three of us."

Paul chuckled. "You've both said pretty much what I was going to say. I'd also be willing to back off if it makes you two happy."

Julia's eyes filled with tears. "Wow, aren't we all being so self-sacrificing here? Anyone would think we loved each other."

Paul cleared his throat. "But we do, don't we?"

"Yeah," Luke said huskily. "We do."

Julia dragged them both into a fierce embrace and sighed as their arms came around her and around each other. "We can make it work, can't we?"

"I don't see why not," Paul said. "We can at least try."

Julia stood on tiptoe to kiss Paul's mouth and then Luke's. "Can we go to bed to seal the deal? The casserole's going to take at least two hours to cook."

Luke grinned. "Sounds good to me, honey, and it's my turn to fuck Paul. Maybe I can do that while he's fucking you."

Julia shivered as Paul picked her up and marched down the hall to her bedroom. Mr. Glynn was gone, she was about to have sex with the two most important men in her world, and dinner was in the oven. Did it get much better than this? Somehow, she doubted it.

Private Eyes

Susan Lyons

Acknowledgments

I had less than twenty-four hours to come up with the idea for this novella, and I loved the premise of a buttoned-up wannabe PI going undercover as a stripper. Except then I had to write the story and I realized I knew very little about either PIs or exotic dancers. So, I'm very grateful to former PI Joyce David, and to current and former exotic dancers Annie Temple, Ryann Rain, Rabbit, and Samantha Mack, for providing me with background information from which I could spin a work of fiction.

Thanks to my critique group for their invaluable input: Elizabeth Allan, Michelle Hancock, and Nazima Ali. And thanks too to Emily Sylvan Kim, my agent, Audrey LaFehr, my editor, and Martin Biro, editorial assistant extraordinaire.

Readers, I hope you'll look for my next book, *Love, Unexpectedly*, an April 2010 release from Kensington Brava, written under the pen name Susan Fox. I love to hear your feedback and invite you to visit my Web site at www.susanlyons.ca, e-mail me at susan@susanlyons.ca, or write c/o PO Box 73523, Downtown Postal Outlet, 1014 Robson Street, Vancouver, BC, Canada V6E 4L9.

1

"**H**ow does she *do* that?" Ry's colleague Tom asked disbelievingly. "Man, if my wife could move like that . . ."

Ry, who'd been paying for the latest round of drinks for their group of six, looked up quickly.

On stage, the stripper, clad in a barely existent red sequined thong, hung upside down on the pole, platinum blond hair cascading toward the stage. Both hands gripped the metal rod, her long, shapely legs spread in a perfect split, and her breasts, huge creamy melons with rosy nipples, defied gravity.

Kari, the younger of the two female PIs who worked at The Private Eye, teased Tom, "If your wife could do stuff like that, she wouldn't be with you." She shook her head in wonder as she studied the dancer. "That is pretty amazing."

"Upper body strength," another female voice said, so softly Ry could barely hear her over the driving beat of a Bif Naked song. "Flexibility, control, and lots and lots of practice."

Surprised, Ry glanced over at Hayley Croft, seated across the table from him. He'd almost forgotten the PI agency's admin assistant was there. Overlooking Hayley was easy to do, she was so bland—like tonight, in her gray jacket and pale blue buttoned-up shirt, her glasses and tightly pinned-up hair.

Her innocuousness made her the perfect person to spell off the PIs on straightforward surveillance jobs. She could sit in a coffee shop or on a park bench for hours and no one would notice her.

She'd surprised him—surprised all of them, he was sure—when she'd joined the PIs at the 4-Play strip club tonight.

The agency's client's wife had taken up stripping when her husband lost his job, and she'd refused to give it up once he found work. She'd withdrawn from him and from her suburban girlfriends. The guy worried she was having an affair, or was into the drug scene.

It was Ry's case, and he'd started with basic surveillance. The wife's life appeared to consist of home, the grocery store, whichever club she was dancing at, and short trips out from the club between shows to the bank, have coffee with other dancers, shop for clothes, and so on.

When he'd reported this to the client, Paul Mortimer, Mortimer had authorized an expenditure for surveillance inside 4-Play, the moderately upscale Vancouver strip club where his wife would be working this week.

At this morning's weekly agency meeting, Ry had reported he intended to make a quick visit to 4-Play to scout out the scene. Unsurprisingly, Tom and Ravi, the two other male PIs, had figured Ry needed a hand—or, rather, two more sets of eyes. Then Evelyn, the head of the agency, and Kari, had insisted on coming along because they were curious. Ry didn't remember anyone asking their admin assistant if she wanted to go, yet she'd turned up.

And buttoned-to-the-neck Hayley was actually watching the stripper. Raptly. With a flush on her cheeks and eyes wide behind her glasses. Prim and proper as she always seemed, she must be embarrassed, yet she didn't glance down or away.

He looked back to the dancer, who was flirting the sides of her thong up and down her curvy hips. A moment later she was naked, but for bright red, very high shoes with platform soles and stiletto heels.

"Oh my God, it's Stripper Barbie," Evelyn muttered, and Kari let out a splutter of laughter.

Ry had to grin. The woman, with her platinum hair, obvious boob job, and full Brazilian wax, did look rather like a plastic doll. Her smile was artificial too, and her performance was more like nude gymnastics than an erotic dance that connected with the music and her audience.

She grabbed a large white towel, tossed it to the stage, and got down on all fours. Crawling, twisting, writhing this way and that on her hands and knees, her stomach, her back, she flaunted her body. Her legs spread, flashing longer and longer glimpses of her naked crotch.

Even if he'd been alone at the club, Ry would have had no desire to join the half dozen men in the front row for a closer view. He sure as hell had nothing against pussy, but this dancer wasn't doing it for him. Maybe because, though she was attractive and athletic, she was only going through the motions.

For him, he'd rather have a woman with a less perfect body and a lot more genuine enthusiasm. Besides, he was a man of action, not a voyeur. If he wanted a woman, he found one and took her to bed.

When the stripper's last song ended and the DJ said, "Let's hear it for the stunning Vivi LeDare," the audience gave her a decent round of applause. But no cheers or whistles.

A male staff member came onstage and wiped down the stripper pole, then the DJ said, "Now you're in for a sexy treat, so please welcome Kat Dancer."

"That's our subject," Ry muttered to the others. Jennifer Mortimer, in real life.

He'd seen her in day clothes and seen her promo photos, but

neither had prepared him for the woman who prowled onto the stage to the sound of "Black Velvet." She wasn't much over five feet, but she had attitude and commanded attention as she went into a seductive dance nicely matched to the music.

Clad in a black bodysuit made out of some gleaming velvety material, her body was compact but definitely curvy. Normally, Jennifer wore her black hair in a simple ponytail, but now shiny waves rippled over her shoulders and down her back almost to her waist. Her makeup exaggerated her eyes, tilting them at the corners in a way that was vaguely catlike.

Her dance had a feline feel too, going from slinky to playful to arrogant, always very sensual. And always, she played to her audience, drawing them in with her eyes and smile as she seductively peeled away one piece of her costume, then another.

Ry's attention shifted as a busty redhead clad in a lacy minidress over a pink bikini strolled up to their table with a flirtatious smile. "Would anyone like a private show?"

"Thanks anyhow," Ry said. Since they'd arrived, a dancer had made a similar offer every few minutes.

She winked at him. "Next time, sugar."

"Don'tcha think I should get a lap dance?" Tom said. "Like, in the name of research?"

Kari snorted. "Your wife would kill you."

Ry and Ravi exchanged grins. Everyone knew Tom was joking. He was devoted to his wife. But he liked to play the goof, a little rough around the edges. It worked for him as a PI. People revealed things to him that they wouldn't to a more articulate, sophisticated man. Ry only wished he'd drop the role when it was just the PIs together.

Ry turned back to the stage. Kat Dancer, now wearing only a black lacy bra and G-string and shiny black high-heeled boots, was working the stripper pole. Her moves weren't as gymnastic as Vivi LeDare's, but to him they were more seductive.

She seemed totally involved, as if the music rippled under her skin, thrilled through her blood, and drove her movements. And always, she connected with her audience, drawing them in with teasing smiles and come-hither gestures.

He could just imagine those lonely guys dreaming of her keeping them company.

Damn, she was good. Good enough that arousal stirred in him.

All the same, she was a stripper. Not that he had anything against strippers; they were doing a job just like everyone else. But the fact that it was a job—even if Kat honestly enjoyed the music and the performance—made the situation too impersonal to be a real turn-on for Ry.

If she'd been his lover, dancing for him like this because she wanted to, he'd have been as hard as that stripper pole by now.

But she wasn't. And in fact, she was his client's wife.

He glanced away from the woman onstage, and again noticed Hayley. Well, wasn't that interesting. Her body was moving as if she, like the dancer, was feeling the music.

A tendril of light brown hair had escaped her normally tight knot. The way it clung to her flushed cheek told him her skin was damp. Her lips were open, then they closed and he saw her swallow hard, her throat rippling above the buttoned-up neck of her tailored blouse. Her tongue came out, licked her lips, then rested between them, tip showing.

She lifted a hand and with one finger pressed her glasses farther up her nose.

Then, with a quick wriggle, she slid out of her jacket. The movement arched her back, made her breasts press against the cotton of her shirt. Her head moved restlessly and she stretched her neck. Then graceful long fingers stroked her throat in a gesture that was innately female and sensual. Not the kind of gesture he'd ever seen Hayley make before.

Or maybe she had, but he'd never looked closely enough. A

PI was supposed to be observant, so how come he'd never noticed that her hair wasn't plain brown but more the color of butterscotch, her fingers and neck were lovely, and her rack was pretty damn impressive?

She stared at the stage, oblivious to his scrutiny. Her lips were parted, a natural pink, moist and gleaming in the dim light. Her hands thrust into her hair, loosening more tendrils. Then she unbuttoned the top couple buttons of her shirt, leaving her hand resting on that slender throat, just by the hollow where her pulse beat.

She looked . . . turned on.

And hot. Hayley Croft actually looked hot.

And he, who'd never paid much attention to her before tonight, was getting seriously aroused.

Not by Kat Dancer onstage—who was now down to just her G-string, boots, and that shifting, shimmering black hair—but by straitlaced Hayley.

Freaking bizarre.

Doubly so, since she was probably a lesbian, getting all turned on by another woman.

Maybe she felt his gaze because she glanced around, catching him staring.

She gave a start, and the color on her cheeks deepened.

He should've looked away, but couldn't. If the woman had any experience with men, she'd read the pure lust in his eyes.

If she was a lesbian, maybe she wouldn't see it. If she was a feminist, she'd probably want to slap him.

Instead, something flared in the golden-brown eyes behind those dark-framed glasses.

An answering heat.

No. Must be his imagination. Light reflecting off her lenses.

She'd never shown the slightest interest in him. Never unbuttoned a button, nor sent him a flirtatious glance. It was the female stripper, not a male PI, who turned her sexual crank.

"Informative as this is," Evelyn said in a dryly humorous tone that made both him and Hayley start, and turn to the older woman, "what exactly are we learning about our subject?"

"That she's one damned fine stripper," Tom said, gaze glued to the stage.

Ry glanced over to see that Kat had discarded the G-string to reveal a narrow strip of black pubic hair. She collected a white towel and flicked it onto the floor.

"Oh, yeah," Kari said. "She's a really talented dancer, and really into it. I admit, I wasn't expecting to see such a high quality performance."

"She sure knows how to perform," Hayley said in that soft, barely there voice, "but she's not that skilled a dancer. I doubt she's had formal training. What she's got going for her is great choreography, knowing how to use her body, and feeling the music."

They all turned to look at the admin assistant.

"How do you know all that?" Ravi asked the question that had been on the tip of Ry's own tongue.

2

Hayley wanted to press her hands to her burning cheeks and retreat to the ladies room. But the five PIs—even Tom had actually turned away from the stage—were staring at her.

Ravi, a really nice man, had phrased his question politely and Evelyn's and Kari's expressions were curious. Ry's face, however, bore an expression that pretty much robbed her of breath, intelligent thought, and the ability to speak.

Which, come to think of it, was his usual effect on her.

It was both heaven and hell, working with Ry Montana. Bad enough he had thick, always-tousled black hair, piercing blue eyes, and a perpetually stubbled jaw. Add in that devil-may-care air, and he was just about the sexiest guy on the planet.

Mostly, he didn't notice her, so she went her quiet way, savoring the eye candy and storing up images to fuel her midnight fantasies. Embarrassed by her attraction to him, she'd been kind of grateful he was oblivious to her, but also a little annoyed. And annoyed at herself for being upset.

Hayley wasn't the type of woman who sought office romances or traded on her sexuality. She firmly believed that in the workplace women should be treated no differently than men. With her abundant figure, the only way she could ensure that attention was on her skills rather than her curves was to dress conservatively and professionally, downplaying her femininity. The one time she'd worn a sexy dress to an office Christmas party, back when she worked for the government, her boss's boss had hit on her in a really nasty way. Remembering still made her nauseous.

Bottom line, she could hardly blame Ry for barely noticing she was female.

But then, tonight . . .

When their eyes had met, she'd felt a distinct sizzle. All the way to her crotch, where steamy arousal dampened her panties.

For a moment she'd thought he was actually turned on by her. Then she'd realized, likely it was the dancer who'd made his eyes blaze that way. She only hoped he hadn't read her own arousal on her face.

She shouldn't have joined the PIs at 4-Play tonight. Shouldn't have indulged her secret craving for adventure.

Her gran, who'd raised her since she was eight, had done her best to stamp out that itch for excitement. She'd drummed into Hayley's head the importance of being practical and responsible, and Hayley really did believe her.

But every once in a while, the itch needed scratching. Only, of course, when there was a practical justification—okay, a way of rationalizing the indulgence. Like tonight. It was research. She'd do more effective work on the Mortimer case if she better understood their subject.

That amazingly sensual, sexy, attractive woman on stage, who held the audience in the palm of her hand.

"Hayley?" Kari sounded concerned.

With a start, Hayley realized they were all still watching her, their expressions varying from curiosity to impatience, waiting for her answer.

"I have some dance training and I've performed onstage," she said softly.

"You dance?" Tom asked disbelievingly.

Ry's brows arched and she had trouble reading his expression. The simple fact that he'd focused on her was enough to fluster her.

"I did. Ballet." She didn't say she'd taken ten years of lessons, dancing until her ever-expanding breasts and hips had become an embarrassment. Nor did she say that, at home alone, she loved to put on some raunchy rock and roll or sultry jazz and get down and dirty.

"Oh, ballet." Tom turned his attention back to the stage.

So did the other PIs. Hayley, too, relieved to no longer be the center of attention.

Kat Dancer finished her act and everyone applauded enthusiastically, including Hayley.

She'd never been sexually drawn to another woman, but she'd sure been aroused by Kat's performance. Even, to a lesser degree, by the one given by Vivi LeDare.

It wasn't the women so much as the combination of music, sensuality, and lack of inhibition. Hayley had almost been able to imagine herself in their shoes, to feel the thrill of performing in front of an audience. Of captivating them. It was something she'd always enjoyed about ballet.

But ballet had been restrictive more than liberating. A dancer had to conform to a choreographer's vision rather than let her body interpret the music. And never had it been sexual.

When she'd come here tonight, she'd expected sleaze. And yes, there was some of that. But there was also sensuality, sexuality, male adoration, the provocative pulse of music in your veins.

What must it be like to be up on that stage? Better, even, than ballet, she guessed.

The next dancer took the stage. Curvaceous and hard bodied, with blond-streaked dark hair, she wore a sexy parody of a biker costume. Music pounded out of the speakers. Hard-driving rock. Def Leppard's "Pour Some Sugar on Me."

The song wouldn't have been Hayley's choice, but the woman onstage was selling it, raunchy and in your face.

"Okay," Ry said quietly, "we've been here long enough. Don't want to be too noticeable."

The others leaned forward so they could hear, and Hayley knew the loud music would make it impossible for anyone else to overhear.

"I'll take the shift tomorrow," Tom said promptly.

At their Monday morning meeting, Ry had suggested that the male PIs make some visits to 4-Play this week to see who Kat Dancer interacted with. To look for sexual vibes with a club manager, DJ, bartender, or bouncer, and to keep an eye out for drug transactions.

"Ry, I've been thinking—" Evelyn started, then broke off when Vivi LeDare, now clad in a skimpy red slip-style dress, came over to ask if anyone would like a VIP dance.

After they'd shaken their heads and she'd gone, Evelyn resumed, voice low. In her fifties, she ran The Private Eye with a nice blend of flexibility and vigilance and they all respected her. "It would also make sense for a woman to try to get close to the subject," she said. "Women confide in other women."

"That's true," Hayley murmured. There were secrets she'd never shared with a man, only with girlfriends. The thought reminded her of how much she missed her best friends, Steph who was back in Victoria and Margaret who'd moved to Toronto.

"Makes sense," Ry said.

"I'm around Jennifer's age," Kari said. "I could bump into her at the grocery store or a coffee shop and try to strike up a friendship."

Ry shook his head. "These days she only hangs out with strippers."

"She's gone over to the dark side," Ravi said in a pseudo *Star Wars* voice, making them chuckle.

"Yeah, in a sense," Ry said. "Her life used to be centered around her husband, home, and friends. Now she's focused on the strip club world."

Hayley glanced toward the stage, where the dancer was now clad in a gold bikini. "Likely she now shares confidences with other dancers."

When she turned back to Ry, his gaze was on her, even though Kari was saying, "Yeah, a girl has to talk to someone."

The man's attention made Hayley squirm in a way that wasn't entirely unpleasant. For once, he was actually seeing her. Was it possible there was sexual interest in those blue eyes, or was she imagining it? The mere possibility sent a charge straight to her pussy.

"Hey," Tom joked, "I could date a stripper, see if she'd gossip about Kat Dancer."

They all laughed and he said, "Yeah, I'd have trouble selling that to my wife."

"Too bad we can't send someone in undercover as a dancer," Evelyn said.

"Ooh," Kari squealed, "what fun! I'd *so* volunteer, but somehow I don't think they'd hire me." She leaned back from the table and patted her seven-month baby bump.

"Don't think they'd hire me either," Evelyn said dryly, fingering a lock of gray hair.

"So much for that idea," Ravi said.

"I could do it." The words burst out of Hayley's mouth without conscious thought.

And again, five pairs of eyes were staring at her. This time with disbelief.

After a moment, Ravi summoned a kind smile. "You're not a PI, Hayley."

Oh my God, what had she done? Now she should politely agree, withdraw her offer, and shut up.

But the same crazy impulse that had made her volunteer now made her say, "You've used me for surveillance."

"Um . . ." Ravi exchanged glances with Ry and Tom. "Because you, uh, have the knack of fitting in."

"Then why couldn't I fit in here?" She glared defiantly at the three men. Damn it, she was an attractive woman, a damned fine dancer, and smart too.

And she'd just used—at least in her thoughts—more damns than she usually did in a day.

"Drugs and gangs might be involved," Ry said. "Can't send you into a potentially dangerous situation."

"Talking to another woman could be dangerous?" she responded. "I doubt it. And don't forget, I'm the one who got that librarian to open up about the straying husband who was meeting his lover in the medieval weaponry section."

"Next time we need someone to go undercover in a library, you'll be the first one we ask." Ry's eyes danced.

Damn the man. He was laughing at her.

"Ry has a point about drugs and gangs, Hayley," Evelyn said. "Who knows what you might run into?"

"Then I'd run the other way. Besides, you know I've been studying kickboxing." That was another activity her craving for adventure had led her to. She'd had no trouble justifying it to herself; a sensible woman should know self-defense.

As for going undercover as an exotic dancer at a strip club, though . . . Why was she being so persistent? If Ry actually let her do it and Gran ever found out . . .

Her grandmother had been delighted when, after getting her BA, Hayley went to work for the provincial government. She had great job security and excellent employee benefits—and lived in Victoria where she'd grown up, nice and close to Gran.

But after three years, Hayley had been bored out of her mind. When she'd seen The Private Eye's ad for an admin assistant, she'd leaped to apply. A PI agency would be exciting, and so would moving from small town Victoria to the larger, more cosmopolitan Vancouver.

She'd justified her decision by saying she needed wider job experience.

Stripping would certainly give her that!

But no, Ry would never go for it. She was safe.

Safe. Again. Just the way Gran wanted.

Kari broke the weighted silence. "I agree with Hayley."

Hayley couldn't suppress a squeak of surprise as the other woman went on. "I think she can do this. She has dance training, she knows about choreography, and she's got a great build."

Ry's gaze drifted down her body, and she resisted the urge to refasten the buttons at her throat. Either that or undo another couple.

"She does?" Tom said.

Hayley gritted her teeth.

Kari bopped Tom's shoulder with her fist, not gently. "Remove foot from mouth, insert beer bottle, and shut up." Then she turned to Ry. "Where's Kat Dancer scheduled to perform in the next month?"

"Next week it's a club in Langley, then it's The Naked Truth downtown for two weeks. That's her most regular gig."

"The Naked Truth?" Kari said. "It's a classy place, isn't it?"

"Yeah," Ravi said. "My girlfriend and I and another couple went there a few months ago. It's only open at night, unlike a lot of clubs that open at noon. It's expensive, nicely decorated, has a dress code. And the security is great."

"That'd give us time to get Hayley ready," Kari said.

Hayley took a deep breath. "Ready?"

She couldn't dance onstage stark naked. Damn, if only she'd

thought before she opened her mouth. "Uh, maybe this was a bad idea. I mean, I'm not exactly stripper material."

Across the table, Ry cocked an amused eyebrow.

Kari grinned. "They didn't think Sandra Bullock was beauty pageant material either."

"Huh?" Tom said.

"*Miss Congeniality?*" Kari said impatiently. "Where the FBI agent went undercover as a beauty pageant contestant."

Hmm. Sandra Bullock's character had gone from being a total tomboy to strutting her stuff onstage in a bathing suit.

"Oh, yeah," Tom said. "But that was Sandra Bullock. I mean, no offense Hayley, but . . ."

"What did I tell you about shutting up?" Kari scolded.

A quick flash of smile lit Tom's lips, making Hayley wonder if he was putting them on. There was more to the man than the bumbling, rather crude façade he presented, or he wouldn't be such a successful PI.

Eyes gleaming, Kari fixed her gaze on Hayley. "Oh, girlfriend, we are going to have so much fun!"

Girlfriend? The word made her smile. Up to now, Kari'd been friendly but only in a businesslike way.

Kari turned to Evelyn. "What do you think? Shall we do this? Will you help?"

This was Ry's case, but Evelyn, as head of the agency, had ultimate responsibility and could veto the idea.

To Hayley's surprise, the stocky woman nodded her head. "I'm in favor so long as we ensure Hayley's safety, and the client approves the expense. I think Hayley can do this. And yes, I'll help in whatever way I can."

"Well?" Kari asked Ry. "It's your case."

Hayley should stop this now. Be firm and say she'd only been kidding, she could never be an exotic dancer. But then she'd look foolish.

Besides, Ry would say no. He'd never believe her capable of doing it.

The thought hurt, and irked her, but it was also reassuring. She'd get out of this with a shred of dignity intact.

The corners of his mouth curled slowly into a wicked grin. "Go for it, ladies."

Hayley's mouth dropped open. He'd called her bluff.

The PIs were offering her an important undercover assignment. Which meant she had a practical justification for saying yes. If she wanted to.

She'd craved excitement. Wondered what it would be like to dance on that stage.

Ry, eyes gleaming, added, "I can't wait to see what you come up with."

The truth—the naked truth—hit Hayley.

If she did this, she'd not only be dancing onstage, she'd be doing it without a stitch of clothing. In front of the world.

Including the panty-meltingly, scorchingly hot Ry Montana.

3

_____

Backstage at The Naked Truth two weeks later, adrenaline pumped through Hayley's blood like the fizz in a shaken-up champagne bottle. She was all set to explode, and only hoped the excitement would spill out in a fantastic performance rather than a quick dash to the bathroom to hork out her guts.

Right now, it was a fifty-fifty toss-up.

She reminded herself she'd felt exactly the same when, at age eight, she'd anticipated dancing her first ballet solo. Then, she'd ended up loving the thrill of performing and the audience's applause.

That dressing room had been filled with girls in pink and white tutus, tights, and toe shoes. Tonight, the dressing room at The Naked Truth held a dozen women in sultry makeup, varying stages of undress, and costumes ranging from black leather dominatrix to cheerleader.

Tonight, Sunday—usually a slow night at strip clubs—was the weekly A&A Night. Amateurs & Auditions.

Their client's wife wasn't here. She was booked to dance

Monday through Saturday. The winner of tonight's audition would receive a contract for the same week.

It was Hayley's goal to become that winner.

If she could manage not to puke onstage.

The scent of warring perfumes and hair sprays didn't help her stomach. And they irritated the contact lenses she was still getting used to.

Over the past days, she'd visited two other clubs with Kari, Evelyn, and Donna, a retired stripper they'd recruited to prepare her. In the audience, she'd analyzed the dancers' performances and used visualization to imagine herself onstage. The PIs said visualization helped them prepare for undercover work. And that's all this was, after all. An assignment.

Yes, she'd be naked for a few minutes. But really, her nudity was simply an undercover disguise.

"Yeah, I'll just keep telling myself that," she muttered nervously. And she'd keep mum when she spoke to Gran.

The woman who shared a mirror with her, a fresh-faced blonde in a sexy nurse costume, chuckled. "Strip virgin?"

Hayley nodded. "You?"

"I dance every few weeks as an amateur. I'm an accountant, and it's fun to let loose." She winked, false eyelashes brushing her cheek. "Let it all hang out. How about you?"

"I'm auditioning for a job here." On A&A night, the club welcomed both auditioning dancers and amateurs.

"Cool. You've got a good look going." She studied Hayley appraisingly.

"You think so?" Hayley gazed doubtfully at her own reflection.

A reflection she barely recognized, in a form-fitting mockery of a business suit. Complete with a chopped-off jacket that left her midriff bare, a micro mini that barely cleared her bum, and a pair of shiny black stiletto heel platform sandals that terrified her.

Her makeover and training had been both humiliating—dancing in ballet shoes was one thing, but when it came to five-inch heels she'd been reborn as a klutz—and strangely affirming, like when the others told her she was gorgeous.

"Oh yeah," the nurse said. "Guys look at a girl like you and all they can think about is getting your hair down and glasses off, and undoing those buttons."

If Hayley hadn't been so nervous, she'd have grinned. Normally, she did wear glasses—real ones not fakes like now, her buttons were buttoned, and her hair was pinned up in the same ballerina's bun as tonight.

Normally, she dressed to avoid crude gazes and comments, the kind she'd heard from boys and some of the other girls when she was an overly curvaceous adolescent. The kind her old boss's boss had made when he propositioned her.

Tonight, though, she wanted men to find her sexy.

An unfamiliar concept. Yet she could accept it because she was choosing the situation, rules were in place to protect her, and she'd be in control.

A dancer burst into the dressing room, fresh from the stage and wrapped in a beach towel, flushed and giggling. Others had returned in tears, some cool and collected, several crowing about what a great time they'd had.

As a striking black woman in a sparkly silver costume headed for the stage, Hayley pressed a hand over her tummy. "I'm after her. I think I'm going to be sick."

The nurse-dancer touched her arm reassuringly. "You'll do great. It's all about attitude. Got any friends in the audience you can dance for?"

When she'd peeked out into the club earlier, Hayley had been reassured to see there were a fair number of women. A lot of the A&A dancers had brought their own cheering sections. In fact, one of the amateurs had said this was part of her stagette.

"A couple," Hayley said. Evelyn and Kari had come to lend moral support. Donna wasn't there. They'd feared someone at The Naked Truth would recognize her from her days of dancing as Roxy Brown, and blow Hayley's cover before she'd even gotten started.

"How about your boyfriend? Mine's out there. He loves seeing me dance." Another long-lashed wink. "Makes both of us horny."

"I'm not dating anyone." She hadn't since she'd left Victoria. There, she'd gone out with a government employee who worked one floor down, but their relationship had been more about convenience than passion.

Unfortunately, the men she attracted didn't satisfy her crazy craving for adventure. She didn't want to settle down with a perfectly nice guy and have a perfectly nice home and kids.

Well, yes, she did yearn for that stuff—love, a home, a family—but she wanted more. Something with an edge, a fizz, a tingle.

A man like Ry Montana.

Thank heavens he wasn't in the audience tonight, or she'd never have the guts to go onstage. She'd made Evelyn and Kari promise not to tell the male PIs when she was debuting.

The middle-aged Asian woman who was coordinating A&A night called out, "Penny Catalina? You're on in five."

"That's me." Hayley's voice squeaked. After brainstorming dancer names from cheesy to outrageous, she and her coaches had played the old "what's your stripper name?" game: put together the name of your first pet and the street you lived on as a kid.

Donna said Penny was friendly and approachable, which customers loved, and Catalina added a California-girl appeal.

The costumed nurse hugged her. "Knock 'em dead, Penny. And have *fun!*"

Carrying her own towel, Hayley walked from the dressing

room on trembling legs. Close to the stage, the music she'd barely been able to hear over the female chatter turned out to be the Police classic "Roxanne."

She closed her eyes and let the rhythm fill her. She'd always loved music. All types of music. Donna had advised, "When you start out, concentrate on the music. Become the music."

Each dancer put together her own CD of four songs, totaling about eighteen minutes. Hayley had asked, "What kind of music?" and Donna had said, "Customers' tastes are all over the place, from country to rock to rap. Pick something that makes you feel sexy."

Eighteen minutes on stage. It seemed like an impossibly long time.

Past the curtain, applause, cheers, and whistles sounded. A few seconds later, the black woman came through the curtain, wrapped loosely in a white towel and carrying her sparkly silver costume.

She gave Hayley a big grin. "That was awesome. Go for it, girl, the audience is great."

Hayley should have smiled back, should have said thanks, but at the moment she needed all her concentration to keep from throwing up.

The DJ said, "Next up is Penny Catalina."

Oh, shit.

What had she been thinking? No way could she do this.

She'd have to withdraw.

But the agency had invested time and the client had invested money in preparing her. Equally important, she had to prove to herself, and to Ry, that she could do this. She might not win, but she damn well wasn't going to chicken out.

On wooden legs, Hayley forced herself to walk toward the curtain. *I've done this before, in my ballet days. Gone onstage. Performed. Soloed. I was good, really good, and I loved it.*

The DJ said, "Penny's a strip virgin, and she's auditioning

for a job here at The Naked Truth. Please give her a warm welcome."

Her music started. Donna had told her to begin with a piece
she totally loved.

It was Irene Cara's "What a Feeling" from *Flashdance*. Hayley had danced to the 1980s movie dozens of times in the privacy of her living room. Donna said she'd never seen anyone
strip to it before, but she'd approved it because the beat was
good, the lyrics were great, and, most importantly, it really
spoke to Hayley.

And it did, as always. First it was the lyrics, speaking of a
dream and fear, that led her forward, one step then another, past
the curtain and onto the stage.

She froze, disconcerted by the stage lighting and by the audience's clapping.

They were waiting for her to perform. Waiting to love her,
or hate her.

She did what Irene Cara told her to in the song, and closed
her eyes, letting the music wind its way into her.

The song started slowly, which was good because her knees
were trembling, her ankles shaky in those ridiculously high
heels. Still, she managed to step forward, the shoes almost forcing her hips to sway and her chest and bum to stick out as if she
was flaunting them.

Keeping her head high was second nature, but she had to
concentrate on the stripper walk Donna had taught her, and on
not falling off the platform shoes.

Gradually, as the music, the lyrics, the emotion of the piece
seeped into her, she loosened up and really began to feel what
she was doing so that the movements started to feel natural. She
was a fit, beautiful woman, dancing to music she loved, bringing her own sensuality to life.

When Irene Cara sang about taking your passion and making it happen, Hayley smiled.

She had a passion for excitement, and yes, right now she was making it happen.

Beaming with pride and the thrill of the moment, she opened her eyes. It took a moment for them to adjust, and then—Oh, my God. There really was an audience out there. She faltered.

The stage at The Naked Truth was teardrop shaped, with a semicircle of seating right beside it, then a mixture of tables and horseshoe-shaped booths going back and up in tiers so everyone could see. And the place was packed.

She felt like a rabbit, pinned by the intent gazes of more than a hundred hungry wolves.

"Go, Penny!" a female voice shouted. Kari, bless her heart.

A male wolf whistle sounded from the back of the room, and Hayley forced herself to move again. To breathe. To try to recapture that connection with the energy of the song.

She should work the whole stage, but she was too nervous so she stayed in the center. Away from the ring of men sitting by the edge in what Donna jokingly referred to as Gyno Row.

Stop thinking, Hayley told herself. *Pretend this is simply another practice session.*

This time she didn't close her eyes, but let her gaze go unfocused, which wasn't hard to do given the odd lighting, her contact lenses, and the fake glasses she wore.

Swaying in what she hoped was a provocative fashion, she followed her choreography and began to unbutton her suit jacket. She and Donna had shopped consignment stores and selected a charcoal and white pinstripe a size too small, then shortened the jacket and skirt.

Under the jacket, Hayley wore only a black lacy bra, also a size too small. Her breasts almost tumbled out the top.

All the buttons undone now, she held the sides of the jacket together with her hands, keeping her whole body moving in a sultry dance. The shoes forced her to move slowly, and Donna had told her to draw out every motion and make it sensual, seductive.

To revel in her own physicality, her sexuality, her female essence and power.

"If the thought of dancing for all those guys turns you on," the ex-stripper had said, "then milk that, ride it, use it."

Mmm. At the moment, the idea of all those eyes—eyes she was avoiding—was more scary than arousing.

"But if it's intimidating," Donna had gone on, "then think about one special guy, one you're really hot for, and dance just for him."

She arched her back, threw back her head, and imagined Ry, with his devil-may-care grin. And a hot, smoldering fire in his eyes.

The fire of arousal. From watching her.

Teasing him, she flirted the front edges of the jacket back and forth to reveal, then conceal, her lace-clad breasts. Feeling the heat of his gaze, the skin of her chest quivered with awareness each time she brushed it.

Deliberately, she let a finger drift across her breast and felt her nipple tighten. Seducing Ry, and seducing herself in the process.

The audience was getting into the act, with cries of approval and, "More! Take it off!"

She ignored the plea. Instead, undulating to the music, she released her jacket and reached up to free the pins holding her hair in its bun. Then she pulled off the elastic and silky waves slid loose. Her hair had always been a mousy light brown, but now it had platinum and gold highlights and she knew they'd catch the light.

Imagining Ry watching, longing to run his fingers through her hair, she tossed her head slowly and luxuriously. The soft, sensual brush of hair against her face made her crave its touch on her shoulders, the tops of her breasts.

She slid the jacket partway down her arms, holding it tight across her chest. Teasing Ry.

The Irene Cara song was ending, which meant . . . Hayley took a deep breath, then thrust the jacket away from her, let it slide down her arms, and tossed it aside, leaving her in her bra as the music faded away.

Voices cheered and Kari called, "Way to go, Penny!" as the music segued into "Brick House."

Hair and jacket during the first song, they'd all decided. Glasses and skirt during the second one.

She concentrated on the upbeat music, the cocky way it made her feel. Flaunting her near-naked torso, Hayley touched one earpiece of the fake glasses, then whipped them off and tossed them aside.

The next moves they'd choreographed centered around the two poles near either side of the stage. Until two weeks ago Hayley had never taken a pole dancing lesson, so this was all new to her. Her hands were still building calluses.

She realized that nervousness had made her quicken her pace. In her head, she heard Donna saying, "Slow it down, Hayley. Slow is sexy."

Yes, sexy. Her body was sexy, her movements were sexy. Her man was watching, getting turned on. Hayley moved toward the pole as if it were a lover. As if it were Ry.

A nice idea, but the shoes threw her off balance and she stumbled. Quickly she added a hip thrust to try and disguise her clumsiness. Thank God for those ankle straps.

When she reached for the pole, her hands were damp with sweat. Wishing she could wipe them on something, she realized she'd almost forgotten an important step in her routine.

The tiny pin-striped skirt had to come off.

She ran her hands over her slowly grinding hips to dry her palms, and let the music carry her. Like the song said, she was stacked, and she wasn't going to hold anything back.

Slowly, teasingly, she slid down her zipper. Imagining Ry's burning gaze on her, she flirted the skirt down a little to reveal the bare skin of her tummy and the lacy black band of her thong as her hips pumped a sultry rhythm.

Donna had told her to get a few coats of fake tan, and under the black light her skin looked healthy. Besides, the tan helped hide the bruises from learning to pole dance.

Though she'd always kept in shape, the workouts she'd gone through over the last two weeks had made her more toned than ever. Oh yeah, she was sculpted, voluptuous.

She gyrated proudly to the music. Ry, seeing her like this, would be so turned on, he'd be hungry—almost desperate—to see more of her. To worship her body with his eyes.

To imagine making love to her with his hands, his tongue, his erect cock.

The thought sent shivers of arousal through her. She let the skirt slide down, proudly stepped free of it, and kicked it away, leaving her in a bra, thong, and stripper shoes.

Oh yeah, she was a brick house, and she was going to let it all hang out and bring her man to his knees with lust.

Finally, she dared to really look at the audience.

"Share it with them," Donna had told her. "Bring them in. Seduce them. Use your eyes and your smile. Those are your two most important tools."

Okay, she had tits and ass, musicality, and dance skill. Now it was time to add eyes and smile. The way Kat Dancer did.

She caught a glimpse of Kari and Evelyn, both waving enthusiastically, and flashed them a quick smile.

But no, if she was going to feel sexy, she couldn't focus on them. She needed a man, one she could pretend was Ry.

There, at the back of the room. He sat in a dimly lit corner, which helped the illusion that he could be Ry. Of course, the PI would never wear that suit and tie, the slicked-back hair, or glasses. But she could pretend, and that would make it easier to fall into the sexy fantasy that she was dancing for her own hot man.

She shot him a saucy wink and her most tempting smile, then turned toward the pole.

As she twined around it—forward and back, in and out, up and down—she worked it as if it were a hard male body. Ry's body.

He'd be watching. Imagining the same thing. She tossed her hair, sent him a steamy glance full of promise.

She wished she could relax into the music and her own sexuality, her imagined seduction of the hot PI, but pole work was too new to her. Donna had kept things simple and Hayley had picked up the moves quickly, but they still took concentration.

And so did remembering to switch from one pole to the other, so everyone in the audience got a closer view of her moves.

As she did a flying spin around the pole, followed by vertical splits with one leg on the ground and the other stretched up the pole, she was so focused on her routine that she could almost forget her body was all but naked.

But when the music changed to George Thorogood's "Bad to the Bone" and she switched poles again, the choreography she and Donna had worked out called for her to tone down the athleticism and make the pole work even raunchier. To make every guy in the audience feel like he was bad to the bone and wanted to make her squeal, just like the song said.

Thank God for the music, the choreography, the numerous practice sessions. The beat of the music was irresistible, her moves fit it perfectly, she felt almost natural as she turned her back to the audience, spread her legs, and bent from the waist to grip the pole.

She ground her hips in time to the music, thrusting her bum toward the audience. Working it, grinding out an invitation.

And in her mind, Ry was watching, wanting to fuck her, almost exploding with need.

And damned if she wasn't flushed and tingling with arousal too.

Having that kind of power over a man like Ry Montana. What an erotic thought.

Almost in a trance, she moved to the other pole and gyrated, imagining herself a sex goddess in Ry's eyes. Feeling the burn of his lust, like actual heated fingers caressing her skin.

She imagined Ry's gaze, his fingers curving around her bare butt cheeks, squeezing her firm flesh. Trailing down the outside of the thong, and between her legs.

She writhed and twisted against the imaginary pressure. Felt the throb and pulse of need in her pussy. Tossed her hair and shot a smoky glance over her shoulder, letting him see what he did to her.

Then she straightened and took the center of the stage, running her hands through her hair, then down the front of her body, lingering as they brushed over her bra-clad breasts.

This experience had become surreal. Yes, she was vaguely aware of the audience, of individual faces and expressions, of a sense of collective appreciation and even lust, but she was distanced from them.

All except for that man at the back, who she'd designated as Ry.

It was as if she moved in a parallel reality, dancing only for herself, for the music, for Ry.

Each motion of her body thrust her breasts into her hands and she wanted to moan with pleasure, and the need for his touch.

She slipped one strap down her shoulder, then the other, then undid the front clasp. Only her hands held the bra in place as she tossed Ry a teasing glance.

The audience cheered, whistled, begged her to take it off.

She knew one of those whistles came from Ry. So she sent him a sultry wink and let the bra drop.

But immediately she replaced it with her hands, feeling the firm plumpness of her breasts, the nipples taut with arousal. The breasts that had embarrassed her as a teen now felt glorious.

The music changed and she heard the opening bars of her final number, Pink's sexy rendition of the Divinyls "I Touch Myself." A song that, right now, seemed absolutely perfect for the way she felt, dancing for Ry and feeling his gaze on her.

Releasing the bra, she raised her hands, twined them in her hair, and gyrated in her thong.

4

Watching from the back of The Naked Truth, wearing a "disguise" of drab business suit, glasses, and slicked-back hair, Ry gaped at the sight of Hayley's breasts. No artificial melons these, they were full, round, lush, sensual, and he'd bet 100% genuine.

He wanted to touch them. To feel that incredible combination of firmness and softness.

Damn, was this really the agency's buttoned-up administrative assistant? God, she was hot.

She swayed to the music as if she was in a cocoon of pure sexuality. Those long, graceful fingers, tonight tipped in red, threaded through her hair, pulling it back from her face and letting it fall again. Then her hands drifted down her body to caress her breasts with aching slowness.

Touching herself, like in the song. Who was she thinking of? Was she getting off on the audience's lust, or dreaming of a lover?

Talk about aching, his own hands ached with the need to

touch her smooth skin, tweak her pebbled nipples, make her gasp with pleasure.

He pulled on the knot of his tie, loosening it so he could breathe.

Did she have a lover?

Evelyn had hired her months ago, yet he knew nothing about her except that all their files—paper and electronic—were in perfect order, and the assignments he gave her were handled quickly and efficiently.

Not exactly sexy stuff. But what she was doing on stage sure as hell was. Ry wished he was closer and could see better, but if she recognized him it might throw her out of her performance.

She and the female PIs had kept quiet about her audition, but the Mortimer case was Ry's and he took his responsibilities seriously. Research had told him the most likely way Hayley could get a contract to dance at The Naked Truth was by winning a Sunday night audition.

He'd tried to tell himself it was a sense of duty that had brought him here tonight. But yeah, he'd been intrigued by the reserved admin assistant's offer to dance.

Being a PI, and before that a cop, it took a lot to surprise him. But when Hayley—aka Penny Catalina—had taken the stage, all he'd been able to think was, "Oh, fuck, is she ever hot!"

His cock had sprung to attention, and now his hard-on was as firm as that pole she'd been gyrating around. If he released it from his pants, it'd lift the fucking table.

As he stared hungrily at her, her hands slid down to hook in the sides of her thong. This time she didn't tease her audience, she skimmed it off in one quick movement, like she couldn't wait to get naked.

Naked, but for those fuck-me shoes.

Her smooth body was decorated by brown curls of pubic

hair that were . . . He squinted. Holy shit. They were trimmed into an arrow shape that pointed the way to her sex.

He'd never seen anything so provocative. The woman was stunning. The sexiest sight he'd ever laid eyes on.

She took a white towel and spread it, then went down on her hands and knees. Back arched, movements fluid and sinuous, she crawled toward the edge of the stage and the guys in the front row howled approval.

Ry tried to whistle, but his mouth was too dry. One hand fumbled for his beer glass but didn't find it, and he sure as hell wasn't going to look away from the stage where Hayley's breasts hung down, full and tantalizing, in front of a row of drooling men.

When he'd agreed she could try out as an exotic dancer, he'd figured she would bail out and confess defeat. But, niggling away in his mind and keeping his cock semiturgid, had been the recollection of the way Hayley had moved to the strippers' music, and the gleam of arousal in her eyes when their gazes had collided.

Tantalizing hints that the woman was more sensual, more sexy, than she let on at work.

But, Christ, he'd never in a million years expected what he'd seen on the stage tonight.

Yeah, she'd stumbled a couple times, looked a little uncertain here and there, but bottom line, she was fiery hot.

And she had a knockout body, just like the one in that "Brick House" song. Why would a woman keep that body concealed under the conservative clothing Hayley wore to work?

Especially if she had it in her to strip onstage.

She'd rolled onto her back and was arching up, as if offering her body to a lover.

Lust slammed through him in a wave so forceful he almost groaned.

Damn, he wanted to be that lover. Wanted to kneel between her spread legs and plunge into her, deep and hard.

The pressure of his fly against his erection was painful, confining. His cock ached to be free. To have one stroke of flesh against flesh. That's all it would take and he'd come so hard he'd—

Fuck, he couldn't think about it or he'd cream his suit pants.

Hayley's music was coming to an end, thank God. Another couple minutes and he'd have been a goner. Last time he'd blown his cork in his pants, he'd been fourteen.

She rolled onto her hands and knees again, this time with her butt toward the audience. Her legs were spread and he could see the plump curves of her ass—man, did she have a spectacular one—and the shadowed cleft between them.

The guys at the front could probably see the folds of her labia.

Shit. This time he had to raise a hand to his mouth to force back the groan.

In a fluid motion, she swiveled around to a sitting position, facing the audience, then rose gracefully as the music came to an end.

Applause, whistles, and cheers broke out.

Ry clapped too, hard, not just because she deserved it but because he hoped to divert some blood away from his ready-to-blow cock.

Hayley's cheeks were flushed, her hair tousled, and there was a gleam in her eyes.

Some of the women, when they'd finished dancing, had looked embarrassed and hurried to wrap themselves in a towel, but she stood straight, naked and beautiful, looking exhilarated by the adulation. He remembered her saying she'd danced ballet and performed onstage. The poise she'd learned then was serving her well.

As the audience settled down, the DJ said, "OK, folks,

Penny Catalina wants a job dancing here at The Naked Truth. What do you think? Does her naked truth measure up?"

Cheers broke out.

It hit Ry for the first time that Hayley might actually win the contest and get a contract.

To dance each night for a crowd of slavering men.

The thought excited him a little, and also pissed him off. He didn't understand either reaction.

But then, he wasn't exactly thinking right now.

His entire being was focused on the driving need to be inside Hayley Croft.

She bent, breasts dangling like succulent fruit, to pick up her towel. After wrapping it around herself toga-style, she gathered up the cast-off bits of her costume, then left the stage.

Ry grabbed his beer and downed half the glass before drawing a breath. He was tempted to pour the other half on his throbbing groin.

No, he'd escape to the men's room and jerk off.

The DJ announced another dancer and a cute blonde in a nurse's costume came onstage.

About to make his getaway and take care of business, Ry's attention was caught by Evelyn and Kari. They had risen from where they were seated closer to the front, and were coming toward him, heading either for the restroom or the bar.

He scooted his lower body under the table, ducking his head and focusing on his beer glass, and hoped they wouldn't see him.

No such luck. In a couple seconds, they were standing beside him.

"What are you doing here?" Evelyn scolded in a whisper.

Getting blue balls probably wasn't the wisest answer. "Wanted to see how Hayley's audition went."

Kari scowled. "How did you know it was tonight?"

"I'm a PI. Didn't take much."

The women exchanged glances, then Kari said, "Wasn't she fabulous? I bet she wins."

"She was, uh, good." He voiced the question he couldn't resist asking. "Are you the only ones who came to watch, or does she have a, uh, date in the audience?" He didn't know whether to say girlfriend or boyfriend.

"It's just us," Kari said. "She broke up with her last boyfriend before she moved to Vancouver." She leaned close to Evelyn, as if she'd lost her balance. Or was poking a surreptitious elbow in her ribs. "Why do you ask?"

To find out if she was straight. If she was committed or available.

If she might be open to a quick fuck in the back alley.

Shit, he was losing his mind.

Did the female PIs suspect what he was thinking? "Wondered if she needed a ride home," he said gruffly.

"We've got it covered," Evelyn said, her curious gaze making him glad for the dim light and the table he'd snugged up to.

"Yeah," Kari put in, shifting from one foot to the other. "We're good. And I really, really need to pee. Not to mention, I'm exhausted. The joys of being seven months pregnant."

He grabbed on to that idea. "You should get home and rest. I'll drive Hayley. I need to apologize for doubting she could do this."

"I'm tired, not dead," Kari said defensively. "But I definitely have to pee." She bustled away.

"An apology would be good," Evelyn said. "And yes, Kari could use some sleep. We'll head home. Give me a call when they announce the winner. And make sure Hayley knows Kari and I didn't spill the beans about her audition."

He nodded, and she went in the direction Kari had disappeared.

Ry watched the last couple of performances—which couldn't compete with Hayley's—impatiently. Once he learned the winner, he could work out a game plan for how to proceed on the Mortimer case.

After all, he had a job to do. And much as he might fantasize about back-alley sex with super-hot Hayley, the chances of her sharing that erotic fantasy were slim.

Finally, the last dancer finished and the club's manager, a stocky Asian guy in a dark suit, came onstage. "First, let's give a big hand to all the sexy amateurs who did such a terrific job of entertaining us tonight."

A group of women in their dance costumes came onto the stage and accepted a round of hearty applause.

"Now," the manager went on, "it's time to crown the winner of the audition. To find out which lovely lady will be gracing the stage of The Naked Truth for the next week."

The women who had auditioned—five in number—took the stage. Hayley's cheeks were flushed and she looked nervous and excited.

She had put her "suit" skirt and jacket back on, but left the jacket unbuttoned and parted at the front to reveal glimpses of her lacy black bra and naked flesh. She'd left the glasses off, and her hair was tousled as if she'd climbed hastily out of a lover's bed and tossed on a few clothes.

She looked amazing. His whole body ached with the need to touch her.

Back at the office, every time he saw her in her buttoned-up clothes, he'd be imagining her onstage. Gorgeous, sexy. Seductive. Arousing.

The manager said, "As I said at the beginning of the night, we identified twelve of you in the audience to judge tonight's competition. Each judge filled in a score card rating our lovely dancers on beauty, demeanor, dancing, sexiness, costume, and music selections, as well as audience response. We've tallied the votes, and here's how it came out."

Another drumroll, then he announced the second runner

up, a striking black woman, and presented her with a bouquet of roses.

Ry held his breath. If Hayley won, it'd be a great opportunity for her to get close to their client's wife. He'd work undercover in the club, making sure she was safe and checking out the staff and clientele, trying to figure out what Jennifer Mortimer had gotten herself mixed up in.

He'd get to watch Hayley dance. Again and again.

But so would hundreds of other men.

The manager announced the first runner up. Not Hayley, but a blonde with tits as big as Pamela Anderson's had been in their glory days.

Ry thought of all those eyes on Hayley, if she won. She'd be a public commodity, naked in front of rich guys and blue collar workers, successful men and pathetic losers.

Tonight, the audience attention had seemed to be a turn-on for her. Hmm, was she an exhibitionist?

Until tonight, Ry'd never thought of himself as a voyeur. Seemed he was, at least when it came to her.

Why did it piss him off to think of other men watching her get down and dirty onstage?

The manager was flourishing a fancy scroll wrapped in gold ribbon. The dance contract he'd award to the winner.

"And the lucky lady—but really, it's this week's audiences who have all the luck, because she's fantastic—is Penny Catalina!"

"Oh!" Hayley gasped, and the audience cheered as she accepted the scroll.

Well, how about that. She'd really done it.

Ry couldn't wait to congratulate the winner.

5

After collecting a few hugs—an especially warm one from the nurse-amateur—Hayley left the dressing room in an exhilarated daze.

Anxious to share her triumph with Kari and Evelyn, she hadn't stopped to change out of her costume, just thrown a light summer raincoat over it.

She'd never really believed she could do it, but the old thrill of performance had carried her through. Along with the audience's approval, not to mention her fantasy about dancing for Ry.

Donna had said each guy in the audience wanted to believe the woman onstage was dancing for him, seducing him, wanting to make love to him. By envisioning Ry, Hayley must have conveyed that message.

Hah! She couldn't wait to see him tomorrow. And Tom and Ravi, too. They'd been skeptical, and she'd proved them wrong.

Humming "What a Feeling," she stepped from the backstage area into the main room of the club, where the audience was dispersing. Where were Kari and Evelyn?

When she'd been dancing, she'd seen them, but they hadn't been at that same table when she'd stood onstage accepting her winner's contract. Maybe they were in the restroom.

As she made her way through the thinning crowd, a few audience members offered hearty—and in a couple cases semidrunken—congratulations.

She gave polite thanks, and kept moving toward the back of the room. The man who'd reminded her a bit of Ry was still there, alone at his small, dimly lit table.

Smiling to herself, she wondered how Ry would react if he knew she'd cast him as a fantasy lover to inspire her performance.

Wait. Was she seeing things? She peered more closely at the black-haired man who lounged in his chair, staring toward her from behind wire-rim glasses. Hair combed back in an unflattering style, a suit jacket folded across his lap, a long-sleeved white shirt and a tie. Not the sexy PI she knew, but . . .

Damn, it was him.

Turned out the PI had a disguise for every occasion. Even for coming to a strip club to ogle her.

Oh, God. He'd seen her naked. Seen her dance, while she'd imagined his heated gaze, his hands on her body, his lust for her.

Embarrassment flooded through her. Quickly followed, thank heavens, by a surge of anger. Anger was easier to deal with.

She closed the distance between them. Hands on her hips, fighting the attraction she always felt when she saw him, she glared down. "How dare you come here."

He shrugged nonchalantly, but, now she was right in front of him, she saw that the blaze of his blue eyes was anything but casual. Was that the heat of arousal? And what lay under that oh-so-casually draped jacket on his lap?

Had she turned Ry on with her performance?

The thought sent another rush of heat through her, recharging every cell that had been so aware, so aroused, when she was dancing. Her breath caught, her nipples tightened, and the crotch of her thong dampened.

A sense of female power emboldened her. "You didn't think I could do it." She waved the contract. "What do you think of me now?"

His jaw tightened. "*Penny*, as a member of the *audience*, I enjoyed your show."

Damn, she'd forgotten they were both undercover. She wasn't supposed to know him. With a big smile, she said brightly, "I'm so glad you enjoyed it, sir. Now, if you'll excuse me, I must find my friends and head home."

Under his breath, he said, "I'm your ride."

What had happened to the female PIs?

Thoughts of anyone other than Ry vanished as he stood. When he reached his full six-foot-three he was, thanks to her stripper shoes, only a few inches taller than she.

Ry was the kind of guy who, when he carried a jacket, hooked it on a finger and dangled it over his shoulder. Yet tonight he held the suit jacket folded in front of him. Hiding an erection?

The thought robbed her of breath. Ry Montana's cock. What did it look like?

Of course she'd checked out his package in those well-worn jeans he favored. She knew he was hung, but she wanted to know the details. Naked, up close and personal.

"I'll go first," he muttered. "You hang back. Say hi to the bartender, tell her you're looking forward to working here."

She'd never imagined that her fantasies about Ry would be anything other than crazy imaginings, but now . . . She was turned on. Maybe he was, too. In a few minutes, they'd be alone in his car.

Moisture seeped past her thong to dampen the insides of her thighs. Her mouth, though, was dry when she whispered, "All right." At first she'd been furious that he'd come tonight, but now the night was full of sexy possibilities.

"Exit the club by the front door, turn left, go down half a block. I'm driving a black Jeep." He raised his voice. "Congratulations again on winning, Penny. You deserved it."

When he walked away, she forced herself not to watch. She was undercover, she had to play her role. Even if her body ached and trembled with lust.

She strolled over to the bar where the bartender, a pretty redhead in her midthirties, said, "Hey, you were awesome. Way to go, Penny." She held out her hand. "I'm Gloria. Used to be a dancer myself."

"Good to meet you. I'm looking forward to working here, though I'm a little nervous."

"You'll do great if you dance the way you did tonight. Tomorrow the manager'll fill you in on the rules. Our customers are pretty good, but just remember, you don't have to take shit from anyone. The bouncers will look out for you. All our VIP booths have cameras."

Donna had told her about the screened VIP booths where dancers took customers for "private shows." Definitely not sex, she'd said, but one-on-one, totally naked, dances.

Anxiously, Hayley said, "My contract doesn't require me to do private dances, does it?"

"No, that's up to you. But that's where the real money is."

It was one thing to create and deliver a performance onstage. No way was Hayley doing a nude lap dance for a strange man. "Thanks for the advice. See you tomorrow."

Heart racing at the thought of being alone with Ry, she left the club. Quickly she found the Jeep and slid into the passenger side.

He had taken off his glasses and tie, undone his shirt cuffs and rolled the sleeves up his tanned forearms, and run his fingers through his hair enough to mess it up. He looked more like his usual sexy self. Except for the suit jacket that rested on his lap.

Oh yes, he definitely had an erection.

"What happened to Kari and Evelyn?" she asked.

"Sent them home."

Because he wanted to be alone with her. Feeling smug, she asked innocently, "Why?"

"Kari was tired." His voice came out in a growl.

She pressed her lips together to keep from grinning. Pregnant or not, Kari, from what Hayley had seen over the last six months, was as tough as Ry. "Oh, that's too bad."

He started the engine and pulled out of the parking spot. "Where to?"

"I have an apartment in Lonsdale near the Sea Bus." Normally she took the ocean bus to and from downtown.

He headed toward Georgia Street, which would take them into Stanley Park and over the Lions Gate Bridge.

Once they reached her place, she could ask him in. Might she actually have sex with Ry? She'd thought he was out of her league, but tonight anything could happen.

"You did good, Hayley." He glanced over and his gaze lingered before he stared back at the road. "How did it feel, up onstage? You looked like you were enjoying it. Or was that just part of the act?"

Remembering, she shivered. "It was scary at first. The idea of all those people watching me while I . . ."

"Stripped." The word rasped out. "And yet you did it."

His vaguely accusing tone made her stick out her jaw. "As a performance. An undercover job where my costume and, uh, nudity were my disguise. Besides, I've gone to avant garde dance, even theatre, where the performers were nude."

"But were they dancing to arouse?"

"Did I do that?" Her voice was little more than a whisper. "Arouse?"

"Hell, woman, you know you did. You must've given every guy in the place a hard-on."

Her heart was pounding so hard she could barely breathe. "Including you?"

"Hell, yeah!" He jerked the Jeep around a corner, driving too fast and narrowly missing another car.

His rough confirmation made her bold enough to admit, "It aroused me, too."

"Shit, Hayley. Oh hell, I can't drive and talk about this."

They were at the entrance to Stanley Park, in the lane that led toward the Lions Gate Bridge. He shifted lanes quickly, to take the one that fed into the oceanfront drive circling the perimeter of the park. His profile looked grim and he had a tight grip on the steering wheel.

Her heart beat even faster and sexual tension knotted her muscles, throbbed in her pussy.

He turned the Jeep into a parking spot above the seawall walk. There was only one other parked car, and no people in sight. He slammed the headlights off and flicked off the ignition.

Then he turned to her. "You looked turned on when you were dancing. That was real?"

She took a deep breath, let it out, and confessed.

"I imagined one man watching me while I stripped for him. Imagined my moves arousing him. The thought of that, of his hungry eyes on me, was a turn-on."

Ry grabbed the jacket off his lap and tossed it in the back. "I'm still aroused. How about you?"

She stared at the fly of his suit pants. Oh, yes! It was all she could do not to whimper at the sight of the massive erection thrusting against the fabric. Her pussy throbbed and she squeezed her thighs together. "Yes. I am."

"Mutual arousal." His voice grated. "Want to do something about it?"

In her wild imaginings, there'd been, if not necessarily romance, at least a little finesse. More than *You scratch my itch and I'll scratch yours.*

But damn, this was Ry, the man she'd fantasized about since she met him. Tonight she'd been naked onstage, naked in front of him, and she was hornier than she'd ever believed possible. Pretty words and gentle kisses weren't what her body needed.

She'd wanted excitement, and this was *It.*

"Yes." As the word sighed out of her, his lips were there, inhaling it and devouring her mouth with a hot, hungry kiss.

She moaned, closed her eyes, blindly grabbed his head. Gripped him as she kissed back.

Hayley had never been a woman who'd get swept away by a kiss. A part of her had always remained analytical. Aware of mingled breath, teeth knocking. Kisses that were too wet, too bland, or too acrobatic.

But Ry's kiss banished thought. It was a total, in-the-moment experience. Passion and bliss, relief and hunger. Sensation that flooded through her body, igniting every pleasure center.

Especially the one between her legs, where she was damp and throbbing.

She and Ry were opposites in so many ways. How could it be that their mouths had been designed for each other?

Their hunger met and matched. Onstage, she'd imagined herself to be a sex goddess in his eyes, and now he made her feel like one. A goddess who drove him wild with need.

Their bodies twisted awkwardly toward each other on the front seat, craving more. His fingers fumbled with the top button of her raincoat.

And car lights strobed through the Jeep, making them jerk apart.

"Damn!" he said. "We can't do this here."

"My apartment?"

"Too far away. I need you now."

Need. He needed her, the way she did him.

"We'll find a place," he said roughly. "Get out."

Too aroused to ask questions, she opened the Jeep door. By the time her shaky legs had found solid ground, he'd come around the vehicle.

She stared at him in the light of a nearly full summer moon. Oh God, he was handsome, black hair in disarray, gaze intent and burning. "Ry," she sighed.

Then, because she was exactly the right height in her high heels, she took a step toward him until her body was flush against his.

Groaning, he pulled her into a tight embrace. Even through their clothes, she could feel his steely erection. She whimpered, squirmed against him, longing to get rid of all the clothes and feel him thrust deep inside her.

She reached down, hiked up her raincoat and short skirt, and pressed her crotch against the front of his pants. Oh God, yes! He felt so good. Exactly what she needed.

A shudder went through him and he pumped his hips.

She wanted to wrap her legs around him, climb him like a stripper pole, rub her clit against him. Just a couple times, that was all it would take, she was so close to the edge.

He grabbed her bum, pulled her tight, thrust against her.

Oh yes, yes. "More," she whispered, grinding against him.

"Shit, Hayley." Voice harsh, he shoved her away. Gone was the devil-may-care guy who was always quick with a quip or ironic comment. Lust had reduced Ry to primal male.

And she loved it. Except, she wanted an orgasm right now.

"Car coming," Ry said raggedly.

Damn, she'd again forgotten where they were.

They stared hungrily into each other's eyes as the car drove by. Then he grabbed his jacket from the back seat of the Jeep, gripped her hand and tugged her across the road toward a grassy stretch of park bordered by bushes and tall trees.

Sex outside? A night of firsts.

It was probably illegal. But that only added to the excitement.

When they reached the lawn, her heels punched holes in the grass, slowing her and making her stumble. Impatiently she bent to undo the ankle straps and pull off the shoes.

Oh, bliss, as her sore feet sank into cool, soft grass. And bliss, again, as she regained her natural posture and stride, hurrying hand in hand with Ry across the lawn.

They found a narrow path through the bushes, and followed it to a smaller grassy area. Semisecluded. Probably no one would be walking through the park in the middle of the night.

Probably.

Ry tossed his suit jacket down, then bent to spread it.

"It'll get grass stains," she protested automatically.

He straightened. "I don't give a fuck about grass stains."

Come to think of it, nor did she. She unbuttoned her light raincoat and tossed it down too.

"Jesus," he groaned, "you're still wearing your costume. Way to make a sex fantasy come true."

"That makes two of us," she murmured under her breath. Then, more loudly, channeling the female power she'd discovered tonight, she said, "Want me to strip for you?"

"Hell, yes. But, I can't take it." He reached for the shoulders of her abbreviated jacket.

She hadn't done up the buttons and it slid off easily. As soon as her hands were free of the sleeves, she reached for her skirt zipper, but he beat her to it. The skirt slipped down her legs.

She arched her back and held her head high. Pulse throbbing in her throat, arousal humming in her pussy, she faced him.

Naked in the moonlight but for her lacy black bra and thong.

6

"You are so fucking gorgeous," Ry said.

This stunning creature was the admin assistant he'd barely even noticed. So much for being a PI and former cop with honed powers of observation.

No woman had ever driven him so wild with lust. Hayley was a grown man's wet dream.

"And you're wearing too many clothes," she said, tossing that gleaming waterfall of hair and reaching for the top button of his shirt.

Her fingers brushed his skin as she undid the top few buttons. That simple touch resonated in his overloaded cock, making him shudder. "That's enough." He pulled her hands away and hauled the shirt over his head.

She let out a soft gasp and her eyes glittered as she studied his naked torso. Her hands followed the path of her gaze, the soft pads of her fingers warm and seductive, the sharper scratch of artificial fingernails pricking arousal.

Every wicked sexual fantasy he'd imagined back in the strip

club was coming true, and he was fucking grateful. But if he got any more turned on, he was going to burst.

He grabbed her hands and pulled them away. "Sorry, Hayley, you're gonna have to live without foreplay this time. I gotta have you. If that's not okay, say so now."

Her eyes, fringed by long, thick artificial lashes, gleamed golden and catlike in the moonlight. She didn't say a word, just grabbed his belt buckle and undid it.

There was a God, and tonight he was looking out for Ry.

Hands getting in each other's way, they struggled to get him out of his pants and boxer briefs. He barely retained enough sense to pull a condom from his wallet and force it over the biggest erection he'd ever had.

She stared. Swallowed. Reached out.

If she touched him, he'd explode.

He evaded her hand. Pulled off her bra and thong.

The sight of her in the park in the middle of the night, stripped nude for his eyes only, made his hips pump and drops of pre-cum surge.

He grabbed her for a deep, tongue-thrusting kiss, then they tumbled down, half on the jacket and coat, half on the grass.

Side by side, their limbs intertwined, she pressed hungrily against his shaft, squirming and rubbing.

He rolled so she was on the bottom.

She lifted her legs to twine high on his hips, opening herself for him.

Bracing his weight on one forearm, he reached between their bodies to stroke her sex. Plump pussy lips, soaking wet. A firm little clit.

When he rubbed it gently, she gasped. "Now, Ry. Come inside me now."

He probed with the head of his cock and she gasped again, legs tightening their grip.

With a groan of relief, he accepted the invitation and surged into her.

On that one stroke she came apart around him, crying out as her body gripped him in the convulsive spasms of her orgasm.

It was more than he could take. His whole body was taut with the need to come.

He pulled out almost all the way, then let go, plunging deep and hard inside her. Exploding so vigorously he almost lost consciousness.

Dimly he was aware of their bodies softening, the tension fading into relaxation.

He'd collapsed on top of her. Firm breasts pressed against his chest and the steamy heat of her sheath gripped him.

Heavy. He must be too heavy.

Summoning the strength to move, he lifted off of her, easing out.

Hayley sprawled, chest heaving, breath rasping softly in her throat. Beautiful. So beautiful.

She watched him with an intent but enigmatic expression. He knew she was waiting for him to say something.

But what could he say? How could he explain what had happened tonight? It had been insanity. Lust.

Magic.

He propped himself on an elbow and stroked the tangled silk of her hair back from her face. "Sorry that was so rough."

She raised her arms, hands behind her head to pillow it, a gesture that tightened her breasts. "Rough worked for me."

"I've never been so fucking turned on in my life." In fact, his cock was stirring again.

A corner of her mouth moved. Not a smile, but a question. "Hmm. Watching arouses you?"

"Not really. Strip clubs, porn movies . . ." He shrugged. "I'm not big into the voyeur thing. Bottom line, I'd rather do than watch." He gave her a rueful grin. "And when I *do*, I usu-ally have a little more finesse."

"Like I said, it worked for me." Her tone aimed for flippant but didn't quite make it. "So, why did tonight's show turn you on?"

There was an edge of seriousness, maybe uncertainty, in her voice that got to him. That made him share the truth rather than joke around. "The show didn't." He leaned over to drop a kiss on her soft lips. "You did."

She didn't respond to the kiss, and her brows rose slightly. "Is that true, Ry? I don't need pretty words. I'd rather have honesty."

Pretty words? He didn't *do* pretty words. "It was you. From the moment you stepped onstage."

"Why?"

He shook his head, stroked the frown line that marred her smooth forehead. "Damned if I know. Because I know you? Yet, obviously, I never knew you. What you did on that stage . . ." He gave a small laugh. "This is going to sound crazy, but it was like you were dancing just for me." That was probably what made a dancer great. She made each man in the audience believe in a personal connection.

His cock was, again, hard.

Both corners of Hayley's lips curved, and her eyes danced with humor. "Uh-huh? Well, maybe I was."

He chuckled. "What did you say about pretty words? I don't need a fake compliment, Hayley. You didn't even know I was at the club."

"True." The amusement was still on her face, like she had a private joke.

"You make me feel like a crappy PI," he confessed. "You've been working for us what? Three, four months?"

"Thereby proving your point," she said dryly. "Six and a half."

Ry winced. "Sorry. I noticed your efficiency, but . . ." He shifted position, the grass cool under his hip, and ran his fingers through the waves of hair tumbling around her face and shoulders, golden highlights almost white in the moonlight. "I never noticed this amazing hair."

"It wasn't so amazing. The highlights are new, and I always wore it up."

"I know you normally wear glasses, and no false eyelashes." With a gentle finger, he drew imaginary glass frames on the delicate skin around her eyes. "But I never really saw your eyes. They're tawny gold, like a lion's."

Still lying stretched out, hands behind her head, seemingly unconcerned about her nakedness, she gazed up at him. "My passport says hazel."

"Gold." Warm gold. Glowing. Dazzling.

It was hard to look away from them, but he did, running his finger down her nose. "I never noticed how cute your nose is. It turns up a little at the end."

She wrinkled her nose and teased, "You were so unobservant, they should probably revoke your PI license."

Grateful she wasn't berating him for being such a jerk, he continued on, tracing the outside rim of her lips, then the center crease. "They should. Any man who's oblivious to these sexy lips has to be blind."

She sucked his finger into her mouth and nipped it. "What else didn't you notice?"

"Your breasts. God, your fabulous breasts. Firm, but so soft and—" He squeezed one gently. "So real. All woman." Now, this was his idea of heaven.

As he spoke, and toyed with her breast, she teased his finger with a swirling tongue, rhythmic sucks, little nibbles.

His engorged cock longed for the same treatment. "I want to make love to you properly. How about we go to your apartment?"

She released his finger. "Let's stay here."

"But someone could come along." He paused as a thought struck him. "Do you share an apartment, and don't want to bring a man home? We could go to my place."

"No. I'd just rather stay here. This is fun, being in the park." Her eyes glittered. "The cops might bust us."

"The cops might bust us?" he echoed, amused and, yet again, surprised by her. "And that possibility turns you on?" Under his palm, her nipple was tight and hard.

She glanced away, then back at him defiantly. "Yeah, it does."

"Jesus, Hayley Croft. You're a wild woman." Where had she been hiding that woman for more than six months?

Hayley smiled a secret smile and studied the gorgeous naked man whose head blocked her view of the moon. "So I'm discovering," she murmured, half to herself. This was, hands down, the absolute best night of her life. All because she'd taken a risk.

Going undercover as a stripper, she'd not only had the thrill of performing to applause and cheers, she'd won the audition.

And she'd attracted the attention of the super-hottie she'd been ogling for half a year.

Attention? More like arousal, overwhelming passion, and some delicious compliments—not to mention, explosive sex like she'd never even imagined before.

Ry had said she, of all the dancers, was the one who'd aroused him, and she believed him. No question he was experienced with women, which meant that his urgency, his lack of finesse when they'd had sex, had to be rare.

"I think you like wild women," she said.

"I sure like this one." He grinned at her, his hand moved to her other breast, then he leaned over and replaced it with his mouth. His tongue laved her areola with broad strokes, heat that turned to tingly chill when he moved on and the night air licked her damp skin. Hot, cool. Both sensations arousing.

She arched her back, ignoring the bumpy texture of the clothing she lay on, and gave herself up to the pleasure of his tongue, the insistent tug of his lips as he sucked her aching nipple. Somehow he knew exactly the right amount of pressure to arouse without hurting.

Now he didn't speak, but the way he fondled her breast, and the seductive brush of his hand as he explored her slim waist, rounded hips, flat belly, spoke of appreciation.

She'd always kept in shape—she loved exercise, motion, being fit—but rarely had there been a lover in her life to enjoy the benefits. Or to give her the kind of pleasure Ry was now bestowing on her.

With her first serious boyfriend, in high school, sex had been a fumbling activity that had never brought her to orgasm. Her second lover, in college, had given her an occasional climax but he hadn't had much clue how to please a woman and she'd been too inhibited to tell him. With the third and last guy, sex had been enjoyable but not passionate.

None of them had understood, reveled in, her body.

But Ry . . . It felt like he worshipped her, turning her on with each lick, suck, breath, stroke. Here was the finesse that had been lacking before.

His exploring fingers moved down to flirt with the small, daring arrow of curly pubic hair, the wax job she'd gotten done at Sugarbox. Raising his head from her breast, he gazed at it. "When you stripped off your thong, all I could think about was following that arrow."

"Feel free," she said breathlessly.

"I intend to." His fingers slipped between her legs with bold assurance.

Hands behind her head, body spread across their rumpled

clothing, she closed her eyes, the better to concentrate on the sensations.

He stroked, smoothing her juices over her labia, slicking the flats of his fingers back and forth, first firmly, then delicately. Each stroke quickened her breath, drew her focus. No man had ever touched her this way before, with such sureness, taking such pleasure in arousing her.

And her body was so responsive to him. The tenderness of her breasts, her sex juices, the aching build of arousal that centered—

Oh God, just where Ry's thumb was brushing now.

7

_____

When he drew away, Hayley couldn't bear it. She opened her eyes and implored him, "Don't stop."

"So impatient." Ry shifted position on the grass beside her. Then he lowered his head and blew warm air against her damp skin, and his tongue took up the same stroking action as his fingers.

As if by accident, the tip of his tongue brushed her clit, then was gone.

He returned. Another flick. Then withdrew.

"Oh," she gasped. Never had she felt so sensitive.

He kept up the rhythm, each flick of her clit driving her toward climax, each withdrawal cooling her down a little. Intense, so intense. Never had a lover, or even her own hand, fueled her need to such a pitch.

She wanted to come, but he wasn't letting her.

As tension built even higher, she whimpered with frustration. "Ry, stop teasing."

He lifted his face enough to say, "It'll be better if it builds longer."

She gave a groan of exasperation as her body hovered on that almost-there edge.

"But whatever the lady wants," he murmured, then lowered his mouth to her again.

She lifted her hips, twisting against his tongue, desperately seeking release.

This time, when he licked his way to her clit, he stayed there. Gently he sucked, flicked his tongue across that sensitive bundle of nerve endings, and—

"Oh, yes!" The tension built unbelievably higher, peaked, then crashed in delicious waves of release.

And somehow his fingers were inside her, pumping into her channel, finding a spot that—oh my God—she'd never known existed, and she was coming apart again.

He kept her there with his fingers, with his tongue, her body spasming with pleasure until she couldn't take it any longer and had to pull away.

Satiated, drained, gasping for breath, she lay back, wondering if she would ever move again.

Dimly she was aware of Ry lying down beside her. She wanted to thank him—for such incredible pleasure and for teaching her what her body was capable of—but speech was beyond her.

Gradually the world realigned itself and came into focus again.

Above them, the moon gleamed serenely. Though she and Ry were only a mile from the center of the city, the smell that filled her nostrils was a combination of ocean and newly cut grass, together with the sultry aroma of sex.

The ever-present hum of traffic passing through the center of Stanley Park, the occasional rumble of a car driving the oceanfront loop on the other side of those bushes, hushed laughter from the seawall walk, all reminded her she and her lover weren't guaranteed privacy.

What if someone had come along when Ry was giving her that mind-numbing series of orgasms?

Then they'd have gotten an eyeful, wouldn't they?

And speaking of eyefuls, what was she doing gazing at the moon when there was a truly hot male body lying naked beside her?

Hayley summoned the energy to roll onto her side, and found that Ry was lying on the grass facing her. A tender, amused smile lit his face and a firm erection nudged her thigh.

Her gaze roamed his hard, lean lines. "You have a beautiful body," she whispered. Just looking at him made her pussy, so recently overloaded with sexual pleasure, stir again.

"That's supposed to be my line."

Delicately she touched his shoulder, ran her hand down his firm pecs, trailed her fingers through the light mat of black curls.

Then she pushed him down so he lay flat and bent over to suck a nipple into her mouth, her hair cascading around her face.

He tasted a little salty, smelled of musky male sexuality. Under her questing tongue, his nipple pulled tight. A shiver rippled through him.

Her sex quivered in response.

She could hardly believe this was Ry Montana. Hers to explore. Hers to arouse.

She trailed her tongue down the center of his body, between those rock-solid pecs, down the middle of a taut ribcage, and into the dip of his navel. There, she circled, feeling his flesh ripple under her touch.

Her tongue bumped against the crown of his engorged cock, gleaming with pre-cum.

With one hand, she eased the shaft gently away from his body. He filled the curve of her fingers, pulsing with burning heat.

This awe-inspiring organ had been inside her. Incredibly, but all too briefly.

And she wanted it back. The throbbing hunger in her sex was building again.

But first, she wanted to explore. Every inch of him.

His hands grazed her face and scooped her hair up, holding it back.

She glanced up to find he was watching her, his eyes glittering in the moonlight.

Oral sex wasn't something she'd had much experience with, but Ry's penis inspired her. Tentatively, she licked the head, then grew bolder, lapping at him as if he were an ice cream cone that was melting with the heat, feeding off his soft moans, the involuntary movements of his hips.

As she made her way down the shaft, paying attention to every bit of naked flesh, Ry shifted restlessly. "Shit, Hayley, that's too good. Enough. Let me find a condom."

Aha! He could dish it out, but couldn't take it himself. "Who's the one who said it'll be better if the arousal builds longer?"

Of course, when he'd gone down on her, he'd set up a rhythm, driving her near her peak then backing off.

Deciding to give him a respite, she eased off. Releasing his cock, she pressed soft kisses against his inner thighs, then she fondled his balls. Enjoying their soft pliancy, she sucked one into her mouth, then moved to the other.

"Jesus, Hayley." His hips twisted and his hands gripped her head.

It seemed this didn't count as backing off.

She freed his balls, then drifted soft kisses up the side of his cock to the crown, giving him a few moments mercy. Then she opened her lips as wide as she could and took him in.

He thrust once, convulsively, then stopped.

Her hands rested on his hips and she could feel how tight his muscles were. Locked. Holding on to control.

She was squirming with need herself, thighs pressed tight together. But, intoxicated by her newfound power, she carried on, sucking on him, then swirling her tongue. With each moan he gave, she grew more confident, more aroused.

He yanked on her hair, pulling her roughly away from him. "I will not fucking come until I'm inside you," he grated out.

Oh yes. She sat up, glorying in Ry's fiercely intense expression.

With jerky motions, he found a condom and put it on, then lay back. "Take me, Hayley."

She straddled him, one knee on her raincoat, one on the grass, and rubbed her damp, pulsing crotch against the base of his shaft, enjoying the titillating friction.

"Inside!" Ry grabbed her by the hips, lifted her.

She reached between them to grasp his cock, then lowered herself, easing the swollen head between her sensitive folds.

"Oh God." She wriggled, feeling herself loosen around him, taking him in slowly. Deliciously slowly. Until he was buried deep in her core.

He groaned, "Oh, yeah," and his handsome face was taut.

"Ry," she murmured, needing to say his name. Then she began to raise and lower herself, growing slicker, hotter, needier as she increased the pace.

His hands caressed the tops of her thighs then slid to the soft inside. Other than that, he didn't move, letting her set the pace.

She tightened her internal muscles then relaxed them, alternately gripping him then releasing as she moved up and down on him.

This was so much better than her wildest fantasies.

When she lifted up, he reached between their bodies and lightly stroked her clit.

She was ripe with sensation, almost ready to burst in a juicy orgasm.

Then he thrust up, hard, plunging even deeper, making her gasp and quiver, eyes glazing over as every cell in her body focused. Wanting, needing, waiting.

He slid out part way then thrust again, his cock, his fingers exerting irresistible pressure on her clit, and—"Oh, yes, Ry!"—she shattered.

He made a wordless sound—triumph, exultation—and drove urgently into her in his own climax.

Legs trembling, chest heaving as she sucked in air, she sat atop him as their bodies gradually settled.

After long moments, he reached for her hand and tugged.

She collapsed down to lie atop him, and his arms encircled her, drawing her close. He rolled them so they were lying side by side, then stroked her tangled hair back from her burning cheeks and kissed her. No passion this time, just gentleness.

Maybe even affection, but she was probably imagining that. More likely, it was sexual afterglow.

And that's what she was feeling too.

Driving lust, then sexual afterglow. That's all that existed between her and Ry.

Except their work relationship.

Oops.

Chagrin filled her. They were coworkers. Why hadn't she stopped for one moment to think about consequences?

Tomorrow, Monday, they'd face each other around the conference table at the agency's weekly meeting. Ry would lay out the strategy for working the Mortimer case, and she'd . . . think about how incredible he looked naked and what an awesome lover he was.

When he gazed at her, would he be seeing the efficient admin assistant, or the naked stripper? Which did she want him to see?

What had they done?

Uncertain now, nervous, she drew away. "We should get going."

His lips twitched. "Thought you were hoping the cops would bust us."

"Uh, not so much. I like the idea more than the reality." Tonight, she'd drawn no boundaries: stripping in front of a crowd and having sex with a man she worked for. Risking arrest for public indecency. Yes, she'd craved excitement, but clearly there was such a thing as too much. Otherwise, she wouldn't be feeling so confused and worried.

She began to get up. "We need to get dressed."

He stretched lazily and reached for his shirt. "I guess."

Turning her back, very aware now of her nakedness, she hurriedly pulled on her skimpy undies and the suit that was a kinky parody of office clothes. The night was too warm for a raincoat, but right now she needed cover. Only when she'd buttoned it did she dare gaze at Ry.

He'd tucked his shirt into his suit pants, but had the sleeves rolled and the neck unbuttoned. His hair was tousled and he looked disheveled and sexy.

"Ry, we work together," she said softly. "Have we broken an agency rule by, uh . . . ?"

His eyes widened, as if the thought hadn't occurred to him. Then he shook his head. "Nope." But he didn't sound 100% certain.

They started walking toward the car, she carrying her shoes and he with his suit jacket hooked over one shoulder. Not touching.

"That's good," she said awkwardly, "but, uh . . . I guess we won't say anything to the others at the agency?" Why would they? They'd had sex; it wasn't like they were dating.

Or, might they hook up again? Her heart lifted with hope. Tonight she'd proved she could bat in the same league as Ry.

"Right. It's no one else's business." He sounded preoccupied, and when she glanced at him, he was frowning.

Her heart sank again. Obviously, his thoughts weren't on the same track as hers.

When they'd both climbed into the Jeep, he started the engine and pulled away. "Hayley, I got carried away tonight." He sighed. "And yeah, it was great and I'm sure as hell not sorry, but we shouldn't do it again. The Private Eye doesn't have a nonfraternization rule, but you're working the Mortimer case. My case. It could look bad for both of us."

He was right, she thought sadly. That was the practical decision, the only one she could possibly rationalize.

Except . . . That was the old Hayley talking. Tonight a new Hayley had been born.

Tonight, with Ry, had been special. Certainly for her. From the way he'd acted, things he'd said—and she'd never known Ry to sugarcoat the truth—maybe it had been for him, too.

Perhaps there was more than strip-induced lust between the two of them.

She'd always assumed Ry was a devil-may-care guy who wasn't interested in a serious relationship, but then she'd also assumed he would never find her sexy. So, assumptions could be wrong. She had a lot to learn about the man beside her.

If she wanted a chance to explore what might lie between them, she'd need to tap into that feminine power she'd discovered tonight.

"Hayley? You okay?" He sounded concerned. "Damn, this is all my fault."

"I'm fine," she said crisply. "And I do see your point."

She just had a better one. Not that she was about to tell him. He was still in the "man, the sex is great" stage. No way was he ready to hear talk about a possible "relationship."

What he was utterly ready for, though, was a seduction.

And the new Hayley was just the woman to provide it.

8

"Okay," Ry said to the group around the conference table, "next up is the Mortimer case." He opened a buff folder and stared at the contents, avoiding looking at Hayley Croft.

The woman who'd revved him up the way no one else ever had.

It had taken all his willpower to drop her at her apartment and tell her to catch a few hours of sleep. He hadn't slept a wink himself, as he replayed memories of how she'd looked onstage, how she'd felt and tasted, the way she'd stroked him and taken him in her mouth.

Fuck. His cock was swelling.

"Hayley auditioned last night," he said, trying to sound businesslike.

"And she won!" Kari cried. "Way to go, Hayley. She was incredible, and now she has a one-week contract at The Naked Truth."

"Really?" Ravi said. "Good work, Hayley."

"You auditioned and didn't tell us?" Tom whined, playing his goofball role as usual. "Now that's just plain mean."

"Oh, sure," Kari teased, "like we'd tell *you?* And have you in the audience leering at Hayley, throwing her off her stride?"

"Children," Evelyn said tolerantly. She ran The Private Eye with a light hand, creating a relaxed atmosphere that had turned the disparate group of PIs into an effective, friendly team. While the others bickered good-naturedly, Hayley didn't say a word. Her silence drew Ry like a magnet. When he glanced at her, he found her gazing right back, golden eyes gleaming behind her glasses. Lovely eyes, fringed with dark lashes. Even lovelier without last night's heavy makeup and false eyelashes.

Did she look different than usual? Her tan jacket and chocolate pants were the typical unremarkable ones, but she'd never worn the top couple buttons of her shirt undone before, had she? Undone, to reveal a hint of creamy lace. Reminding him of her full breasts last night, barely contained by black lace. Of how they'd looked in the moonlight. Of the incredible softness of her skin, the way her nipples had hardened when he sucked on them.

His cock, predictably, swelled again.

Ry dragged his gaze from her chest and noted that her hair was pulled up in the usual tight knot. Yet it glowed with highlights and a few soft curls had drifted loose—they'd never done that before, had they?—reminding him of the long silky waves she'd tossed seductively as she danced. Of the way her hair had caressed and teased his body when she went down on him.

Damn, but he wanted to free her hair, rip off her glasses, unbutton her. He shifted, his cock now uncomfortably hard within the confines of his jeans.

Her lips twitched. Full, rosy pink lips, still a little swollen from last night's passion. She straightened them quickly, but there was a twinkle in her eyes.

Forcing himself to refocus on the conversation, he realized

Kari and Evelyn were telling the other men about Hayley's makeover and training. Rigorous training, from what they said.

"Oh, come on." Tom grinned. "All that work just so you can swing around a stripper pole?"

"I'd like to see you try it," Hayley answered evenly, eliciting a giggle from Kari.

Ry smiled. How had he never noticed Hayley before? Last night, when he'd come to his senses, he'd decided they needed to keep things professional. But damn, his thoughts kept wandering in a far more intimate direction.

He glanced around the table. "With Hayley dancing at the club, she'll be able to talk to our subject and try to make friends." He shot her a cautionary glance. "Just talk. You're not a PI. Don't put yourself in the way of anything that's potentially dangerous."

"I understand. And I appreciate that you're trusting me with this assignment." Now she looked totally serious.

But still sexy, damn her.

He tore his gaze away. "We'll need eyes and ears in the rest of the club. It's the place where Kat Dancer performs the most. If she's having an affair or into drugs, it's likely happening there. And of course we need to make sure Hayley's safe."

"I'll volunteer to keep an eye on her," Tom said with an exaggerated wink.

Something primitive and male inside Ry made him snap, "No, I'll do it."

Evelyn raised an eyebrow, and he realized how abruptly he'd reacted.

Tom had pushed his buttons. Rather than admit it, Ry justified his response. "You're the wrong type for this club. Their clientele's mostly businessmen."

"I can spell you off," Ravi offered.

The young Indo-Canadian was professional and a genuinely

nice guy, but all the same, raw instinct made Ry reject the idea of him watching Hayley strip. "No, thanks. It's my case. I'll handle it."

Kari and Evelyn exchanged glances. Hopefully they didn't suspect he and Hayley'd had sex, and just thought he was being considerate of her. After all, he'd already seen her strip, so what was the big deal about a few more nights of it?

Arousal pulsed thick and heavy in his blood at the thought of seeing her naked, night after night.

"What's your cover story?" Hayley asked. "Are you a stranger or does Penny know you?"

Know him? As intimately as any woman ever had. His cock throbbed at the memory of her mouth teasing him. Of plunging deep inside her sweet moist heat.

He cleared his throat, trying to ignore his erection. "I'm a businessman from Edmonton who's here for a couple weeks work. Alone, looking for entertainment. Lonely and chatty. I'll try to build rapport with the bartender, waitresses, security people."

"Are you planning on covering all the hours Hayley's working?" Evelyn asked. "With no one else taking shifts? And what about the expense? Has the client authorized it?"

"I'm hoping it'll only take two, three nights, then Hayley can fake illness and quit. As for the hours, The Naked Truth is only open at night and . . ." He turned to Hayley. "Your safety comes first. I don't think there's much to worry about between eight and ten thirty or eleven, so I could come in later and stay until the club closes. But if you'd like someone there all the time—"

"No, I'm not worried," she broke in, shaking her head so the loose curls bounced around her face. "And I'd rather no one else took shifts. As Kari said, it might throw me off and I might blow my cover."

"Take your cell and put my number on speed dial," he told her, wishing he could reach out and twine one of those shiny curls around his finger. Or his swollen cock.

Sweat broke out on his forehead. "Go to the club by public transit. No vehicle with a tag that'll trace back to you."

"And take a taxi home after?"

"Ry will be at the club," Kari said, "so he can give you a ride. It'll give you a chance to compare notes." There was an undertone in her voice that made him look at her suspiciously.

"Good idea," Hayley said. "He can debrief me."

Into his mind flashed a vivid image of peeling off her black lace thong. He almost groaned as his erection thrust against his boxer briefs, seeking release. Craving Hayley's soft hand, her wet mouth, the welcoming grip of her tight, warm pussy.

How would he find the willpower to resist having sex with her again?

Hayley entered the dressing room at The Naked Truth dressed as Donna had suggested, in jeans and a T-shirt, hair in a ponytail, wearing contact lenses. She lugged a gym bag with four costumes: the one she'd worn for her audition, a white lacy peignoir set, a purple harem outfit with gold trim, and a rhinestone-laden black evening dress. It was so much fun—and so enlightening—to explore different personas.

But right now, she was here to work for The Private Eye and she wanted to impress Ry with her competence. As well as seduce him, of course, but she wouldn't think about that until she was dancing for him.

In one corner, a pretty young Latina, also in jeans and a T-shirt, sprawled in a chair with a heavy textbook and a yellow highlighter. She didn't look up.

Two other women were pulling clothing from their bags: Jennifer/Kat, looking wholesome in a pink blouse and khakis, her black hair in a ponytail, and a buxom blonde in a tight black track suit. They turned assessing gazes on Hayley, and the blonde drawled, "Oh, goodie, it's the new girl."

Donna had said most dancers thought rookies should shut up and learn, so humility would be the best approach.

Hayley nodded, letting her nervousness show. "Hi. I'm Penny and I'm a total newbie. So if you see me doing something stupid, would you tell me before I make a fool of myself?"

A snort from the corner told her the student was listening.

"Don't be bitches, you two," Kat said. "We were rookies once." The gaze she turned on Hayley was neutral. "Why are you here? Was it just a whim, auditioning last night, or do you really want to be a dancer?" As she spoke, she unbuttoned her blouse and took it off.

Hayley launched into her cover story. "My boyfriend lost his job and he's having trouble finding another. I'm a salesclerk, but that's not bringing in enough money for us to live on. Someone mentioned dancing." She shrugged. "I worked up some routines and here I am."

The blonde, who had stripped down to an underwire bra and a thong, rolled her eyes. "Another one who's supporting her guy. Ladies, wise up, it's supposed to go the other way around."

"No," the Latina girl said, closing her book. "It's about being independent. Which is why I'm getting a law degree, so I can support myself in the style to which I fully intend to get accustomed."

"Sounds like a good plan," Hayley said. Might Kat be doing the same? Saving money to further her education?

The other women had been pulling off clothing casually, and the blonde was naked now, but for a large butterfly tattoo on the upper curve of her bum.

Hayley didn't know where to look.

If Gran could see her now, she'd be shocked. This under-cover job, like her kickboxing, was best kept secret. She didn't want to worry her grandmother, or get another lecture.

"There's nothing wrong with dancing," Kat said tartly, skimming off bikini panties so that she, too, was naked. "Don't be a snob, Lolita." To Hayley, she said, "She thinks lawyers are better than strippers."

"They make a hell of a lot more money," Lolita shot back, rummaging in her bag and pulling out a tiger-striped bra and G-string. "This job pays well, but not great. You know British Columbia guys are crappy tippers."

Out of her bag came a black leather whip. "And law isn't an age-limited job like stripping. And lawyers get way more re-spect."

The Private Eye had a number of lawyer clients. "Yeah, the profession gets more respect," Hayley said, "but lawyers are like anyone else. Some are good people, some are scummy. I imagine that's the same with dancers?" The other women seemed so comfortable with their nudity, it encouraged her to start taking off her own clothes.

"Exactly," Kat said. "By the way, I'm Kat, Penny. So, how was it last night? How did you feel up onstage, peeling off your panties?" There was a challenge in the question.

How should she answer? She had no idea whether Kat en-joyed stripping or did it to be close to a lover or a drug connec-tion. Rather than guess, Hayley went with honesty. "Before I went on, I was so scared I thought I'd puke. But then I got into the music, and I realized the audience was really into it. Like, I was performing and they were . . ."

"Worshipping you?" the blonde asked. "Yeah, that's cool, isn't it?"

"Very. I'm not used to men worshipping me."

"I know that feeling," Kat said dryly, stepping into a silver G-string. "Here's another thing that's cool. Power. You're in control. You hold those guys in the palm of your hand." Like she'd felt with Ry. "Feminine power. Yes, it's pretty heady."

"What's your boyfriend think about you dancing?" Lolita asked. "Guys can get nasty about it. Jealous, possessive."

Kat nodded. "Not to mention buying into the negative stereotype and thinking there's something wrong with you."

Ooh, very interesting. Hayley was dying to pursue that line of conversation, but another couple dancers came into the dressing room and there was a flurry of greetings.

As she listened, Hayley realized that some of the women would be dancing onstage like her, others would only be doing private dances, and some, like Kat, would do both. Soon she was absorbed into the noise and bustle, the female scents and abundance of nude, toned flesh.

The ambience was relaxed and bawdy and, once she got used to it, pretty fun.

Yes, there were some crude, often hilarious jokes. As well as bare crotches and women checking each other for unclipped tampon strings and clingy bits of toilet paper that would glow under the black light in the club. And discussions of boob jobs and sequins, rug-burned knees and flashers.

But the bottom line was, these were women like any others. With baby pictures, menstrual cramps, and laments about dry skin and oily hair.

Hayley was a bit of a Girl Scout—always prepared—and by the time she'd given ibuprofen to one dancer, produced a Band-Aid for the blister on another's foot, and loaned tweezers to a third, she was feeling almost like part of the gang.

When it was her time to take the stage, she performed the same number as last night, feeling much more confident. It was early and Ry wouldn't have arrived, so this time, rather than dance for him or a fantasy of him, she instead tried to connect with the very real men who were watching.

And damned if she didn't have one hell of a good time. Yes, as the tattooed blonde, Candy, had said, it was cool to be worshipped. And, as Kat had mentioned, Hayley did have a sense of power and enjoyed being in control.

Dancing was a turn-on, but where last night it had been sexual, imagining Ry, tonight it was about finding her power as a woman. A sensual, sexy woman. She'd use that power later, to seduce Ry.

When she came offstage, she laughed exultantly. "Wow, I could get hooked on this!"

Kat, who was ready to go onstage, grinned. "You know it!"

She seemed so natural, so nice. Hayley had trouble believing she'd cheat on her spouse or get into the drug scene.

Candy, who'd been onstage before Hayley, had changed into a skintight minidress. "I'm going to see if I can rustle up some VIP dances. You coming?"

"I-I don't think I'm ready for that."

"Hey, you want power, girl, that's where it is. You get them all worked up and they can't even touch you. And they pay you for the privilege."

Hayley knew the liquor licensing laws prohibited touching in an area where liquor was served. She appreciated the rules and clear boundaries in the club. Too bad men outside in the real world didn't have to obey the same ones.

"Lots of guys don't even want the dance so much as the conversation," a petite brunette commented. "They're lonely, just want some company. Half the time, I think we're more counselors than dancers. You should give it a try, Penny."

"Maybe later."

Hmm. Perhaps she'd offer a private dance to Ry.

There were cameras in the VIP booths to ensure the rules were obeyed. What a test of self-control it would be, giving Ry a lap dance if neither of them could touch the other. With foreplay like that, he wouldn't be able to resist having sex later.

And, as she was coming to believe, the way to a man's heart was through his cock.

9

Ry had come to the strip club earlier than he'd told Hayley he was going to. Rationalize all he might about being concerned for her safety, the naked truth was that he couldn't wait to see her dance again.

His disguise wouldn't fool her twice, so he'd remained partially hidden behind a pillar and watched every second of her first routine.

Tonight she was less nervous, more polished. More deliberately seductive, he thought. She was truly performing for her audience, and getting off on it. There was definitely an exhibitionist side to Hayley.

And a voyeur side to him, because he sure as hell was getting off on this too, damn it. A man's anatomy wasn't designed to be achingly hard for this long without any relief in sight.

Only thing was, he wished she was dancing for his eyes only. It pissed him off to see other men gaping at her naked body.

She was a coworker, doing an undercover job. If it had been

Kari—a nonpregnant Kari—up there, he wouldn't be feeling aroused *or* possessive.

What the hell was it about Hayley? Was this just because they'd had sex?

When she finally left the stage, he let out a sigh of relief and drained the rest of his beer.

A scantily clad waitress promptly appeared, smiling warmly. "Another drink?"

"Please."

By the time she returned, he'd recovered his composure. Her "Didn't I see you here last night?" was the perfect opening to launch into his cover story.

For the next hour or so, he played the lonely out-of-towner, chatty but harmless. He talked to the waitress, the bartender, one of the bouncers, and a couple of the dancers who were offering private shows.

He kept an eye on Kat Dancer as she chatted with customers, disappeared toward the VIP area with a couple of them, and exchanged comments with other people who worked at the club. Never did he get a sense of any special, clandestine relationship.

She made her way over to where he sat. "Hi there," she said, smiling. "Enjoying the dancers?"

"Sure am. I'm from out of town, and the concierge told me this was the best club. I think he's right."

She leaned close. "I bet you'd enjoy it even more if you had a private dance."

He deliberated. It would give him a chance to talk more intimately with Kat Dancer. Then the DJ's voice caught his attention, announcing Penny Catalina.

His pulse quickened. "Maybe another time. I'd like to watch the next dancer."

"Penny? She's new tonight, and seems like a nice girl. Cheer for her, okay?"

So, Hayley was succeeding at ingratiating herself. Good for her.

And right now, his full attention was needed onstage. She appeared, wearing a full-length white robe that was more lace than fabric, and white stripper shoes trimmed with fluff. The white glowed alluringly under the black light, calling attention to every bit of her fine body that was displayed, and every bit that was hidden.

The word boudoir—one he'd never used in his life—popped into his mind.

Her hair was pinned up, loosely this time, all soft and messy. She looked semivirginal, semiwicked. Like every red-blooded guy wanted his bride to look on his wedding night.

Whoa. Wedding night? Where the hell had that thought come from?

Not that he was against marriage—hell, his parents were still in love after forty years—but as best he could recall, he'd never before looked at a woman and thought about a honeymoon. His problem was, the women he found sexually appealing tended to have personalities that bored him, and the women he really liked, people like Kari and Evelyn, weren't usually the ones who turned his crank.

Hayley moved seductively across the stage and he forgot about all other women he'd ever met. The female singer—Beyoncé?—teasingly said she was feeling like a naughty girl.

Oh yeah, Hayley was a naughty girl. Instantaneously, Ry was hard again.

Mouth dry, pulse pounding, he watched as she danced, playing with her robe, then slipping it off to reveal a short see-through nightie. Underneath it, he could clearly see a white lace bra and thong, and lots and lots of bare skin.

She glanced around, as if maybe she was looking for him, but, not wanting to distract her, he'd chosen a seat where she'd have trouble seeing him. Soon she focused on others in the audience and settled into her performance. Each time she danced, she gained confidence, working the stage more effectively and connecting more intimately with the audience.

And that tweaked his jealousy. Yet, what a turn-on that the seductive beauty onstage who was flirting the straps of her nightie down each sleek shoulder had been in his arms last night.

His. Only his. The other men could watch, but Hayley was his.

Well, she had been. Maybe could be again?

Last night, satiated from incredible sex, his brain had finally kicked into gear and he'd decided they shouldn't have a repeat performance. Now, the insistent throbbing in his groin begged him to reconsider. The Private Eye had no rule against colleagues dating; it was left up to people's judgment.

Right now, all his judgment had surged to his cock. Which meant, he'd better stick to the decision he'd made back when he was thinking straight.

Hayley pulled a clasp out of her hair and the glossy waves tumbled free, messy and glorious. Then she twirled around the pole, hair flying and nightie lifting to reveal her near-naked bottom half.

Back on the ground again, she strutted, hips swinging in a sultry dance, over to the other pole. She eased down both nightie straps and, with a sensual shimmy, let the garment slip to the stage.

Clad only in a bra and thong, she worked the pole, worked the audience. Her eyes sparkled, her smile was seductive, and she seemed to glory in her sexuality and in the audience's admiration.

As she twined around the stripper pole, he remembered her legs twined around his body, his cock embedded deep inside her.

He watched from within a haze of desire as her bra came off.

Her dance became more sexual, more provocative. He could barely breathe. All the blood in his system had surged south.

She was on the floor, hands stroking her body. Crawling to one side of the stage, she displayed her assets in a sequence of seductive poses. Running her tongue around her lips—lips that last night he'd owned—she smiled intimately at the men seated close to the stage.

Then, each movement drawn out and erotic, sultry, and full of sexual promise, she crawled toward a different group of men, arching, spreading her legs with amazing flexibility, flashing her naked crotch.

Last night, she'd spread her legs and welcomed him in. Her body had risen and fallen with him in a passionate drive to climax.

He could barely stifle a groan.

When she finished her show, he joined the rest of the audience in applauding energetically, but he wondered how he'd survive the rest of the evening.

Forcing his mind back to work, he continued to observe the club, its staff, and its patrons, but he wasn't seeing anything to account for Jennifer Mortimer's transition from a sweet-tempered wife to a loner who refused to give up stripping.

He wondered if Hayley was having any better luck backstage.

And then, there she was, wandering around the club in a white halter top that glowed in the light and a denim skirt that barely cleared her butt. What the hell was she wearing under it? Her assignment required her to strip onstage, not expose herself intimately offstage.

She exchanged words with a few customers, a waitress, seeming casual in her progress through the room. When she reached his table, she smiled, eyes twinkling. "Hi, I'm Penny. Are you enjoying your evening?"

Enjoying being tormented by her? Yes, and no. "Very much," he said, playing his role. "You're a very good dancer."

"Why, thank you. It's a pleasure to dance for a man who appreciates it." There was a twinkle in her golden eyes.

"Oh, I appreciate it." His groin ached from appreciation.

"In that case, maybe you'd like a private dance?"

Shit. His voice rasped, "No," as his body screamed *Yes!*

"You wouldn't? You don't want to be all alone with me, and have me dance just for you?" she teased.

Of course he *wanted* to. "That's not a good idea."

Her chin lifted. "No problem, sir. Enjoy your evening. I'm sure I'll find another man who's more receptive." Swinging her hips, she turned to go.

Jesus. She wouldn't, would she? "Hayl—" He stopped himself from saying her name and from grabbing her hand. "Hey, Penny, wait."

When she turned back, brows lifted, he muttered under his breath, "Private dances aren't part of the job. You should be talking to Kat."

She tilted her head and he realized Kat was across the room, chatting to a patron. "Or one of the other dancers," he said lamely. "Maybe they'll gossip."

"Mmm." She sauntered away. Backstage, he was thankful to see.

Hayley, giving another man a private, naked dance? Hell, no.

A flashily dressed pair of guys sauntered through the club and took seats at a table near the stage. Hmm. They had the look of drug dealers or pimps.

He made a trip to the men's room, and when he came back chose a table where he might overhear some of their conversation.

Snippets of talk drifted his way, with words like "deal" and mention of ritzy cars, enough to make him think he might be right. When Kat Dancer approached their table, his attention sharpened, but he didn't see any items change hands and the pair turned down a private show.

He'd just relaxed again when Hayley took the stage. Now she wore a gauzy harem costume made of flimsy purple fabric with gold fringe, embroidery, and sequins. Her music was Middle Eastern and sultry. Belly dance music.

This time, though she did smile at other men, he got the feeling she was dancing for him. Or maybe that was wishful thinking.

He shouldn't want her to focus on him, to draw attention to the two of them, yet a primal instinct made him want to claim this woman as his.

He toyed with his beer and tried not to watch her sultry, hip-swiveling movements, but that was as impossible as stopping an orgasm once he'd reached the point of no return.

By the time she left the stage, he was biting back curses. Damn, they had to solve the Mortimer case. His body couldn't handle any more nights like this.

The flashy guys had downed a few drinks, and got louder. Good for eavesdropping, but he quickly realized what they were dealing was cars, not drugs or hookers.

Time to change tables again, or go sit at the bar.

He was about to get up when Hayley drifted over again. She was back in the denim skirt and halter top.

With a public smile, she leaned close and whispered, "Kat and the others are after me to try a private dance." Her warm breath tickled his ear. "It's a challenge. I can't refuse. But if I do one and say it makes me uncomfortable, they'll back off. So, it's either going to be you or some other guy."

Hell. He swallowed hard.

She held out her hand invitingly.

No way was she going to dance naked in a tiny VIP booth for some other man. Ry had no choice but to rise and take her hand.

His own tingled at the contact, a tingle that spread up his arm and straight to his crotch. "Thought the customers and dancers weren't supposed to touch," he muttered.

Hell, how could he survive an intimate dance with sexy Hayley when he couldn't touch her? Couldn't have sex with her?

"Not during the actual dance." Her hand squeezed his. "But it's tradition to hold hands on the way to and from the VIP booths." She stretched up, lips close to his ear, to whisper, "Smile, Ry. You're supposed to be into this."

Oh yeah, he was into her. Into doing her, here and now.

He forced a public grin. "Okay, Penny, let's see what you've got."

When they'd left the main room and she was leading him down a corridor, he reminded himself that, before his cock had taken control of his brain, he'd decided they shouldn't have sex again. In which case, engaging in no-contact foreplay would be sheer torture. "We'll just sit and talk." He kept his tone low, so it couldn't be overheard above the music from the stage. "I want to hear how things are going with Kat."

"There are video cameras in the booths," she whispered back. "I'll have to dance or it'll look suspicious."

Damn, he'd researched this club thoroughly. How had he forgotten the cameras?

Or had he wanted to forget?

They walked into a room containing booths, some with the curtains pulled for privacy, others open to indicate they were empty. Hayley led the way into an empty one, and decisively whipped the curtain shut behind them. The booth contained only two chairs and a small table. He put down his beer and hung his jacket on the back of the chair, noting the video camera's eye staring at him. The music from the stage was piped in here and, though it was loud, he could hear a woman's husky laughter from a neighboring booth.

Privacy was an illusion, and the men who came here must know it.

Ry sat down, jaw clenched. He'd had a lap dance once, when a friend had bought one for him for his twenty-first birthday, and had concluded he'd rather have real-life sex instead.

His feelings sure as hell hadn't changed, even if he'd decided he and Hayley shouldn't share that particular pleasure again.

She gave him a flirtatious smile. "I'll dance to the next number when it starts. This one's almost over, and I want to make sure you get your money's worth."

He gritted his teeth. "Okay. But you don't have to, uh, be too enthusiastic."

Her false lashes batted. "I take my job seriously. Of course I'll be enthusiastic."

Oh, shit. He was fucked.

Belatedly it dawned on him that maybe she hadn't been impressed with him dictating the terms of their relationship. Was that why she was determined to torture him?

The song ended. They heard applause, the DJ's voice, and a few voices from other VIP booths. "I wonder what they'll play for us?" Hayley asked.

When the music started, he recognized Lady Gaga's "I Like It Rough." Reminding him of last night, the first quick-and-dirty sex. Unable to resist, he teased, "Does that suit you, *Penny*? Do you like it rough?"

Hayley began to sway to the music. Hips and pelvis, shoulders and torso, head. "I think you know the answer to that. I like it rough, I like it tender. Just so long as it's *good*." She drew the word out, glossy lips pouting seductively.

Her hair shifted and glimmered and her body shimmied and undulated in front of him—full breasts, narrow waist, curvy hips gyrating in front of his eyes.

He wanted to grab those hips and yank her down on his lap where his cock was rising to meet her. His hands twitched with the need to touch her. Instead, remembering the camera, he gripped the seat of his chair on both sides and vowed not to let go. "God, you're beautiful."

Her lips curved. "Thank you."

"And so sexy. It's killing me that I can't touch you." He spread his legs so she could dance closer—and so she could see the erection tenting his suit pants.

She sucked in a breath, then moistened red lips. "I wish you could. It would feel so good." Her eyes were half-closed, heavy lidded. Smoky and sultry. "So good for both of us. Mmm, I can just imagine your hands on me."

Slowly, sensually, she ran her hands through her thick hair then down her body. The slender column of her throat. The lush breasts that pressed against the silky halter top. The sleek expanse of skin between the bottom of the halter and the low waistband of her skirt. The outer curves of her hips, then in to her center and back out to her firm, sleek thighs.

Her golden eyes glittered with excitement. Sexual excitement.

Swaying her hips, she slowly rotated, arms above her head, graceful hands weaving a spell. Enthralling him. When her back was to him, she bent down, legs spread, and grasped her ankles. Her butt thrust toward him, just out of reach.

The question that had been plaguing him was answered. Under the tiny skirt, she wore a scarlet thong.

The skirt rode high, revealing curvy cheeks that begged to be squeezed. His finger wanted to trace the line of the thong, and his cock wanted to slide through the vee of her legs and drive into her pussy.

Still bent down, she twisted her body to one side so she could smile at him, her face framed by long, rippling waves of hair. "Is this good? Am I doing it right?"

"Shit, yeah. But come a little closer."

Lithely, sinuously, she rose and, keeping the dance going, slowly rotated until she was facing him again. Her arms, tipped by nails that matched her thong, swirled in the air, drifting past his body. Close, so close. Teasingly making him imagine her touch.

His blood throbbed. If only he could strip naked and feel the caress of her bare flesh against his.

"I like the way you look at me," she said, gazing into his eyes. "All hot and intense. Like I'm the sexiest woman alive."

"That's because you are."

"Aw, you say the sweetest things."

She thought he was teasing. But the truth was, while he'd been with lots of attractive, sexy women, none had had the innate sensuality, the exciting spark, of Hayley Croft.

Still shimmying, she rotated so her back was to him. Her whole body rippled and undulated, mesmerizing him, then her hands skimmed her hips over denim. A moment later she'd undone the zipper and was sliding out of the skirt, putting it on the spare chair.

With her back still to him, she put her hands on the edges of his chair and, still gyrating, lowered herself so she was almost sitting on his lap. So close that her silky hair tickled his nose.

His swollen cock ached and the need to grab onto her gorgeous butt and pull her down that last crucial inch was overwhelming. "You're killing me," he groaned.

She straightened, shook her hair to one side, and toyed with the ties of the halter, then undid them and tossed the scrap of silk on top of her discarded skirt.

When she turned to face him, her beautiful breasts were naked.

"It's a turn-on for me too," she said. With those sensual, provocative moves, she shimmied partway down, leaning forward so her breasts were only a tantalizing inch or two from his face. Her nipples were pebbled with arousal.

"Especially," she said, "because I know how good you can make me feel."

Now she was almost sitting on his lap again, this time facing him. She arched her back, ran her hands caressingly across her breasts, along her thighs. Up close, her golden eyes were glazed with passion.

Oh yeah. Give him ten minutes alone with her and he'd make her feel very, very good. Multiorgasmically good.

He'd give it to her tender, give it to her rough, give her anything she damned well desired. "God, I want you."

"Me too," she breathed.

One little tug and she'd be seated on his lap. He could unzip his fly, shove aside the crotch of her thong. Embed himself in her.

His hips thrust uncontrollably and his distended fly pressed her crotch.

She gave a soft gasp and pure need burned in her eyes.

"Shit," he said under his breath, and they jerked apart. "Sorry," he muttered. "But you really get to me." In fact, he had to clench every muscle to stop himself from coming.

She levered herself off his lap, careful not to brush him again. The music was ending. "Darn, I timed it wrong," she said.

"Huh?"

"I was supposed to get naked." Her fingers flirted with the side straps of her thong. "Want to buy another dance, so I can do it right?"

"Fuck, no." She was toying with him, and he was the wrong

man to mess around with. "Put your clothes on," he growled. "We'll finish this later."

She gave him a long, considering look, then ran the tip of her tongue around her red lips. "Oh, yeah. And in the meantime, remember that camera and fork over thirty-five dollars. Plus a tip, because I'm worth it."

10

After her last show, Hayley wanted to rush out of the club, find Ry, and demand a screaming orgasm. She was pretty sure her seduction had succeeded, and he'd be just about dying to oblige.

But Kat was in the dressing room too, getting ready to leave, and for the moment the two women were alone. No matter how badly she craved sex, Hayley couldn't turn her back on this opportunity.

So, Hayley began to change into street clothes as Kat slowly removed her makeup. The other woman looked subdued. Tired, perhaps.

Trying to empathize, Hayley said, "It's been a long night. I'll be glad to go home and put my feet up."

"You find it tiring? I guess, but it makes me feel so alive."

"Dancing does? Performing?"

"All of it." The other woman gazed at her own reflection, the sweetly pretty face of Jennifer Mortimer emerging from under Kat Dancer's dramatic makeup. "Having men think I'm beautiful. Being in control for once. Earning my own income. Doing something I'm good at. Something fun and exciting."

Dressed now, Hayley sank into the chair beside her. "Oh, yeah. I can identify. I've only been onstage a few times, but already I've changed."

Jennifer gave an understanding smile. "You feel like a whole new woman?"

She smiled back. "Exactly." And in that moment of sharing, she had a hunch. No, she didn't think Jennifer Mortimer was hooked on drugs, or having an affair with another man.

Ry was outside in his Jeep waiting. Hopefully, waiting to have fiery hot sex.

But right now, she was going to follow her hunch and see how Jennifer responded.

Half an hour later, Hayley hurried out of the club and rushed to the spot where Ry had said he'd pick her up.

When she leaped into the Jeep, he grabbed her arm. "Are you okay? I was getting worried."

"Sorry, but I finally had a chance to talk to Kat alone."

"Great." He pulled away from the curb and drove quickly, leaving the area where they'd be likely to run into anyone from the club.

All ready to tell her story, she noticed he was heading in the wrong direction for her apartment. "Ry, where are you going?"

"My place. Gastown. Tonight, we're gonna have a bed."

Oh, yes! He was so hot for her he didn't want to talk about the case, just get her into bed. She put her hand on his leg and trailed her fingers upward.

His thigh was warm and hard, powerful muscles shifting as he varied pressure on the gas pedal. The bulge under the fly of his pants was growing.

Work could definitely wait, even though she'd cracked the Mortimer case.

"Thought you didn't want us to have sex again," she teased.

He rested his hand atop hers for a moment, then returned it

to the steering wheel. "Turns out I can't be with you and not want you, Hayley."

Nice phrasing. He might mean that he couldn't watch her dance, see her naked, and not want to fuck her, but she'd like to believe that the actual words he'd spoken were true. Or, even if they weren't yet, that they'd become true if he spent more time with her.

"I feel the same." Her exploring hand curled over his erection and he groaned again.

If she was right, that there could be something real between them, something much bigger than sex, might it cause problems at The Private Eye? If so, she'd quit. She had a feeling her days as an administrative assistant were nearing an end anyhow. It was time to find a job with more responsibility, more excitement. More independence.

Mostly for herself, but also because she wanted to be the kind of woman who truly deserved a strong, sexy man like Ry. For the past six months she'd believed he was out of her league. Now, damn it, she was ready to create a league of her own.

As he pulled into an underground parking lot, she stroked his firm erection through his pants, feeling an answering tug of hunger in her pussy. "I know you mentioned a bed, but how about I give you a lap dance? Both of us naked this time."

His cock jumped under her hand. "You do that and I'll last all of a minute."

Hmm. She wanted longer than a minute.

She glanced around as he pulled the Jeep in between a SUV and a Smart Car. The parking lot was stark and unromantic, the lighting neither bright nor dim. No doubt a security guard patrolled it.

Still, what she had in mind wouldn't take more than . . . oh, probably a minute. She unzipped his pants. "Then let's take the edge off."

A second later, his warm, throbbing cock was in her hands, then she bent and closed her lips around the crown.

"Jesus." He groaned, fisted her hair.

He was all musky, turned-on male, his scent in her nostrils, his taste in her mouth. Arousal perked her breasts and quivered between her thighs as she sucked rhythmically, swirled her tongue around him, and pumped his shaft.

He'd been right about not lasting more than a minute. He gave another deep, wrenching groan, and surged to release.

She swallowed every delicious drop, then lifted her head. "Now, how about that lap dance?"

He chuckled. "Woman, I like the way you think."

Gingerly he zipped himself up and, hand in hand, they hurried to his apartment.

His place was a top floor loft, she discovered, open and informal. A little messy, and definitely a place he'd made his own. "I like this. It suits you."

"You suit me." The words came out gruffly. Like he really meant them, and felt embarrassed to admit it.

Her heart warmed with hope.

He pulled her into his arms, hard and tight, then he kissed her. Passionately, lingeringly. The way she'd always dreamed a man would one day kiss her.

After endless minutes, he broke for air. "It's been one hell of a long night." Then he was kissing her again.

The next time their lips separated, they hastily peeled off their clothes.

"Go sit in that chair." She picked a straight-backed solid one.

He obeyed, cock eagerly erect.

She picked up his suit jacket and searched the pockets, finding the tie he'd been wearing at the club.

"Uh-oh," he said, looking intrigued.

"Full contact," she said, "except you can't use your hands."

"Man, Hayley." But he didn't object as she secured his hands to the back rails of the chair.

"Condom?"

"Cabinet under the bathroom sink."

She went to get one, and grabbed a couple more for good measure.

He looked so sexy she was tempted to skip the dance and leap straight to the conclusion. But he'd been right when he said building arousal higher and higher resulted in stronger orgasms.

So, after sheathing him, she flicked quickly through his CDs. Who'd have guessed that, among the harder-driving guy music, there'd be some mellow stuff like Harry Connick Jr. and Diana Krall, and some classics like Leadbelly and early Joni Mitchell?

Aha! He had Boney James's old album *Body Language*. The music would be a perfect accompaniment to the body language she intended to speak to Ry.

When the music started, she sauntered over to where he sat spread legged, hands bound behind him, erection fully alert.

Letting the music move through her, the power of her own sensuality fill her, she danced slowly, close to him but not touching, caressing her body and reveling in finally knowing she was beautiful. Sexy. A woman who could captivate Ry Montana.

She saw it in his rapt expression, the skim of sweat on his brow, the tautness of his muscles.

Teasingly she turned her back, sent him a flirtatious look over her shoulder, then bent down, spreading wide to give him a clear view of her curvy butt cheeks all the way through to her damp pussy.

Slowly, sinuously, she rose and moved closer, almost sitting with her bum on his lap. Her back brushed his chest, the bottoms of her legs grazed his thighs. Between them, his cock jutted insistently, pressing hard against her backside. Her body's hunger urged her to grab hold of him, ease him between her legs, and ride him to climax.

Resisting, she shimmied her bum, stroking back and forth against his rigid organ until he begged for mercy.

She raised herself, turned to face him, and caressed both his thighs. Then she slid them together and put one leg on either side of his, not sitting on his lap—not yet—just gyrating with her unconfined breasts close to his face.

Resting her hands on his shoulders for balance, she slid forward until he could take a nipple in his mouth and suck on it.

Pleasure streaked through her body, a hot rush of need.

Rotating her hips in the air above his thighs, she brushed against his cock. No matter how good his lips felt on her breast, she knew something that would feel even better.

Lowering herself to sit on his lap, she kept up her seductive gyrations, but now his cock rose proudly between her legs, and each swirl of her hips pressed her pussy tight against him. Her juices slicked both of them so their bodies slid against each other, swollen and aching.

Her movements grew uncoordinated as tension coiled tighter inside her, demanding release. If she moved just right, his cock nudged her budded clit, and the need grew and grew.

She whimpered, and he said, voice hoarse, "Take what you need, Hayley. Or untie me, and let me give it to you."

Grabbing his shoulders, she squirmed, pressing harder, not caring about the dance, the music, only about her need. Staring down, she loved seeing how ripe and swollen his cock was.

Ry's cock, rising between them, all hers to use for her pleasure.

She ground hard against him, then cried, "Ry, oh God!" as the tension burst in surges of climax.

"Now," he grated out. "Now, Hayley."

Fingers clumsy with urgency, she reached down to grasp him, lifted herself, and guided him to her entry. She was so sensitive, still on the edge of that first climax, that when he plunged into her in one hard thrust, she burst apart again.

His hips jerked as he drove into her, hard, over and over. Somehow, amazingly, she kept coming around his rigid shaft. Then he shuddered and shouted out with his own release.

She clung to him for long minutes.

"Hayley, for God's sake untie me."

Oh, right, he was still bound.

She freed him and they embraced silently for long minutes. Finally he said, "Gotta deal with the condom. Sorry."

Untangling themselves, they rose. Her legs ached—from dancing, from stripper shoes, from spreading wide for Ry. But it was a wonderful ache.

"What an incredible night," she said with satisfaction when he returned.

"Oh, yeah. You're fantastic, Hayley, Penny, whatever your name is."

She laughed softly. "And I haven't even told you what Kat said."

"How about a glass of wine and a snack in bed, and you can tell me?"

Her heart quickened. "Are you asking me to spend the night?"

He touched her cheek. "Can't think of anything I'd like better."

Oh, yes. They were only just beginning and there was everything to learn about each other, but the tender light in his eyes told her there was a lot more to Ry than that devil-may-care attitude he showed the world.

A few minutes later, settled cozily in the loft bedroom with wine, salty pretzels, and the man of her dreams, she clicked her glass against his. "I solved the case."

"What? You're kidding. Already?" He was reclining, propped against pillows, strong torso naked, covers draped casually at his hips.

She sat cross-legged facing him, wearing one of his T-shirts. "It's not what her husband feared, but all the same he may be losing his wife. Not because of another man, but because of himself."

Ry punched up the pillows behind his back so he sat straighter. "Go on."

"Paul's almost ten years older than Jennifer and he married her as soon as she graduated high school. She never had a job and he didn't want her to get one. He prided himself on taking care of her, providing everything. The guy sounds like something out of the fifties."

He grimaced. "Believe me, some women want that kind of life."

"Jennifer was too young to know what she wanted. Paul looked after her, but he never told her she was beautiful or smart, never gave her fun, exciting, or sexy gifts. She always felt second class and dependent. She wasn't unhappy, but she wasn't happy either."

"Why didn't she do something about it?"

"She was passive, stuck in her rut, and Paul liked things the way they were. Until he lost his job and couldn't find another. Jennifer had to work, and discovered stripping. She was good at it and made good money. Men adored her, she was the center of attention. The one in control."

Slowly, he nodded. "I can see that."

"Dancing gives her a high, then she goes home and it's a letdown. She wants to get back in costume and dance." Hayley reached for a pretzel from the bowl resting between them. "From the beginning, Paul wanted her dancing to be a deep, dark secret. She couldn't tell her girlfriends, and besides she's afraid they'll think it's immoral. Now she feels like she has more in common with the other dancers."

"She can't talk to her husband about this?"

"No. He hated that she was stripping, so she could hardly tell him it turned her on way more than he did. She just withdrew."

He gave a low whistle. "That's a pretty unhealthy situation for both of them."

"Yeah. And it won't get better unless she's honest with him. Even then, I don't know if they can work things out, but at least they'd both know what the problem is."

"You're sure there's no other man? No drugs?"

"Yes. She's faithful to Paul, though they rarely have sex. As for drugs, a couple of the girls use them, but Jennifer says they take away your control, so she's against them."

He lifted his glass to her. "Job well done, Hayley. I'm impressed." Then he grinned. "Hey, you can call an end to your career as a stripper. Gotta say, I'm not unhappy about that. I don't like all those guys gaping at that gorgeous body of yours."

She toyed with her own glass. Some of the dancers had talked about boyfriends who got jealous and possessive. Surely Ry wasn't the kind of man who'd try to control what she did. "I think I should finish out the week."

"In case there's something else going on that Jennifer didn't tell you about?"

"Partly. And I want to encourage her to come clean with her husband, maybe get counseling."

He frowned. "So have coffee with her."

"I could, but . . ." Ry needed to know the truth. She took a deep breath. "I want to dance. For me. I'm learning things about myself. Good things. I'll do this on my own time; it won't be an expense for our client."

He studied her for a long moment. "You're not thinking of becoming a stripper, are you?"

She tilted her chin. "Would that be so bad?"

"Jesus, Hayley."

"You think there's something wrong with stripping?"

"Uh . . . No, I guess not, but—"

If she'd ever had the slightest prejudice against strippers, she'd lost it tonight. "It's a job like any other job, with pros and cons. And it's dance, performance, and I'm pretty darned good at it."

One corner of his mouth kinked. "You're damn good at it. Too damn good. But hell, it's hard to think about my girlfriend being naked each night in front of a roomful of guys."

His girlfriend. Oh, yes! Warmth flooded her heart.

"Okay. Finish out the week," he said. "Just make sure I'm the guy you come home with."

"No question about that." She'd wanted Ry since she first saw him, and now they were boyfriend and girlfriend. It was her dream come true.

She was flattered that he wanted to keep her for himself. Besides, she wasn't likely to decide she wanted to become a stripper for real, so there wasn't going to be any issue between them. They weren't going to be like Jennifer Mortimer and her husband.

11

Saturday night, after Hayley finished the last show of her contracted week, she felt an odd mix of feelings. Relief, triumph, regret.

Satisfaction, primarily. She was a different, much stronger, woman than she'd been a week ago.

Kat, wearing her slinky black costume, watched as Hayley, now totally comfortable with nudity, dropped her towel and reached into her gym bag for the bra and panties she'd wear home. "I'll miss you, Penny."

"Me too. Good luck with the counseling." Kat/Jennifer had sat her husband down for a tell-all, and they'd decided to go to marriage counseling. In Hayley's opinion, there was a fifty/fifty chance they'd either fix their marriage or part company. Either resolution had to be better for both of them than the status quo.

Once Hayley was dressed in figure-hugging jeans and a tank top that showed off her cleavage—she'd made a few additions to her wardrobe—she gave the other woman a hug. "Be strong. Be happy."

A couple other dancers who'd come in to change costumes

hugged her too and wished her well. In the last few days, she'd developed a real fondness for these women, and for the dressing room cluttered with sequins, makeup, and stripper shoes.

She'd also developed more than just fondness for the man who waited outside. After six months of fantasies, the reality was even better than she'd imagined. Ry was tough and capable, smart and witty, tender and considerate.

Of course, no man was perfect. Ry's biggest flaw was his attitude toward her stripping. He treated her temporary job with amused tolerance—and undisguised impatience for the week to end.

How would he react when she told him about her plans?

Fifteen minutes later, when he ushered her into his condo, she gave a pleased, "Wow!"

Beside the big window with its view of Vancouver Harbor sat a small table decorated with a vase of purple orchids, two champagne flutes, and an ice bucket containing a bottle of Lanson bubbly.

She only hoped they'd still drink it after she told Ry what she had in mind.

She only hoped they'd still be together.

He took a platter from the fridge and put it on the table.

"Oh, yummy." They were Lebanese lamb meatballs with yogurt sauce and pine nuts. "Kari made these?" When the PI had brought them to the office a couple times, made from her grandmother's recipe, Hayley had loved them.

"To congratulate you for a job well done."

"Does the fact that she gave them to you mean she's on to us?" she asked as they sat down across from each other.

"She says she saw it coming before we did."

And she'd sent her special meatballs as a symbol of approval. Hayley smiled and tasted one. "Mmm. Delicious."

He eased the cork from the champagne and deftly poured two glasses.

She clicked her glass to his. "What are we toasting?" If only he didn't say the end of her stripper career.

"You. You and me, and the best week of my life."

Her heart melted. "I'll definitely drink to that." Even with their occasional differences of opinion, there was a sense of rightness about her and Ry together.

It gave her the courage to tell him what was in her heart. "I fell for you the first day I met you, Ry. And I've been falling a little more each day."

Across the table, his blue eyes were soft. "It took me way longer, Hayley. But when I fell, man did it happen fast and hard." He leaned over to give her a slow, sensual kiss.

This was bliss, and she wanted to relax and savor it. But she had to tell him about her new job and see how he reacted.

"Ry, I have news. I'm tired of being an administrative assistant. I want a job with more challenge and excitement."

His eyes narrowed. "Tell me you don't want to be a stripper."

Damn, she really hated his attitude. So she said, "The other dancers told me their agency would be thrilled to represent me, and the manager of The Naked Truth said he'd have me back anytime."

"Shit, Hayley."

Deception was bad, so she told the truth. "I chose something different, though."

His face brightened. "Whew. You had me worried."

Troubled, she studied that handsome face. Would he be any more approving of the career she'd decided on?

If not, it would be the end of their relationship. No matter how much she wanted Ry—was even falling in love with him— she'd never be with a man who tried to control her. This week had taught her that.

Feeling stronger, yet more vulnerable, than ever before, she said, "I talked to Evelyn today. I'm going to study to become a PI and she'll be my supervisor."

"A PI?" He looked a little stunned, then delight lit his face. "Hayley, you're perfect for it."

Relief made her a little giddy. "I think so too." She had the attention to detail and patience to do the tedious tasks like research and surveillance, and the intelligence and people skills to do the more challenging work. And her craving for adventure would be satisfied on a regular basis.

She'd even discovered she had her fair share of courage. Enough to strip onstage and enough to take on Ry Montana. Hopefully, enough to tell Gran about the changes in her life. As she'd told Kat/Jennifer, you shouldn't try to deny who you really are, and you should be honest about it with the people you love.

"And you're perfect for me," he said, sounding content.

Who'd have known that big, tough Ry Montana could sound content, and be so happy about it? Something told her Gran might well approve of this man.

"So, here's to your short-lived career as a stripper," he said, hoisting his glass again. "Thank God it's over."

She took a deep breath. Her career change had been only the first hurdle. The second promised to be even more problematic. "I don't intend to give it up completely."

"What?" His face darkened.

"It's fun." She spoke softly, but with determination. "Choosing the music, putting together a costume, working on the choreography. Getting out there onstage and feeling . . . like a goddess."

"You're my goddess. Isn't that enough? Why the hell d'you have to take your clothes off for other men?"

"I don't have to, but I want to. It's a thrill."

"You sound like Jennifer Mortimer," he said disapprovingly. "Living life from one thrill to the next."

"No. I do like having some excitement in my life, but I'll

never be addicted to it. And I want it to come from a number of places, like my job, being with you, and every now and then dancing as an amateur at The Naked Truth on Sunday night."

"Damn, Hayley."

She stuck her jaw out. "What's your big problem with this? Do you think there's something wrong with stripping?"

The challenge kept him quiet for a few moments. Then he said, "Shit. Okay, it's not just stripping, I'd be pissed if you modeled for Victoria's Secret. I guess I'm being chauvinistic and possessive. But hell, would you be okay with a bunch of women gawking at my naked bod?"

Her lips twitched at the thought of Ry stripping. He'd sure make great eye candy. But when she thought of other women drooling over him, maybe tossing their panties onstage, she did feel a surge of jealousy. Fear. Insecurity.

Insecurity? Was Ry actually insecure? Did he think she might choose another man, or feel like such a goddess that he wouldn't be good enough for her?

Maybe that's how Paul Mortimer felt about Jennifer's work.

All the same, insecurity was no basis for a relationship.

"Maybe I'd feel a little uncomfortable," she admitted. "But if you and I had a committed relationship and you really wanted to be a stripper or model, I'd try not to be jealous or possessive. I'm not like Paul Mortimer. If it was important to you, I'd do my best to understand and be supportive."

He studied her face for a long moment, then made a rueful sound. "Point taken. Hell, I don't want to be a jerk like Mortimer. If it's what you want, then you should do it. You're damned good at it." A grin started. "Can I be in the audience?"

She let out a relieved sigh. Oh yes, things were going to be okay. More than okay, they were going to be wonderful. Thank heavens Ry was willing to see her point of view and change his mind. "I'd love it if you were in the audience. It would give me extra motivation."

"So, stripper girl," he said, eyes twinkling, "it'll just be an occasional stage show? No private dances?"

"Oh, I might be persuaded to do a private dance now and then. For a very, very exclusive audience."

"A wet dream come true." He shoved back his chair and patted his lap. "My own private dancer?"

She rose and went over to straddle him, pressing her jean-clad crotch against the bulge behind his fly. "Mmm, that's pretty selfish of you. But I might consider it."

Shifting her a little, he reached into his pocket for his wallet. "Now, let me see if I remember. It's thirty-five dollars a dance, right?"

He opened his wallet and pulled out a wad of bills. "If I want all your dances for the foreseeable future, will this cover it?"

Heart full of relief, joy, and a feeling she very much suspected was love, Hayley reached over and extracted his charge card. "Lover, you're going to need this."

Cherry on Top

Anne Rainey

For my editor, Audrey LaFehr. I cannot thank you enough for making this dream come true.

and

Jen, Kelley, Rita, Moran, Pat, as well as those extremely valuable beta readers, you know who you are. There's been quite a bit of ranting, hair-pulling and even a few tears along the way. I will always treasure your generous offers of wine and chocolate, not to mention your unwavering support. You all rock!

My loving and supportive husband and my two very patient daughters . . . you make my life tremendously rich!

1

The hot water jets massaged and soothed her muscles, bringing her fully awake. "I'm *so* not a morning person," Cherry muttered to herself as she slapped a hand against the tile wall of the shower to keep herself upright.

As the heat continued to do its job, Cherry grabbed her pink puff and spurted some bath gel onto it. She ran the sponge over her arms and shoulders, down her ribcage, then dipped it between her thighs. The instant the soft sponge touched her clit an image sprang to mind.

Dante Ricci. The man who haunted her dreams and drove her crazy with his intense blue eyes and dark good looks. They'd never shared more than a few hellos and yet she always had the impression he saw right through her, as if reading her thoughts. He was a dangerous man to any woman, but that didn't stop her from wanting him. Craving him. His sculpted body, square jaw, and sensual mouth were pure sin. Fantasy material for sure. And she'd had plenty of fantasies over the last four months since moving to Zanesville, Ohio.

Cherry dropped the sponge and grabbed the removable

showerhead from the hook on the wall, then ran it over her body. She closed her eyes and let her mind conjure up an image of Dante, nude, kneeling in front of her, taking her clit between his teeth, licking and suckling her pussy.

She let the pounding streams drift over her breasts, increasing her pleasure, then down to the juncture of her thighs. She gasped and flung her head back when the water hit her throbbing center. Each nerve ending came alive. She imagined Dante's fingers plunging deep inside her aching hot core as she stroked and petted her glistening pussy, her body convulsing. She laid her head back against the shower wall and lifted her foot to the ledge, exposing her flesh, then dipped two fingers deep as the water teased her clit.

Cherry trembled with anticipation, her entire body alive with sensation. She squirmed against the onslaught, as she envisioned Dante's mesmerizing gaze, dark, tousled hair and powerful body. Her lower body started a sweet rhythm that drew a whimper out of her. Cherry pulled her fingers free and cupped her left breast, squeezing and massaging with the sort of force she imagined Dante using. She pinched her own nipple, torturing herself further. She slid the water jets over the inside of her thigh, coaxing a moan from deep inside her chest, her soft, wet pussy throbbing and aching for release, then back to her clit again. The swollen mass of nerve endings pulsed as wicked images of Dante fondling her, licking her to completion, drove her over the edge. She slammed her palm against the wall and rode out the climax, shouting Dante's name as she came.

Cherry placed the shower head back on the hook and took a moment to catch her breath, legs shaking, her body still pulsing with little aftershocks. It wasn't the first time she'd started her day this way, and it wouldn't be the last. She wished she had the nerve to approach the sexy owner of the business next to her massage therapy center. One of these days maybe it really would be him in this shower with her.

"Yeah, and I'll suddenly sprout wings and fly." Whom was she kidding? She was too damn shy to approach a man like Ricci! Thanks to her jerk of an ex-husband, she was just way too unsure of her own appeal.

She finished washing and turned the water off, then forced herself to forget about things that could never be, and concentrated on the task at hand, which was making Serene Comfort a success. She had clients coming in who needed her to be in top form and she refused to let them down. Word of mouth was a powerful promotional tool and Cherry hoped the more people who left her center happy, the more business she'd have. She wouldn't let anyone derail her from making her business a success.

"There, that's the last box. Now it's official."

"You've been doing business for two months and *now* it's official?"

Cherry laughed. "Wade, it's never official until the last box is unpacked. Surely you knew that."

Wade picked up another donut and took a large bite, then mumbled, "By your way of thinking, I've yet to be moved into my apartment and I've been there for three years."

"You just don't understand the female mind."

"And no man ever will, baby."

Cherry stopped and stared at her friend. He'd been there for her through it all. The divorce, the tears, and the worry of what she was going to do with the rest of her life. He'd never once complained. Heck, she wouldn't even have the shop if it weren't for him. He'd been the one to show her the empty space, then he'd helped her set up the loan at the bank. She owed him so much. Tears welled in her eyes. "I can never repay you for everything you've done for me these last four months."

Wade's head shot up. It was always like that with him. He picked up on the slightest hint of sadness. She'd never quite understood how he could read her so well.

When he placed the chocolate iced donut back in the container and strode across the room, she knew what was coming and welcomed it. His big strong arms wrapped around her shoulders and pulled her against him in a tight embrace. "Don't you worry about repaying me. I'm just glad we found this building so cheap. It worked out perfectly."

"Yes. It was the first good thing to happen since Brody decided I was in the way of his happiness."

"Brody is a bastard. He's out of your life, and if you ask me you're better off."

"Thanks, Wade. It's odd, but I do feel like there's been a weight lifted. It's scary to think I could spend three years with a man and not really know him for the snake he is."

"Just remember, not all men are like Brody. There's a gem out there for you, I know it."

"My white knight," she murmured.

"Damn straight."

The bells on the door chimed and she stepped out of Wade's arms to see who it could be; she didn't have another appointment for an hour. When Cherry saw the man filling the doorway, she cringed. Dante Ricci from the financial consulting business next door, and if the scrunched brows were any indication, he wasn't any happier to see her than she was him. Her morning foray in the shower sprung to mind and her cheeks heated. Dante's mouth curved, as if he knew her naughty little secret. Damn annoying man.

She stiffened her spine. "Can I help you?"

"I'm here to schedule an appointment."

Her eyes shot wide. "You are?"

He stepped forward. "Got a problem with that, Ms. DuBois?"

She had to step back. It was pure suicide to stand so close to a man like Dante. He exuded power and masculinity. Cherry wanted nothing to do with either. At least that's what she kept chanting to her overactive libido.

"I'm booked up today."

"I'm free tomorrow," he countered.

On shaky legs, she walked around the counter and grabbed her appointment book from the shelf underneath. When she flipped it open and realized she had a slot open at the end of the following evening she winced. "I can fit you in at five, does that work?"

"Great. See you then."

He started to leave and for a moment she was distracted by the way his black suit pants stretched over his tight buttocks. My God he was delicious to look at! The bells on the door brought her out of her lustful musings. "Wait! I need to know how long you want. I offer a half hour, forty-five minute, and one hour massage."

His gaze moved south, had Cherry not been watching him so closely she would have missed the quick peek at her cleavage. "Definitely an hour," he growled, then walked out.

"Wow," she breathed.

Wade snapped his fingers in front of her face. "Earth to Cherry."

"He's really . . . something."

"He wants you. Bad."

Cherry's cheeks heated, again she thought of her little masturbation session that morning. "He wants a *massage* bad, not me."

Wade tapped her nose and murmured, "No, babe, he wants you. The massage is a ruse."

She frowned. "In that case, maybe I should cancel the appointment. It's not appropriate."

"Listen to yourself. Not appropriate? You aren't married anymore and you did nothing wrong by giving him an appointment. If things get hot and heavy, you'll handle it."

"You have more confidence in me than I do, Wade, because I'm not sure that man can even *be* handled."

Wade laughed and grabbed his bottle of apple juice. "Trust me, with a body like yours, you'll handle Dante Ricci just fine."

"Are you flirting with me, Mr. Harrison?"

"Hell no! That's like flirting with my sister." He gave a mock shudder. "Gross."

Cherry shook her head. "Gee, thanks."

Wade took one last swallow of his apple juice then handed her the empty bottle. "Thanks for breakfast, Cherry darlin', but I need to scoot."

She took the bottle and rose on her tiptoes to place a kiss on his cheek. "It was the least I could do considering all the work you put into this place. I still wish you'd let me pay you for the wallpaper you hung."

"No. And if you dare bring up payment again, I'll spank your ass."

"Ooh, kinky," she teased.

He leaned down and whispered into her ear, "You have no idea, baby, no idea."

As he turned and left, Cherry could only stare. In all the years they'd been friends, Wade had never once said anything sexual to her. It must have been the August heat getting to him. And while he was a handsome devil, it wasn't his voice and mesmerizing eyes she'd been dreaming about for the last few weeks. No, that dubious honor went to Dante Ricci. The dark haired Italian with the brooding good looks and dangerous aura, who just happened to own the business next to hers. And now he wanted a massage. She'd have his flesh beneath her fingertips, his big, hard body on her massage table. The thought sent a shiver of awareness to her core.

As she placed a clean sheet on the table she thought of how hard Brody had worked to make her feel inferior. When he realized she would never be the meek little wife he so badly craved, he'd sent her packing. She'd been left floundering with no home and no money. Thankfully, Wade had stepped up and given her a place to stay. Once it sank in that she was going to have to find a job, it had been Wade who'd reminded her of the massage therapist license she'd earned before marrying Brody. The one smart thing she'd done in the three years of marriage to the jerk was keep her license renewed. Thank God for that at least.

The divorce hadn't been pretty, but thanks to the lawyer Wade had hired, she'd been compensated nicely for the way Brody had treated her. She'd found a place of her own and took out a loan to open Serene Comfort. Now all she had to do was keep it open.

She glanced at the clock on the wall and realized her client would be there soon. She put thoughts of failed marriages and gorgeous looking Italians to the back of her mind and got to work. After all, making Serene Comfort a success was sure to be the best sort of revenge against Brody.

The next day, Cherry's nerves were shot. She'd been anticipating Dante's massage all day, even contemplated canceling it to keep from having to face the man who sent her thoughts scattering and her body rioting out of control. As the clock struck five, Dante strode through the door. Right on time, she wasn't surprised. He seemed like a precise sort of man. She instructed him to undress to his own personal comfort level and wrap the folded sheet around his lower half, then lie facedown on the table. Five minutes later she returned to the massage room and saw that Dante had done exactly as instructed. She noticed his clothes folded neatly on the chair. He'd stripped down to his birthday suit. She really wished he hadn't done that.

Cherry took a fortifying breath and said a silent prayer to get through the massage without fumbling, then went to work. First, she turned on the music and dimmed the lights just enough to create a relaxing atmosphere. Then she grabbed her oil out of the warmer and squirted a small amount onto her hands and rubbed them together.

"I'm going to start on your back and work my way down. The sheet will cover you at all times, except for the part I'm working on. If I'm using too much pressure, say so. This should feel good, not painful."

He nodded and somehow even his silence seemed dangerous. She worked on his deltoids first, then the trapeziums. The heavy muscles proved difficult. He was much stronger and thicker than any man she'd massaged. She had to use more pressure than what she was used to, and Dante had a lot of tension. She frowned. "You should come in at least twice a month. You have knots on top of knots."

"Mmm, I would have been coming once a week since the moment you opened had I known how good you were."

A zing of delight ran through her veins. "I've had my license for a while, but I've only put it to use recently since I opened two months ago."

"I know how long you've been here. You bought the space that I wanted to use to expand my business."

"Oh. I didn't realize."

"I know."

She worked her way over each vertebra, taking great care to massage each one. As she reached his gluteus medius, she covered the part of his back she'd just worked on and asked, "Are you comfortable with me working on your buttocks?"

"Go for it, I'm not the shy type."

She choked back a laugh. Yeah, she'd just bet he wasn't the shy type. Cherry started on his buttocks. She removed one side of the sheet at a time, keeping his other buttock covered. He groaned several times and she grinned. There was something about giving another individual this type of stress release that always had her smiling with pride. She loved her job and when she made people feel good, made them forget their cares, it was a rewarding feeling.

"So, Mr. Ricci, what do you do exactly. I know your business is financial consulting, but what all does that entail?"

"I help people select the right sort of investments. Showing them how best to save for the future, dealing with pensions and the like can mean retiring early or working until you can't work any longer."

Cherry slowly but methodically made her way down his thighs, finding and massaging several pressure points along the way. "So why did you want the space?"

"I'm considering bringing in other certified advisors, which will hopefully expand my client base and theirs."

She noticed his low voice, as if he was nearly asleep. She carefully massaged each foot, then broke contact and said, "Now, you can turn over. Just drag the blanket as you go."

Dante slowly slid to his back, his eyes closed, a drowsy expression on his face. He looked . . . boyish. Wow, he really was getting the most out of the massage. Cherry squirted more oil on her hands and began to work on his forehead and temples. With easy, flowing movements, she made her way down his jaw, where she carefully massaged the chords in his thick neck. She kept going, keeping her pace precise, her inner timer warning her that she needed to keep moving or she would get off schedule.

"That scent, what is it?"

"Cherries."

He muttered something she couldn't quite make out, then said, "I told you about my business, now you tell me about massage therapy."

As she made her way over his torso, she talked. "When I received my license I got a job working in a chiropractor's office and slowly built up my clientele. After a few years, I met Brody."

"Who's Brody?"

"My ex-husband. After we married, I quit working and we began trying to have children. It never worked out, though."

"I'm sorry."

"Me too." She mentally pushed the sadness away and focused. "Anyway, after the divorce, I moved here."

"Where did you live before?"

"Columbus. Not a huge move, but one that seemed necessary at the time."

"A fresh start."

She smiled. "Pretty much."

"So, do all your clients undress completely?"

The question seemed so far out of left field, but she answered him anyway. "They always have the option of leaving their undergarments on. Knowing in advance how thorough they want me to be helps save a lot of embarrassment."

"Have you ever had a man insist on keeping his boxers on?"

She rolled her eyes. "Of course. Most men aren't very modest, but there are a few who are."

"How many people do you massage a day?"

Cherry noticed his voice wasn't quite so steady. He was so relaxed she doubted he even knew half of what he was saying. "Depends. As you know, I offer one hour massages, but I also offer half hour and forty-five minute massages. The shorter times are basically targeted towards a specific problem area. For instance, I have a few clients who deal with carpel tunnel syndrome, the half hour is perfect for that. Also, one pregnant woman comes to me for her feet. She has a lot of swelling so I focus on her legs and feet. On average anywhere from ten to fifteen people a day."

"And you work Monday through Friday?"

She finished the massage by smoothing out the tension in his arms and hands. "Yep. Five days a week keeps me afloat."

"That's a lot of work. It can't be good for you to be on your feet like that."

Cherry stepped back and admired her handiwork. He was oiled from head to toe. With his tousled dark hair and sleek muscles, he looked like a calendar model. Sex and sin. And he was noticeably aroused. Oh my, he was huge!

"We're through," she managed around the rock in her throat. "I'll just, uh, let you get dressed."

Dante's hand snaked out and grabbed on to her arm. A single tug and she was practically lying across his chest. "Mr. Ricci!"

"If you do this with all your male clients you can bet your sexy ass you'll have a thriving business soon." She started to protest, but he stopped her with a hard kiss. His lips were rough and commanding. When he pulled back, they were both panting. "I came here in the hopes of finding out that you're a fraud. I want this space and I was all prepared to do whatever necessary to get it. But, I can see you're very good at what you do. It's obvious you love your work. My only question is, are you dating anyone?"

"That's none of your business. Please let me go."

He released her at once, which caused her to lose her footing. She stumbled backward, just barely keeping her balance. When she moved to leave, he stopped her with another quick demand.

"Have dinner with me tonight."

"Why? So you can talk me out of my lease?"

He sat up, keeping the sheet in place. "No. I won't deny I want this space, but I also want to spend more time with the woman who stole it from me."

"I did no such thing!"

He stood, one hand clutching the white sheet. He was the most forbidding man she'd ever seen. His sheer size alone made her feel vulnerable.

"Whether you realized it at the time doesn't matter. Not anymore. I just want to spend an evening with you. Is that so much to ask?"

"You're a client. It's not ethical."

"You're an MT not a doctor, Cherry. Besides, having dinner with me is perfectly innocent."

She rolled her eyes at that bit of nonsense, then spared his growing erection a quick glance. "There's nothing innocent in your invite and you know it."

He had the gall to grin. "Okay, so I want you, but if all we have is dinner then it doesn't matter how I feel, does it?"

"No. I don't date my clients."

He was silent a minute, then he said, "We'll see."

On shaky legs, Cherry left him to dress. His words flitted through her mind late into the night. The next morning she found herself in the shower again, attempting to stamp out her own wild cravings. And as usual, it wasn't working for crap.

It'd been a month since that first massage and Dante hadn't let up once. He had a standing appointment every Friday. His gentle coaxing was whittling away at her strength. He was simply too damn gorgeous. Too dangerous and exciting. It was like saying no to a slice of chocolate cake. No woman had that sort of strength!

Today marked his fifth massage and once again he asked the same question.

"Will you have dinner with me, Cherry?"

It'd been a long time since she'd enjoyed a man's company. Well before the divorce in fact. Who could blame her if she caved? "Dinner, nothing more. Are we clear on that?"

"Clear as glass, Ms. DuBois." The grin that curved his sensual lips wasn't at all reassuring. "Now, go so I can dress in private."

"Yes, Master," she answered sarcastically.

His eyes narrowed and she was sure he was about to say something more, but he stayed silent. She took the advantage and left him to dress and went about closing up. When he came out of the massage room, his perfectly sculpted body once again encased in a pair of navy trousers and a white dress shirt, she all but drooled. God, he was one gorgeous man.

2

It hadn't taken him long, she'd give him that. They'd shared a lovely dinner at a small, quiet Chinese restaurant, then she'd somehow found herself agreeing to a nightcap back at his apartment. Was she just that easy or was he that good? She couldn't decide.

"I barely know you. Tell me more about yourself, Dante."

He kept his eyes on the road, his hands firmly wrapped around the wheel of his sleek black BMW 5 Series. "Let's see. I grew up in Florence, Italy. I came to the States after turning eighteen, when my father had been transferred."

That sure explained the delicious accent that made her bones melt. "It must have been a serious culture shock for you."

He nodded. "It was difficult at first, but I grew to love it here. A few years ago my father died of a heart attack. It was hard on my mom, she and Dad were very much in love."

"I'm so sorry, Dante."

He looked at her then, taking his gaze off the road for a second. "It's okay. I was raised to believe that death doesn't mean the end, merely a change of location."

"I've never heard it put quite that way, but it's a very nice way to think." She glanced at his ring finger, noticing not for the first time that there was no glimmer of a gold band. "So, you never married?"

"No. I'm not opposed to marriage, but I've been busy getting my business off the ground. Mom says I'm a workaholic."

"Are you?"

He shrugged as he turned a corner. "Maybe. Maybe I've just never found the right distraction."

She had nothing to say to that so she stayed silent and watched as he pulled into a parking garage.

As he maneuvered the car into a space, he shut off the engine and turned to her. "We're here."

"I barely know you," she blurted out.

Dante leaned forward and took her face in the palms of his hands. "I've watched you every day for the last three months. I've wanted you since the first moment I saw you. I can't stop wanting you, believe me I tried."

It'd been the same for her, but she wasn't about to give him that sort of leverage. "But you want my shop. You want to close me down. You admitted that yourself."

He shook his head. "It's true I wanted the space. Hell, look at it from my viewpoint. I go away on a two-day business trip only to come back and find it already leased. I won't lie to you, Cherry, I wasn't real thrilled."

"Yeah, I thought as much."

"I had that place all planned out before you came along," he murmured. "And I had thought to coerce you into giving it up, but I still would've compensated you so you could open Serene Comfort elsewhere."

"And now?"

"Right now the only thing I can think of is *you*. What you look like underneath those conservative slacks and that silk blouse. I have a fair idea, but I'd really like to see for myself."

"You're much too bold, and I'm way out of your league."

"How so?"

"For three years I was married to a man who tried his best to destroy my sense of self-worth by cheating on me."

Dante's face hardened, as if angered on her behalf. "Why did you stay with him?"

She shrugged. "When you love someone you don't give up at the first sign of trouble. I wanted to make it work, no matter what."

"What changed?"

"I realized that some men are better off single."

Dante's grin lit her on fire. "He was an idiot. I never would have looked at other women if I had you in my bed."

She leaned back, to preserve her sanity if nothing else, which forced him to drop his hands. "Don't flatter me. I'm already here so obviously flattery isn't necessary."

His features changed, turned hard. "I don't lie. I say what I mean."

She faltered at the seriousness in his tone. "I'm not perfect, Dante, I have just as many flaws as the next gal."

"Maybe, but I like you just as you are. I wouldn't expect you to be anything other than *you*."

"You don't even know me."

Dante closed the gap she'd created. "You're Cherry DuBois, the sexy massage therapist who managed to snap up the space I'd been eyeing for the last six months. You're the woman I've craved so bad I go to bed smelling that damn cherry oil you use on your clients. You're the woman in my car arguing over whether you deserve compliments or not. You're the only thing I want and everything I need."

Every bone in her body seemed to gel, her blood heated and her mind went blank. She couldn't counter an attack like that. No woman would be capable of speech after such a statement.

Dante didn't seem to require words from her though, he

simply placed two fingers against her lips and murmured, "Just follow me and you'll see."

She blinked, then nodded. They left the car and he took her hand in his and led her to an elevator. They rode up in silence. Once inside his apartment she knew the truth. She was about to sleep with Dante Ricci. She would no longer be imaging his kisses and touches, she'd be experiencing them. Oh, my.

When they entered his bedroom, Dante flipped a light and the room instantly came into view. "Wow," Cherry cried.

"You like it?"

Like was too tame a word. She was floored. He'd decorated the room to the hilt in romance. Tiny red rose petals littered the bed. White candles sat atop the dresser and the bedside table. On the nightstand stood a crystal bowl full of cherries. The most sensual ruby-red nightgown lay across a corner chair. Long flowing satin with spaghetti straps. Simple, but elegant. She'd never worn anything so exquisite. She'd given him so much grief and he'd gone to such trouble.

She turned, needing to say something, anything, but he was killing her further with more thoughtful gestures.

"I took the liberty of buying you several items from the store. In the bathroom there's a toothbrush, hairbrush, scented soaps and creams."

"You planned this. All of it. But why?"

He reached up and smoothed a hand through her hair, letting the long, silky strands sift through his fingers. "I started buying things the minute I realized I'd never get you out of my system by simply willing it," he murmured. "You have no idea how much I've wanted you here, just this way. It's Friday, Cherry, and I had hoped you would spend the weekend with me. Just the two of us. I want us to get to know each other. Would you like that, little one?"

She'd been unsure and scared when she'd accepted his dinner invitation, but this went beyond anything she'd experienced. Brody had certainly never taken the time to romance her. Never once had she felt this wanted, this craved. For once Cherry knew exactly how to respond.

"I would love that, Dante. Very much."

His eyes darkened as he looked at her from head to toe. "First, I want to run you a hot bath. I have a need to sample all these scented soaps I bought."

"I wouldn't want you to buy something you aren't completely satisfied with. We should definitely test everything."

"My thoughts exactly. Including the cherry flavored oil."

"You bought *edible* oil?"

His eyes twinkled with mischief. "Yep. And I can't wait to try it out."

"You are a very bad boy, Dante Ricci."

"And you're all mine, Ms. DuBois."

Cherry went still. Hearing the statement of possession from his lips made it real. She really was spending the weekend with the big, gorgeous, Italian hunk.

Hot damn.

Dante made damn sure Cherry didn't have a chance to change her mind. He moved swiftly around the small bathroom and prepared everything before heading to the tub and running the water. She was still in the bedroom, getting naked he hoped. Once he had the water temperature just right, he looked at the scented bubble bath. He'd bought a variety, but he had no idea what sort of scent she liked. He didn't want to ask and sound like an imbecile. So, he closed his eyes and randomly selected one. He opened them again and realized he'd picked the strawberries and cream. He popped the lid and inhaled. Mmm, yeah, good choice. It reminded him of the Cherry scent that seemed such a part of her. His mind conjured an image of her creamy skin topped with luscious berry nipples. His body hummed to life. She wasn't even in the same room and he was getting a hard-on! She'd been a fire in his blood for too long. It was high time to do something about it.

Dante poured the scented soap into the bath. How much of this gooey shit was he supposed to use? He shrugged and dumped in a good portion. Bubbles started to appear before his eyes. He'd never taken a bubble bath with a woman, but he was already picturing Cherry's long, lean frame surrounded by the white fluffy stuff. Her dark hair swirling around her body like a black curtain. He loved her hair. He'd watched her each morning opening her shop, she'd start out with her hair down, but by the time she left for the evening it would be up in a ponytail. At first he'd been angry that she'd gotten to the empty space first. The more he watched her, the more he realized she'd been innocent. It'd been his dumb luck that she'd come across the FOR LEASE sign while he'd been away on business. Once he'd come to the conclusion that she'd not duped him, he'd allowed his mind to wonder what it'd be like to make love to the luscious beauty.

Dante's cock felt strangled in his restricting pants. He reached down and unbuckled his belt, then popped the top button. Better, but not by much. The only thing that would relieve his ache was getting his dick as far into Cherry's hot little cunt as he could. He wanted to be balls deep. Damn! And she'd agreed to the entire weekend. Thank God, because a quickie with Cherry would only be a teaser. It would take a good long time to get his fill. He wanted her naked. Eager. Screaming with pleasure. A little taunting voice inside his head kept egging him to get on with it already. He wished he could shut that damn voice up.

Cherry was jumpy as hell already. She would need to loosen up if he was going to get her to drop her guard. He had ideas. Very specific ideas of how he wanted their first time to go. He wouldn't let his dick derail his plan now.

Dante turned off the water and left the bathroom. He

stopped dead at the sight that greeted him in the bedroom. Cherry, sitting naked on the edge of the bed, legs pressed together tight, arms over her pretty tits. Damn, if he didn't already know she'd been married, he would've taken her for a virgin with the way she appeared. Her black hair covered her like a protective shield, eyes downcast. The sweetest temptation he'd ever seen.

And she's all mine.

He crossed the room with purposeful strides and sank to his knees in front of her. She looked up at him finally and Dante's heart squeezed tight in his chest. In her expression, she conveyed a volatile mix of anxious wanton and hopeful innocent. He wanted to get her past her shyness though. He ached to see the wanton beauty that lay beneath the layer of protection.

Her husband must have done a real number on her sense of worth. She needed to get over that psychological bullshit. He wanted her in fighting form. Ready to give him a piece of her mind, even while he fought to get a piece of her succulent little pussy.

She seemed to be beating herself up for being in his bedroom, but he wouldn't let her hide behind guilt. Taking her hand in his, Dante whispered, "Your bath awaits, Ms. DuBois."

He saw a sparkle light her eyes for a brief second before she hid it. "You like pampering me, don't you?"

"Yes, and knowing how much you're going to enjoy my pampering makes my cock a very happy camper."

She laughed and loosened her arms a touch, which was all part of his plan. Soon, she'd drop her arms altogether. Then, he could get a good long look of the sexy woman he'd desired for the last three months.

"Well, I'm glad you have a happy cock."

Dante reached out and placed his hand on her arm; her eyes grew as big as quarters. "My cock will be even happier when you let me look at you."

Cherry bit her lip, worried, anxious, but in the end, bravery won out. "I will, but I want to look at you too."

Ah, now they were getting somewhere. "You want me naked, little one?"

She closed her eyes tight and blurted, "Yes."

In an instant, Dante was on his feet and shucking his clothes. Her eyes opened and her mouth dropped as she watched his efficient striptease. Soon, he wasn't wearing a stitch, his cock mere inches from her face. He had the insane urge to wrap a fist around his stiff erection and rub it all over her. Cheeks, lips, chin, then lower. He wanted to kiss her nipples with the slit in his penis. He wanted so many things with Cherry.

"You don't mess around, do you?"

He crossed his arms over his chest and pointedly looked down at her still-covered chest. "I'm naked. Now you."

Cherry's spine stiffened. Again, her fearless streak appeared to come to the rescue and she dropped her arms.

Dante's libido shot into overdrive. He dropped his own arms and clenched his fists at his side to keep from jumping her. "Now your legs."

Cherry looked down at herself, then back up at him, frowning. "What's wrong with my legs?"

"They're pressed too damn tightly together. Open them for me. Let me see what's mine."

A regal brow rose. "What's yours?" she repeated.

He knelt down and looked directly into her blazing green eyes, then slowly spread her open himself. He let his eyes dart quickly over her darkly covered mound, then he leaned in and kissed her there, right over the clitoris he ached to suck and tease. "This is mine. Same as my cock belongs to you," he growled. "This weekend we belong to each other."

Her voice was decidedly weaker when she replied with a demand of her own. "Then I should get a kiss too, shouldn't I?"

She wasn't really asking, she was telling. Cherry reached out and wrapped her slender fingers around his biceps and tugged, indicating she wanted him to stand. He stood and she pulled him forward. When her pink lips barely grazed the swollen red head of his cock, it was all he could do to stay upright. She leaned back and stared at him there, then her eyes traveled up his body to his face.

"You taste very nice."

"That wasn't a taste. That was a tease." Her answering grin was that of a naughty imp. Oh, yeah. Much better than the scared innocent moments earlier.

He held out a hand. "Come on, before your bath gets cold."

She rested her palm in his and Dante guided her to the bathroom. He heard Cherry inhale sharply at the sensual sight that greeted her.

"Do you like it?" He was more anxious than he cared admit.

"I love it. You've outdone yourself. I'm truly bewildered by you."

Candles were the only light in the small room. The flickering glow caused the bubbles in the tub to dance. It was so strange, being seduced and cherished. Cherry didn't know how to handle it.

She turned, wanting to say something, anything, but her attention was caught on the object in his hand. A remote control. He pushed a button and the soft masculine voice of Frank Sinatra filled the room. The tune Dante had chosen: "Mind If I Make Love To You."

"Dante," she murmured. His name and nothing more. She couldn't begin to put into words the way he so easily got under her skin.

Dante set the remote on the bathroom counter and stepped into the tub. Once seated, he spread his legs wide, knees peaking out of the water, then lifted a hand in silent invitation. She stopped thinking and followed his lead. He'd asked for the weekend. She'd agreed. All the reasons why she shouldn't be here could wait until Monday.

Cherry dipped her toes in, testing the temperature. It was perfect, of course. She slipped one leg over the rim of the tub, right between his hard, muscular thighs, then the other. A rush of heat swept over her when he took her hips in his rough palms and tugged. She melted and sank into the warm frothy water. Dante hummed his appreciation and drew her back against his powerful chest. His cock nestled against her ass.

"That's it, just relax and let me take care of you, little one."

"I'm six-foot-one, not exactly little."

Dante stroked both his large hands over her hips clear to her stomach. He massaged her lower belly and whispered against her ear, "I'm six-foot-four and have about a hundred pounds on you, you're little compared to me."

His fingers began to find their way south. He sifted through her wet curls and slipped his long thick index finger between her folds, teasing her by sinking only to the first knuckle.

"Your skin has such a pretty glow and your tantalizing breasts are so full and ripe." His finger moved in tiny circles and she arched against him. "You're sexy as hell. It's been nearly impossible resisting you."

"Please, Dante."

He moved his finger all the way out and flicked her clit. "Please what?"

"I need you. Stop teasing me!"

Dante took her clit between his fingers and pumped it. Her body sizzled with little shock waves that only he seemed able to create. His other hand came up and cupped her right breast and squeezed. She'd always been extra sensitive there and Dante zeroed in on the fact immediately. The man was intoxicating.

When his finger dipped between her slippery pussy lips again, she pushed forward, telling him without words what she wanted. He complied by sliding two fingers in. This time he sank them deep and began pumping her hard, his thumb swiping back and forth over her clit, his other hand torturously pinching her nipple. His head dipped down and licked the side of her neck and shoulder, then he bit down. Hard. Cherry jolted and her pulse throbbed, as if eager to be tasted. Dante was everywhere at once. Cherry couldn't hold back.

Her orgasm began a slow climb. Water splashed over the edge of the tub as she gyrated against his palm and fingers. He slipped three fingers in and Cherry lost it. A mass of heat welled to the surface as Dante finger-fucked her, his words pushing her over the edge.

"Let go. Take what you want."

And she did. Her right hand reached beneath the water and behind her buttocks. She found his heavy cock and she squeezed him tight.

"Fuck, yeah."

Her body took over and suddenly she exploded. Her orgasm went on and on as Dante wrung every bit of pleasure from her he could.

They stayed that way, her hand wrapped tightly around his rigid length, his fingers still deeply embedded in her vagina. When she wriggled her bottom, they both groaned.

"Do you remember after my massage, when you called me Master?"

Cherry could barely breathe, let alone think. It took her a minute to recall the episode. "I was being sarcastic because you were way too arrogant."

"But I still liked it. I want more of it."

Cherry swiveled her head to look at him. She couldn't turn around completely, because his fingers were still buried inside her pussy. He seemed content to leave them there indefinitely. She couldn't quite figure out why the notion seemed so appealing.

"You want me to call you, *Master*?"

"In the bedroom, yes."

She should not be turned on. Every instinct screamed in outrage. "What if I don't want to? What if I can never do that?"

"I happen to know you've at least thought about it. That magazine you subscribe to is proof."

He couldn't possibly know. How could he know? *Oh, God, please tell me he doesn't know.* "What magazine?"

He quirked a brow and said, "*Whips and Gags* ring any bells?"

Her cheeks heated with equal amounts of embarrassment and anger. "You stole my magazine?"

"It was delivered to me by mistake, imagine my surprise to see who it belonged to."

"You had no right, Dante."

"Hey, it wasn't my fault the postman got the wrong address." She started to protest, but he placed a finger against her lips and murmured, "I find I'm quite intrigued by your secret fantasies, baby. All you have to do is open yourself to me and those fantasies can be reality. Are you willing?"

Say no. Scream no! "Yes."

Dante's mouth came down hard. His possessive, untamed kiss curled her toes. Nothing she'd ever experienced could have prepared her for such a force of nature. In her gut, Cherry understood what he was showing her. He wanted her to see how pleased he was by her acceptance of their new game. She was being rewarded for her trust in him. She'd read a little about this sort of thing, but never experienced it. She hadn't really had a lot of time to look over the *Whips and Gags* magazine with all she'd had to deal with since the divorce. Besides, Dante was oh, so much better than anything she could have found in those magazines.

His lips forced hers open and his tongue delved deep. His fingers slid free of her wet channel, then came to her throat and squeezed. In a flash, her body was ablaze with sensations. Cherry didn't let herself think as she surrendered herself to Dante.

She clutched his stiff penis as her own need mounted, then began to massage his silky length. Up and down, the water giving her the right amount of slick pressure. Dante broke the kiss and squeezed her throat tighter.

"You do not touch me until you've been given permission. Move your hand."

Cherry froze. She didn't know what to do. Was he serious? The darts of fury in his eyes said he was deadly serious.

For an instant his gaze gentled. "You need to learn the game. Move your hand away and ask permission to touch your Master."

She saw it then. The arousal as well as the tenderness. He was ready to take them both to the next level of pleasure. All she need do is move her hand and do as she's told. Could she? Would there be no turning back if she did?

Cherry closed her eyes and removed her hand. For good measure she mumbled, "Sorry."

"Sorry what?"

She took a deep breath and spit the words out. "Sorry, Master."

Dante's grip on her neck loosened and his grin both excited and frightened. She'd affectively stepped into his wickedly erotic world. There would be no going back.

3

Dante was so primed it was difficult to maintain his composure. As soon as Cherry had shyly uttered the word *Master*, he'd gone from zero to sixty. That she was willing to try this form of love-play stimulated the hell out of him.

"Stand up," he demanded.

Water sloshed back and forth as Cherry did his bidding. He watched in quiet fascination as streaming bubbly lines dripped enticingly down her body. She was facing away from him. Hiding? Maybe, but he wouldn't let her get away with it. Tonight was going to be an eye-opener for her.

He reached up and fondled her ass cheeks, filling his palms with her warm, wet flesh. Her understated curves had been the lure. He'd been like a fish on a hook the instant he'd spotted her. As he'd watched her from afar, it had been her determination that had him wanting to get up close and personal with the cute owner of Serene Comfort. Dante ached to bring her to heel. He knew instinctively his attitude was crude and primitive. But no other woman had ever made him feel so wild.

Cherry brought out a side of his nature he'd never even known existed.

In his seated position, he could see Cherry's trembling legs. He loved her legs. Long, slim, sexy columns that he wanted wrapped around his waist as he fucked her. Yeah, he'd thought a lot about her legs over the past three months.

Dante quickly stood and left the tub. After grabbing a towel off a steel shelf, he ordered her to step out. She kept her eyes averted as her feet landed on a fluffy rug. He knelt down and began massaging the soft white cotton over her feet first. Her toes curled in, as if attempting to escape his touch. For now he'd let her get away with the little bit of insolence. He was too anxious to get to her other slippery parts.

The towel made a slow route upward as Dante took great care in drying her ankles and calves. When he reached her thighs, he frowned.

"Open your legs."

Cherry licked her lips and widened her stance.

A few inches of space and no more. Dante's voice hardened as he ground out, "Farther."

Cherry looked at him then, her expression full of defiance. Had he not also recognized her eagerness to please him he would've been forced to punish her. His already painful erection pulsed with the idea of bending her over his knee and spanking her delectable ass. He wouldn't give her a light pat either. He'd want her to remember the lesson. Dante would make sure her ass turned a nice shade of pink. Knowing Cherry, he didn't think he'd have to wait long for such a punishment to commence. He let a grin slip as he watched her move her feet farther apart for him.

Like a laser beam, his gaze went straight to her cunt. He wanted to lick it. To feast on her juices. But that wasn't supposed to happen just yet. It was torture for him to lift the towel once more and begin drying her thighs and the tempting juncture in between without leaning in to kiss her there. Did she even realize how difficult it was for him not to stop right then and drag her to the floor? In a heartbeat, he could have his dick buried to the hilt and they'd both enjoy a good hard fuck. Instead, he kept to the game. Intent on claiming Cherry in a way no other man ever had.

He made his way over her hips and buttocks, then to her stomach and chest. Cherry labored for breath as he dragged the towel over her round, perky tits. Her hands clenched into fists at her side when he took extra care to dry her erect nipples. Still she never said a word, never reached out to touch. She was being such a good girl and Dante wanted to reward her.

After quickly drying himself, he dropped the towel and pointed to the doorway. "In the bedroom."

Cherry bit her lip and turned away, ass swaying as she walked swiftly out of the room. Dante groaned and wrapped a fist around his cock and squeezed. He was so close to getting himself off. He needed the relief. With great effort, he dropped his hand and went into the bedroom. Cherry stood in the middle of the room, looking around as if unsure what to do next.

Wanting her to stew a little, he went to the dresser first. He opened the third drawer and took out the items he'd bought from the adult fetish shop. He'd begun accumulating things after he'd noticed Cherry's name on the naughty magazine. Still, fantasy wasn't the same as real life. If she balked at what he'd bought—or worse, laughed—he'd feel like an idiot.

Only one way to find out.

Dante dropped everything, but the leash and collar, to the dresser top. He turned around, letting them dangle from his right index finger. Cherry's mouth formed a shocked 'O.' In two long strides, he stood in front of her. He held her gaze as he wrapped the red leather collar around her throat, so the word engraved into the supple leather was clearly visible. He secured it and attached the leash to the ring hanging from the front.

"Dante?"

He let the leash go, fascinated by the way it hung between her breasts, tempting him. In the next breath, Dante spun her around so she faced away from him, then he brought his palm down hard onto her ass. Cherry yelped.

"What did you call me?"

Silence.

He spanked her two more times in the same spot just as hard, then he leaned down and whispered, "Say it."

"Master," she bit out.

"Good girl," he murmured with a kiss behind her ear as her prize. His tongue made a wet path down her neck and his fingers smoothed over the place on her ass where he'd smacked her. When he dipped his fingers between her legs and found her dripping wet with arousal, he smiled. Her mind might be rebelling, but her body had already given the go ahead. She liked the game they were playing and he'd just been given the green light to continue.

He moved backward, letting his hand slide slowly away from her supple flesh. Her unhappy little whimper lit him on fire.

Dante walked around her so they were facing each other, then he picked up the leash that rested against her belly. "Get down on your hands and knees."

He could tell she wanted to protest, but then stopped at the last second. Maybe it was the threat of another spanking, maybe not. Either way, she slowly melted to her hands and knees. With her head back, Cherry stared up at him, waiting.

The leash tight in his fist, Dante tugged her forward and demanded, "Suck me."

Cherry crawled toward him, her lips tilting upward when she looked from his face to his groin. Mouth wide, she took him in and clamped her lips around him so tight he nearly came.

He wrapped the leash around his fist several times so there was no slack, no way for her to retreat, then with his other hand he grabbed a handful of her long hair and guided her head over his cock, showing her how he liked it. But she only had half his length and he wanted more.

"All the way in, Cherry. I want to feel the back of your throat, little one."

She frowned and tried to take more, but gagged. She pulled back and stared at his cock, as if trying to figure out a way to do what he wanted.

Dante's hand came out of her hair and he stroked her throat. "You're tensing up. Relax your throat."

"Easy for you to say," she groused.

Dante tugged on the leash, gaining her attention. "Careful what you say. I'm not a merciful Master. One more smartass comment and your ass will be so red you won't be able to sit for a week."

"Sorry, Master."

"Mmm, that's sweet," he purred. "I love seeing you submit to me, baby. You won't regret it. Now, do what I said and loosen up."

She nodded and licked her lips. Dante grabbed her head again and pulled her mouth to his cock once more. This time she swept her tongue over the engorged head and hummed eagerly, then pulled him balls deep into her mouth. Dante's entire body shuddered. Her head bobbed back and forth, her tongue circling his tip, then she took him deep again. Her eyes drifted closed, face flushed.

The hand Dante had fisted in her hair tightened. "You like that don't you, little slut?"

She wiggled her ass and moaned. The slurping sounds she made had his sac drawing up tight. Her tits bounced as she pulled him all the way out. Her mouth made a popping sound, then she drew him in again and started the process all over.

"Mmm, such an eager little thing. I knew when I saw the collar I'd have to have it engraved with your name in big bold letters. I think my pretty Cherry should suck me every morning. You can drink my come for breakfast."

Her only response was a delicious humming sound that vibrated over his length as she continued her sweet torture. He flung his head back and closed his eyes, savoring the moment.

He was so close to coming. Too close. When he felt her tongue probe the slit in the end of his penis, he yanked hard on the leash.

"Enough," he warned.

She pouted, but obeyed and released him.

Overcome by both tenderness and lust, Dante dropped the leash, bent forward and took her head in his hands. "You are being such a good little girl, Cherry. You'll get a sweet treat very soon, I promise."

Dante kissed her gently and went to the dresser. He picked up one of the other items he'd purchased from the adult shop, walked on stiff legs to the bed and sat on the edge.

"Crawl to me."

Cherry looked at his hand, no doubt trying to see what he held. Between the dim lighting and the distance separating them, it would be impossible for her make out exactly what he had in store for her next. She squinted suspiciously and began slowly inching toward him. Uncertain, but still curious enough to follow his orders. When she came close enough to touch, he held up his hand and let her see the silver chain.

"Nipple clamps?"

He didn't answer, only crooked his finger, indicating that he wanted her up on her knees.

Cherry lifted herself up and kept her hands at her sides. Dante saw real fear in her eyes. What was that about?

"Did your husband ever use these on you?"

"Yes."

Her eyes darted to the silver clamps, then away. He knew intuitively that the asshole hadn't used them correctly.

"They aren't truly painful when they're used properly, little one. There is no need for fear."

Her eyes blazed angrily at him. "In my experience there is every need for fear . . . Master."

Scared, and yet she still kept to the game. Dante cupped her chin in his hand and stroked his thumb over her plump lower lip. "Your ex didn't know what he was doing. I do. And there's no way I would ever cause you pain."

Her eyebrows shot upward. "Oh, really? Then what was the spanking about?"

He grinned. "You enjoyed it."

She snorted, and Dante nearly laughed. She was such a defiant little witch. He jangled the chain and forced them both back to the game.

"Do not forget your place." He picked up the leash and waved it in front of her face. "This means I own you and until I'm through you'll watch your tongue." She stared green fire at him. He cocked his head to the side and threatened, "Maybe your ass needs another reminder?"

Cherry bit down on her lip, as if forcing herself to hold back words that would get her into trouble. He could so easily picture her as a child, so willful and full of spirit. If he wasn't careful he was going to fall in love with the little beauty.

"Sorry, Master."

Damn, he loved when she called him that. It did things to him. Crazy things. Never in his life had he played games of this magnitude in the bedroom. With Cherry, experimenting, playing the dominant to her submissive seemed perfectly natural. It seemed right.

"Take your pretty tits in your hands and squeeze them together for me."

She cupped the undersides of both creamy swells, then lifted and pushed them together. He loved watching her touch herself. Sometime during the weekend, maybe he could talk her into letting him watch her masturbate.

Using the tip of the leash, Dante rubbed it back and forth over both nipples. They tightened and extended for him, begging to be suckled. He obliged and leaned forward to pull one raspberry tip into his hungry mouth.

Cherry quivered and arched her back, smashing her tits against his face. He flicked his tongue over her nipple, then released it with a pop. As he rubbed his face over her satiny skin, chafing her with his five o'clock shadow, Dante played with the leash, dragging it over her belly, up and down, teasing her with the red leather.

When he licked and bit her other nipple, he saw Cherry's eyes flash open, watching him with heated interest. He did it several times before he leisurely brought the metal clamps into play. Her nipples needed to be good and hard. The clamps would enhance her pleasure if she was turned on, they'd cause pain if she wasn't.

When he was certain she was in the right frame of mind, Dante leaned back and looked into her eyes. She was breathtaking. Her green eyes so full of desire. The upper swells of her breasts pink from his rubbing, her nipples perky and tempting.

"Now you're ready," he confirmed, then began adjusting one of the clamps. "You should feel a pinch, but nothing more."

Not a single protest from Cherry while Dante worked. Once he had them both adjusted right, he carefully secured one over her right nipple. He watched closely, gauging her reaction. Unwilling to bring her any pain.

"Is it okay, baby?"

Cherry nodded and bit her lip.

Not good enough. He needed to be sure she was aroused and not hurting. "Is it too much?"

"No, Master."

He leaned forward and kissed her, then whispered, "Good." He applied the other clamp and let go of the chain. It hung between her breasts invitingly. When he cupped her mound and encountered dewy heat it was his turn to shake. Dante wanted Cherry to remember this moment. To ache and throb with need whenever she thought of the clamps and the personalized collar.

Standing to his full height, Dante instructed, "Get onto the bed. Hands and knees."

Cherry scrambled to obey and he took a moment to catch his breath and slip a condom on. With her ass facing him, he gave up all pretense of control. His cock needed to feel the silky clutch of her pussy or insanity would surely set in.

He practically leaped onto the bed.

Behind her now, Dante clutched her hips and nudged her ass with his engorged cock. She arched and cried out his name. He was beyond caring about the game anymore.

"Reach back and guide me in."

Her right hand went between her legs and she grabbed hold of his length, squeezing tight, then she rubbed the bulbous head over her fat pussy lips and clit. He groaned his approval, spread her ass cheeks and watched the erotic show. Back and forth, Cherry rubbed herself with his length.

"Oh, Dante, that feels so good."

"Make yourself come like that, baby. Do it now, while I watch."

Given permission, Cherry let herself go and rubbed faster, the head of his dick dripped with pre-cum. He reached beneath her and tugged on the chain hanging from the metal clamped onto her puckered nipples. Cherry moaned and pushed hard against him, then came, screaming his name in wild abandon.

Not giving her a chance to come down from her peak, Dante took over. He wrapped a fist around his heavy erection and drove into her so hard she fell to the mattress. He grasped her hips and pulled her ass into the air, forcing her to stay on her knees, then he pounded into her. Fast and furious. He sank all the way in, slapping her clit with his balls. Over and over, hammering her. When her soft moans became shouts and he felt those delicious inner muscles of hers grip him tight, he knew another orgasm was fast approaching.

Her hips slammed against his, giving him the full blast of her passion, her wet cunt pulsing all around his dick as she finally burst apart. Little aftershocks continued to squeeze him and Dante lost it. Two more strokes and he erupted.

They both collapsed to the bed, sweaty and exhausted, her body squished under his. He should pull his cock out of her, but he wasn't ready, may never be ready.

Dante smoothed her hair back from her damp face and kissed her cheek. She smiled, eyes closed, as if content to stay under him the rest of her life. He growled his approval at that idea and praised her good behavior.

"You've performed beautifully. Your Master is very happy," he whispered. "Next time, I think I'll show you the other items I bought from the adult shop."

"Good God, I'll never live through it."

He chuckled at her disgruntled response and reluctantly pulled free of her body. He leaned back on his haunches and kissed her ass, then flipped her over. She stared at him with such a mixture of emotions it startled him.

No more words were shared as he removed the clamps and massaged her nipples gently, then kissed each one with reverence. She convulsed as blood rushed back into the tight peaks. Next he unhooked the collar. He dropped everything to the floor, then kissed his way over her torso. Her breasts received extra special attention. When he reached her clitoris, he growled, "My pretty cunt." Then he kissed it too. Cherry mumbled something and clutched his hair, holding him against her mound. A few flicks of his tongue and she flew apart all over again. Damn, she was such a responsive little thing. He was a lucky bastard.

Once she settled, Dante lifted up and waited for her to open her eyes. As soon as her green gaze landed on him, he said something he'd never said to another woman.

"I know this weekend was made in haste, but for me this is about more than satisfying desires. You're important to me, Cherry."

Cherry blinked and looked away. He let her. She wasn't ready to take that step with him, but soon.

Even though she saw their weekend as a temporary reprieve, Dante wasn't so cavalier. He would use the rest of their time together to prove to her that he was a better man than her husband. He would earn her trust if it killed him. In all his years of dating, he'd never found a woman he could imagine spending his life with . . . until now. He'd been too driven to make his business a success. Relationships had always taken a backseat to hard work and long hours at the office. He suddenly saw his existence as a never-ending stream of meetings and financial documents. He wanted more. Somewhere along the line he'd become an empty shell. She, on the other hand, appeared vibrant, eager to grab life by the horns. He'd been drawn to her like an ant to sugar.

Dante wrapped his hands around Cherry's thighs and pulled her legs wide. Her eyes darted to his.

"What are you doing?"

His answer was crude, but truthful. "Looking at your cream dripping from your pussy. I had thought to wash you, but I don't think I want to anymore. I like seeing you all wet."

"Oh."

Dante winked at her small, shy response and kissed her belly. "This will be an exciting weekend, baby."

Cherry relaxed against the sheets and murmured, "I have no doubt."

He moved her over and stretched out beside her, then pulled her back against his chest. She settled in and let out a soft sigh.

"Sleep, little Cherry. You'll need it for tomorrow."

She laughed. "I believe you."

Dante smoothed his hand down the satin curtain of her hair and listened to Cherry's deep breathing. Once she was sound asleep he left the bed, covered her and went to the living room to make a few phone calls. He needed to make plans for Lee, his manager, to handle things at the office should anything come up over the next forty-eight hours.

Dante wanted no interruptions this weekend. Saturday and Sunday would be spent pleasuring Cherry. He grinned, looking forward to the challenge already.

4

Caresses. Someone was smoothing a hand over her belly and breasts. By sheer force of will, Cherry pried her eyes open. Dante stared down at her, drowsy and hot with desire. Cherry slapped his hand away.

"I'm not a morning person."

"Learn to adapt," he grunted, a hint of a smile playing at the corners of his lips. Then he went back to caressing her. Maybe he didn't believe her.

"Get it straight. I do not do mornings. Back off."

He leaned down until his nose was touching hers and said, "No."

Cherry growled. "Ever see the movie *The Exorcist*?"

"I think everyone's seen that movie. Why?"

"The little girl, Regan I think, was a gentle lamb compared to me first thing in the morning. Now, get your horny ass off me so I can get back to sleep." Then she flipped over, facing away from him, pulled the covers up to her chin and closed her eyes.

She heard him chuckle, then she felt his hands coasting over her butt cheeks. Clearly the man had a real hard time with the word no.

"Go away, Dante!"

His hands kept right on moving as he replied, "Not a chance, baby."

Maybe she should kick him or something. She was thinking of how best to get rid of him, when his questing fingers found their way over her clitoris. Suddenly, she wasn't so tired anymore. As he wriggled a finger in between her swollen labia, wringing a small moan from her, Dante softly sighed and positioned his body against her back. He'd won again. She was forever letting him win. What was wrong with her?

With his chest against her back, Cherry could feel his morning erection. Does the man never get enough? She'd never be able to keep up with him!

"Aren't you tired?"

"Not with you lying next to me I'm not."

"Gee, that's real sweet, but I'm tired." Her body wasn't used to so much activity and as he pushed two fingers into her, she also realized she was a little sore. "Besides, I'm too tender at the moment."

Instantly Dante stopped his explorations and pulled his fingers free. He nudged her shoulder, forcing her to turn and look at him. He looked concerned, his brows creased into a worried frown.

"Was I too rough, baby?"

His concern went straight to her core. He kept doing that. Shocking her with his kindness. It was disconcerting. "Not too rough. I'm just not used to so much . . . activity."

He leaned over her and kissed her. It was so brief, so gentle, Cherry wanted to scream for him to come back and do it up right, but she never got the chance. Suddenly he was leaving the bed and heading toward the bathroom.

"Where are you going?"

"Relax. I'll be right back."

Who was she to complain? Cherry closed her eyes and was nearly asleep by the time she heard Dante come back. She opened one eye and peeked as her curiosity got the better of her. He had a towel hanging around his neck and a bottle in his hand.

"What's that?"

"The cherry flavored oil I told you about." Ah, now this she could totally get into. "Scooch over and lie on your tummy. Your Master wishes to soothe your aches and pains."

God, why had she let him talk her into the Master thing? She'd never played the submissive before. Heck, Brody hadn't done any playing in bed at all. Their sex life was all about getting him off. Her pleasure hadn't been a real big concern. The prick. Dante was the exact opposite. He seemed determined to bring her to new heights each time he touched her. And he did have the most wicked imagination.

With the thought in mind to make what she could of their weekend, Cherry turned over and waited for Dante's healing touch. She didn't have to wait long. His gloriously nude body straddled her legs and warm, oiled hands rubbed her shoulder blades. Smooth, firm circular strokes, his rough palms giving just the right amount of friction. He eased his way over her spine, massaging each vertebrae carefully, before moving to the small of her back. He spent a great amount of time kneading the tiny indentations just above her buttocks. She groaned and sank into the mattress, her muscles going lax.

"That feels so good. You're very skilled at this."

"Mmm, I have reason to do this right."

"What's that?"

His fingers found their way over her left butt cheek and she felt him digging his fingers into her flesh, not too hard, but with enough pressure to have her muscles humming with gratification. "If I properly pamper you, then maybe you won't be so sore anymore. And if you aren't sore anymore, then maybe I can get you to play around."

She laughed at his phrasing. "Play around?"

He kept kneading, moving to her other butt cheek, and then he positioned his big body lower and her thighs got a good rub-down. "Yeah, I want to play hide the salami."

A laugh burst out. "You did not just say that!"

"Yep. I've got a big fat salami and no place to put it."

As his clever hands made their way over her calves, Cherry surrendered. "With a massage like this, you could get me to do just about anything."

Dante's hands stilled for a moment, then he continued working his way down to her ankles and feet. "Careful what you say, baby. Words like those are dangerous. I'm the kind of man who would happily take advantage of such a statement."

She didn't say it aloud, but it was her opinion that all men were that way. Ruthless and willing to do whatever it took to get what they wanted. She pushed those maudlin thoughts aside and remembered her vow to enjoy the weekend.

He massaged each toe carefully, even got a few giggles out as he hit a particularly ticklish spot, then his hands released her feet and he moved to the side. "I've reached the end of the road. Turn over so I can start on the front."

She turned, her body more sluggish then ever. He'd effectively relaxed nearly every muscle in her body. Amazing. Since she was a massage therapist, Cherry shouldn't be so surprised at how good it felt to be pampered in such a way. But, it wasn't very often that she was the recipient. Usually she came home sore from digging into people's flesh all day long. It was nice to be the one taken care of for a change.

She watched while he squirted more of the fragrant oil onto his hands and rubbed them together, then straddled her again. Her heart sped up as she looked down at his jutting cock. Wow, he was big. She simply couldn't get used to the sheer size of the man.

Fingers dug deep into her scalp and she let her eyes close once more. Her hair would be an oily mess, but she didn't care. It felt too good. Every care, every worry fled at his healing touch.

"You're beautiful in the morning, Cherry."

Her eyes flew open at his sensual words. He was looking at her with so much blazing heat, she was robbed of breath. Her throat tightened. No man had ever looked at her like that before.

"Thank you, Dante."

His fingers moved down to her temples. He gently massaged them as he continued his seduction. "I only speak the truth. Waking up next to you is a pleasure."

She needed to inject some lightheartedness into the conversation or she was going to fall in love with him right then and there. And that was truly the most frightening idea yet.

"I hog the blankets."

"I'm a walking furnace, you can have the blankets."

What else could she say? He was an immovable object! As his talented hands moved over her face to her neck, she lost track of the conversation. Her eyelids became too heavy. His heated kiss against her pulse brought out a sigh of contentment. Large, calloused palms found their way to her shoulders and arms, totally bypassing her breasts. She would not beg for him to play with her nipples. Cherry refused to give him a bigger head than he already had.

"Stay still."

On that soft command, her eyes flew open. "I am still."

His smile was slow and intimate. "No. You were wiggling around."

She refused to believe it. "Dream on."

He didn't dispute her, only took great care in stroking each of her fingertips, before moving to her belly. His palms roamed over her torso in little circles, up and down, barely grazing the undersides of her aching breasts. He was teasing her. The wicked gleam in his too-sexy eyes said it all. Cherry forced herself to stay still. It was a toss-up who would give in first.

As he moved his hands over her ribs, taking a good long time to massage each one, Cherry forgot about the game and a whimper escaped. In a heartbeat, Dante was there, drinking in her surrender with a kiss. His tongue forced its way into her mouth. He wasn't asking for permission. She was helpless to deny him. Her body had long since decided for her. It was like standing a woman in front of a fresh batch of chocolate chip cookies. Of course she was going to dive in!

His tongue played tag with hers, his lips soft but insistent as he drove her body into high gear. The hands he'd been so generously using to relax her were now flat against the mattress beside her head, holding her captive for his invasion. With his muscular torso pressed against her, Cherry knew he'd caged her in. No escape. She wrapped her arms around his neck and pulled him in for an even deeper kiss. He groaned his approval and sucked her tongue into his mouth, as if wanting to gobble her up. Her legs opened and Dante pushed his heavy cock against her entrance. She lifted up, needing him to fill her, aching to feel his girth stretching her. He refused her, pulling away just enough to have her frowning.

"You're sore."

"I'll live," she muttered. "Come back here."

He only shook his head, holding firm. "You need a few hours to recover, baby." When she would have protested further, he placed two fingers against her lips. "It's time for breakfast."

Her eyes shot wide. "How can you think of food at a time like this?"

His gaze roved over her lips, watching in apparent fascination as his thumb stroked her lower lip. "Not food. You."

Instantly, blood rushed from her head to her hot center and her clitoris pulsed in readiness.

"I wouldn't mind being your breakfast, lunch, and dinner," she admitted daringly. Then she dipped her tongue out and licked his thumb, excited and encouraged by Dante's narrow-eyed gaze.

He slipped it between her lips and let her suck it. She closed her eyes and laved his salty skin, giving him a good idea of what she'd like to do to his other tasty parts. His lower body came into contact with hers again as he rocked his pelvis back and forth, rubbing his dripping length over her swollen labia and clit. When she swept her tongue over the tip of his thumb, Dante pulled it free of her lips and growled, "Such a little tease. I think you deserve a mouthful of cock."

He lifted off her and turned over, laying on his back on the mattress, his head at the foot of the bed. Dante reached a hand to her and urged, "Climb on top of me, baby. I'm hungry and I want my Cherry on top."

She wasn't bold enough for this in the bright light of day. The sixty-nine was completely new to her. Her inner wall-flower came to life and she froze.

He knew. Somehow, Dante knew she was fighting a bout of bashfulness and he took over, grasping her hips in his steady hands and pulling her onto his chest, positioning her just the way he wanted. Once she was flush against him, her mouth inches from his cock, her pussy in his face, Dante issued one more demand. "Be a good little slut and suck it."

As if he'd flipped a switch, she was back there again. Last night's adventure into dominance and submission came rushing back. She helplessly obeyed.

Levering herself with her right hand on Dante's thigh, Cherry wrapped her other hand around the base of his length.

He was so big, she couldn't get a good grip. His skin was scorching hot and the veins traveling the length pumped with life. She dipped her head and kissed his wet tip. She tasted his salty fluid, inhaled his musky scent. Suddenly she was starved. Her lips parted, eyes closed, she took him into the wet cavern of her mouth, sucking strongly. She angled her head forward, opening her throat and took him deeper. His hips flexed beneath her, his stomach shuddered. She pulled him free and licked him up and down, tasting him like an ice-cream cone. That's when she felt his tongue probing her entrance. She jolted at the contact and Dante's arms wrapped around her middle, holding her still for his sensual torture.

"Mmm, cherries and pussy juice, my favorite blend," he murmured, then he took her clit between his teeth and flicked it back and forth with his tongue. She slammed her hips against his face and drew his cock into her mouth, bobbing her head up and down in time with the thrust of his tongue into her tight channel. His arms loosened and she felt him coasting his hands over her oil-slick flesh, until he reached her ass. He parted her buttocks and probed her tight pucker with an oily finger. Cherry gasped at the shocking nature of what he was doing. He released her clit as his finger slipped into her anus. "All of you, Cherry. I own every inch of this beautiful body."

She knew then. Dante was marking her. He wanted her to know that she was his territory now. Two could play that game.

Cherry slipped his cock out of her mouth and sucked on her finger, getting it good and wet, then she fondled his balls. He moaned his approval, even while he slid his finger in and out of her ass and ate her pussy as if starved. Rhythmically, she moved her hips up and down, increasing her own pleasure as she slid her finger beneath his heavy sac to his tight, puckered opening. When she dipped in and explored him in the way he'd done her, he went utterly motionless.

"Cherry," he warned.

"All of you, Dante," she countered. "I own every inch of this delicious body." Then she drove her finger deep, clear to her knuckles.

Dante's ass shot off the bed as he pushed against her face. "Fuck, baby."

He went wild after that. Tongue-fucking her, his finger pumping in and out. Cherry moaned as she sucked on Dante. Her finger sliding all the way in, then she'd pull it out and do it all over. Soon, they were both reaching their peak. She pushed her finger in one more time and rubbed it along his inner wall. Dante shouted her name and flexed his hips, filling her mouth with his hot, creamy load. He flicked her clit one last time and pumped her ass hard and fast. Then it was her turn to scream as electricity shot through her body, forming a glorious ball at the very heart of her, muscles tightening while her body burst wide open. At once, her pussy flooded with wet heat and Dante licked her dry.

The little pulsing jolts lasted for an eternity and all the while Dante held her still, finger firmly imbedded in her tight opening. Once she went lax against his hard length, he pulled out of her and kissed her clit tenderly, worshiping her with words of approval. Eventually, he lifted her off him and laid her down on the bed, then he stood and said, "Come, baby. We'll shower, then we can get some sustenance."

Feeling ornery, she mumbled, "Nope. I'm full, thanks anyway."

Dante laughed, then leaned down and lifted her into his arms. "And you were a very good little girl to drink every last drop," he stated. He kissed her as he carried her to the bathroom, where they spent an hour exploring each other all over again.

Cherry had surely died and gone to heaven.

5

It was late Saturday night and they'd been watching a movie, some old sixties crime thriller and Cherry had never felt so wonderful. She'd called Wade, not wanting him to worry about her. He'd been curious, but content to wait until Monday for all the juicy details.

It was strange to be so happy. She'd spent her childhood trying to please her parents, only to leave them disappointed that their only child was merely average. Then she'd married Brody and he'd been equally disappointed. With Dante, she felt as if it was enough to be herself. As if he were content to be in her presence, eating popcorn and watching a movie. Go figure.

When she noticed his touch on her thigh moving higher, she held her breath, aching for more. Aching for him to touch her very center.

"Have you been enjoying the weekend so far?"

"You know I have."

"Are you sore anymore?"

She felt her cheeks fill with heat. All they'd done and she still blushed. "No, not sore."

"I thought not. How about I take you to the bedroom."

"What about the movie?" She didn't really care about the movie, but she thought she should protest a little.

He stood and held out his hand. "The movie is a rental. It'll be here when we're through. Come."

Cherry took his hand and he pulled her to her feet. He started walking them toward the bedroom, when Cherry thought of something else. "Dante?"

He went straight to the bed and sat down, then pulled her between his thighs. He cupped her ass and they both moaned in pleasure. "Yeah, baby?"

"You said there were other things you bought from that adult store. What are they?"

Dante's hands stilled and he looked into her eyes. "Do you want to see them?"

She swallowed hard and went for broke. "Yes."

Dante's predatory grin filled her with heat. "I think you're going to enjoy them quite a bit. I know I will." He stared to get up, but stopped. "Are you willing to submit to me again? Am I your Master, baby?"

Cherry shook with anticipation, her entire body revved at the notion of playing the submissive for Dante. How had he so easily tapped into that side of her when she hadn't even known it was there herself?

Dante stroked his hand down her cheek. "It is your choice, you know. It's always your choice," he reassured. "I'm fine leaving the games out for tonight."

She blurted out her answer, lest she lose her nerve altogether. "Yes, I will submit." Dante's entire stance changed. His muscles appeared larger, his body bigger. His incredible blue eyes spoke of an untamed panther, barely caged.

"Good girl," he praised. "Get undressed and lie down on your back while I get your toys."

Cherry quickly did his bidding. She'd already learned what

the consequences were when she didn't obey. As she stripped out of her shirt and bra, her mind conjured up several scenarios and discarded every one. She had no clue what Dante had planned for them this time. As she shimmied out of the shorts he'd let her borrow, she nearly laughed. Her sexual experience just wasn't extensive enough. She wished now she'd taken more time to explore the *Whips and Gags* magazine because she was still sorely lacking in the imagination department. What toy could he have for her now? She'd thought the leash and collar pretty wild. She got up onto the bed and lay down on her back. Cherry tracked Dante's movements across the room. He'd already turned the lights down, bathing them in a soft glow. The closer he moved the better she could see what he had in his hands. But his gorgeous, nude body kept distracting her.

Never mind the toys. She wanted him.

When he reached the side of the bed, his erection was now at eye level. Or mouth level rather. She really wanted to reach out and touch him. But, she was the submissive and as such she needed permission first. As he dropped the toys to the mattress her eyes bulged out. At least one item she recognized.

"Is that a ball gag?"

"Something like that. It's called a cock gag," he explained in a voice gone hoarse. "Now, enough talking," he ordered, "come here."

Cherry wriggled across the bed until she lay along the edge right in front of him, his heavy erection and balls inches from her eager mouth.

"I'm going to wrap the strap around your head and the small purple cock goes into your mouth." He paused then asked, "Can you handle it, baby?"

Cherry gulped. Holy hell, what had she gotten herself into?

Dante rubbed the purple jelly tip of the gag over her lips. "Come on, be a good little girl and open wide."

Said the bad boy to the trusting innocent. "What if I can't handle it? I'm not sure about this." She eyed the gag with both uneasiness and anticipation. Dante did that to her. Just when she thought she was in control of her emotions, he did something primitive and sent her spiraling out of control again.

"I'll know and we'll stop. There's nothing exciting in it for me if you aren't deriving pleasure from this."

"Okay," she said, still reluctant but willing. "Go ahead."

Dante leaned down and kissed her, then whispered against her lips, "You're forgetting the game. Let me hear you say it right."

"Sorry, Master," she bit out.

Dante chuckled. "You're very obstinate."

"Just another of my many charms."

"And I look forward to discovering each and every one of them," he murmured, then he loosened the buckle and wrapped the black strap around her head, positioning the cock gag in between her lips. Once it was tight enough, he asked, "Is it comfortable?"

She nodded, unable to speak. The silicone was warm and smooth and her mouth had to stretch a little, but it wasn't uncomfortable. And the wild look on Dante's face drove her pussy wild. Her dewy center throbbed for his touch.

"I want to fuck you like that, baby," he growled, then grabbed her legs and moved her around. Now her feet were over his shoulders and her ass was on the edge of the bed. His gaze held hers as he drove into her cunt with one hard thrust. Cherry gasped at the intense pleasure and threw her head back. Dante pulled all the way out then drove in again, burying himself deep.

"I can't get enough of you," he gritted out as he fucked her faster, flinging her into another world. "I look at you and it makes me want to shut you away in a cave. Somewhere no one can see you. So no other man can ever touch you." He pulled out and bent to lick her dripping cunt, then admitted, "I want to own you."

She moaned her displeasure when he didn't fill her again with his hard length. Instead, Dante kissed her mound, then shuffled her around so she was once again lying on the bed. She made a sound of protest, already frustrated with the inability to speak.

Dante came down onto the bed beside her, holding the other adult toy he'd bought her. "I know what you want, because I want it too. You'll get it, I promise. But first I want you to let me try something. Will you?"

She wanted to shout she was so turned on. To show him how annoyed she was, Cherry placed her own palm over her mound and rubbed. He stopped her instantly with his hand over hers. "None of that. You need to learn restraint. Discipline. It's all part of the pleasure."

Inside, her body screamed with the need to come. But, she made a valiant attempt to regulate her breathing and nod her consent.

"You're such a mix of innocent and vixen. My body is at war each time we make love. I want to eat you whole, but I also want to stick you in a protective little bubble." His calloused palm roamed over her curves, lighting her on fire. "You make me say and do things I've never even imagined."

She knew the feeling. As she lay there, her body liquid lava, her mouth stuffed full with the cock gag, Cherry could easily understand what Dante was saying. Her thoughts scattered though as he showed her the other item he'd bought. It was a crystal box. Inside were two round pearls. Big pearls. Huh? Her confusion must have shown on her face and Dante was quick to explain.

"Have you ever heard of Ben Wa balls?" She shook her head, lost and a little scared. "They're designed for a woman's pleasure. They go inside your pussy. Once they're in, I'll fuck you. Slow. Teasingly. I'll hold onto the silk string attached to the end. It makes the experience for you much more stimulating."

She was *so* not sure about this. Cherry shook her head adamantly and started to move away. Dante was faster and stronger, he held her still with one palm against her belly.

"Easy, baby. I won't hurt you." She was still reluctant and he added another plea to his growing argument. "Remember the nipple clamps?" She nodded, squinting up at him. "You were worried then too, but I showed you how good they could be when used properly."

He was right. She'd been terrified of those torture devices, but Dante had made them exciting and erotic.

He placed a protective hand over her pussy and murmured, "I would never hurt this pretty cunt. It's mine and I treasure it, little one."

Cherry bit the bullet and nodded. Besides it wasn't as if she were restrained. If she didn't like it, she could always stop him. Dante coaxed and pleaded, but he never forced.

"Mmm, such a sweet little thing. Your Master is very happy."

His whispered words floated over her flesh and Cherry found her desire rising higher. He took the shiny, white balls out of their crystal box and knelt between her thighs. After positioning her legs over his and spreading her thighs wide, he slid a finger inside her. She watched him bring it to his lips and suck her juices off.

"Damn, you taste like heaven. I could suck you dry when you're like this, baby." He snared her gaze in his and murmured, "My Cherry deserves a reward."

Then he carefully placed the first ball against her labia and slowly glided it inward. It wasn't painful, as she'd suspected. She wasn't sure what to think yet. As he started to slide the second ball inside her, she noticed he was watching her face, as if ready for any change in her expression. She reached a hand up and wrapped it around his forearm, needing the small contact. He pushed both balls deep, but still held the black silk string attached. When he wrapped his hands around her hips and wiggled, the balls moved. Her breath caught in her throat at the new sensation.

"Are you okay?"

Was she? Truth be told, she was better than okay. She tightened her vaginal walls and felt the balls move again. Holy hell. They seemed to touch nerve endings she never knew existed. Going with the moment, Cherry arched her back and clenched up again. She let loose a moan.

Dante swept a hand over her breasts and made little sounds, worshiping her body. "I'm going to put my cock inside you now, and I'll move the balls in and out that way the pleasure for you will increase."

She was beyond caring. Her hips twitched again and her body rioted out of control as the balls rolled around inside her womb. With one hand, Dante held her down as he inched his way into her tight passage. He forced her to remain still as he slowly moved in and out, pulling on the string so the balls moved in time with him. "Lift up," he ordered, "I want to suck your nipples."

Cherry pushed herself upward and wrapped her hands around his neck. Now she practically sat in Dante's lap. His cock and the Ben Wa balls still seated inside her hot core.

He leaned forward and sucked one peak, then the other. She smashed her tits against his face and moaned her approval when he bit and laved at each one with slow precision.

"Reach down and make yourself come. Do it now, baby. Once I pull the balls out I won't have the control to hold myself back."

Cherry rose up and down on his shaft, fucking him slowly, leisurely, then she slipped her right hand between their bodies and began playing with her clitoris, flicking and tugging the swollen button over and over. As her orgasm began to build, Dante pulled out all the way, then he slipped the balls free and laid them on the bed.

With both hands free now, he wrapped his fingers around her waist and shoved her onto his engorged length once more. "Yeah, baby, that's what I need. I love the way your body wraps around my dick. So tight. So mine."

Cherry's blood raced and her legs tightened around his hips, as she continued to rub and pump her clit. Once. Twice. Her pussy clenched. It was too much. It was all she needed, all she could take. Throbs turned to spasms as Cherry moaned and threw her head backward, coming apart and flying over some imaginary cliff. Dante was right there with her as he shouted her name and found his own release. Hot seed filled her as his cock pulsed and emptied into her limp body.

It was a few minutes before Dante loosened his hold on her enough to place a kiss to her forehead and cheeks. He unbuckled the cock gag and dropped it to the bed, and worshiped her with sweet words.

He grabbed her head in his hands and growled, "You're amazing. I've never met anyone who drives me so wild. There is no way I'm ever giving you up, Cherry. Never."

Cherry was breathless and too exhausted to bother removing herself from Dante's firm embrace. She wanted to protest his statement, but she just couldn't muster the strength.

"I just sat here, Dante. You're the one with all the naughty ideas."

Dante kissed her lips and slipped his tongue into her mouth. His hands sifted through her hair and held her still for his intimate invasion. Cherry tasted his warmth and masculinity. It was a flavor she wanted on her tongue every morning.

Lifting away, his hands still wrapped in her hair, Dante said, "What you do to me . . . it's not like anything else. I don't know what it is yet, but what we have is unique, little one. It's special."

Cherry blurted the first thing that came to mind. "You wanted the weekend and you admitted you wanted the office space. You like having sex with me, but is it really any more than that? Can you honestly say there's more than just lust, Dante?"

He was silent. Staring at her with eyes that saw way too much. She looked away, unable to face the awful truth. That he enjoyed her body, but may never want *her*.

"It's more than lust. And the office space doesn't mean shit to me. Not anymore."

His harsh tone had Cherry swinging her gaze back to his. The blue of his eyes had gone icy with anger. She didn't know what to say. She lifted off his lap and went to the bathroom. After she washed up and came back into the bedroom, she noticed Dante was now lying on one side of the bed beneath the covers. His gaze tracked her movements as she slipped into one of the T-shirts he'd let her wear.

"Why don't you wear the nightgown I bought you?" His rough voice had the affect of a caress.

"It's too pretty to sleep in."

When she came back to the bed and slid under the covers, he turned the light off. A long time passed, neither of them talking, neither of them touching. Her heart felt hollow and cold without Dante holding her. Had she grown used to being in his arms so quickly, his strength and heat surrounding her in a safe cocoon?

The bed shifted and an arm came around her middle as Dante effortlessly dragged her across the expanse separating them. He pulled her into his body, her back against his chest and slung one muscled thigh over her legs. "You're a stubborn woman, Cherry DuBois, and I have a feeling you're going to lead me on a merry chase."

Cherry's eyes burned with unshed tears, her voice shook when she answered. "Everyone gives up eventually and I always disappoint in the end. Eventually, I always disappoint."

Dante's lips brushed the back of her head. "Sleep. It will be okay, little one. I promise."

Cherry didn't bother to dispute him, even though she knew firsthand that to believe in a promise, was like buying into false advertising. The consumer always ended up the loser.

6

This time when Cherry pried her eyelids open, she was alone. She sniffed the air. Ah, coffee. She slipped out of bed and went to the bathroom for her morning constitution. When she finished she washed up and took a moment to stare at her reflection in the mirror. Her hair was all over the place. It'd take a week to get rid of the tangles. This was it, the final day of their weekend of frivolity. It was time to be all sophisticated. Thank him for a good time and leave. Of course, that'd be a lot easier to handle had she not fallen for the gorgeous hunk somewhere along the line. Why couldn't she do anything right? Have sex, leave. That was the way to do it. Not, have sex, fall in love, and hope he shared the same feelings. She was too much of a romantic. That annoying trait is why she'd ended up married to Brody. She wouldn't make that mistake twice.

Cherry left the bathroom and searched out Dante. She found him at the kitchen table, bent over a newspaper, a cup of coffee in his hand. She cleared her throat. He turned his head and stared, his gaze scorched a wicked path from head to toe.

She fidgeted under the onslaught. The T-shirt she'd put on covered all the important parts, but barely.

"Got more of that black stuff you're drinking?"

He stood and came toward her. "A whole pot actually."

"Wonderful," she managed around a suddenly very dry mouth.

His palms cupped her cheeks and he leaned in. Lips touched and Cherry melted. He lifted his head a few inches. "*You're* wonderful," he asserted.

"Thank you, for everything."

"Everything? That sounds like a good-bye to me."

She looked away. "Are you going to get me a cup of coffee or not?"

"Cherry, look at me."

She forced her gaze back to his. "What?"

"Are you saying good-bye?"

She pushed an unruly lock of hair out of her face and said, "The weekend is nearly over. Tomorrow we both go back to our normal lives."

"And you can't have a normal life with me in it somewhere?"

That stunned her. "You wanted the weekend," she reminded him.

"Yeah, and now I want more. I want you, all of you."

She hadn't been prepared. Damn it. She just hadn't been adequately prepared. "*Don't say things like that, Dante. Please.*"

"Why? Because it forces you to own up to your feelings?"

That stirred her anger. She stepped forward and pointed a finger at him. "You don't know a thing about it, so don't presume to know how I feel."

He grabbed her finger and tugged, she landed against his chest. His arm came around her middle, holding her in a tight embrace. "I know the way you quiver when I touch you. I know how hard you work at being a success. I know your ex was a fool to lose you. And I know that I'm not a fool. I care about you. In the last three months since you moved here, I've watched you, baby. You work hard and you take very little time for yourself. I think this weekend was an eye-opener for both of us. And if you'd quit being so damned stubborn you'd see that."

Tears filled her eyes, blurring her vision. "I'm just not cut out for this sort of thing. I don't know what to say."

"Say you'll think about me. I won't push you, but at least give me a chance. Isn't love worth that?"

"My marriage sucked. The divorce was even worse. My entire life I've been one big disappointment. I'm tired of never measuring up."

He swiped a tear away with his thumb and murmured, "You measure up just fine."

She buried her head in his chest and cried harder.

"It's true, baby. Just look at how you stole that office space away from me. You're one crafty lady."

That had her laughing and crying at the same time. She pulled back and stared into his blue depths so full of tender affection. "I told you that was just an accident. I didn't know you wanted the space."

His smile filled her with warmth. "My point exactly. Just imagine what you're capable of when you try!"

He was being so sweet, but she was still too afraid of being hurt all over again. "So you want a chance with me?"

"Yes," he growled.

For the first time since she'd confronted Brody with his indiscretions, hope bloomed. "And you're content with not getting the space?"

"I've already been scouring the city for a bigger building. Serene Comfort is safe from my evil clutches."

"I can't make any promises. It's just been four months since the divorce was final." she noticed his shoulders stiffen. "But I'm willing to . . . give this . . . give us a chance."

Dante's dangerous grin filled her belly with butterflies. "That's all any man can ask for, baby."

"Okay then. Since that's settled, how about that coffee?"

He backed up, taking her with him. "Later for that," he ground out as he sat in the chair he'd vacated earlier. He picked her up as if she weighed no more than a feather and plopped her onto his lap, then coasted his lips over hers.

Cherry got into the game quickly, drifting her hands down his nape to his shoulders, then his pecs and ripped abs. He was so hard and muscular all over it nearly melted her every time she touched him. He was a bronze, sleek god. Regal and arrogant and too good looking for his own good. Feeling wild and impetuous, Cherry slid her palm over the bulge in his faded jeans, cupping his rigid length. She was way too happy to note he was as turned on as she. As he continued to eat at her mouth, Cherry played. Soon, his free hand was sliding up her calf, beneath the T-shirt she wore. He caressed his way up her thigh and cupped her mound. Cherry lurched at the feel of him there.

By sheer will, she forced her mouth off his and moved her hand away from his crotch. "Dante?"

He growled. "Be still and let me have some fun."

His mouth moved to her neck and he began to nibble and lick. "Oh, God, that feels so good."

Dante drifted his lips to her ear and whispered, "I've only just begun."

His talented mouth pressed against hers and Cherry forgot about everything else. There was only Dante and Cherry. All her worries and fears fell away. She opened her mouth and danced her tongue over his lips. At his rumbling of approval, Dante opened up and took her in. Their tongues mated and

Cherry's hands clutched on to Dante's biceps, excited and eager. Her body was on fire. She wanted him. Inside of her. Around her. Drinking her in, filling her up. He was a craving in her blood, one she could no more deny than she could her next breath.

Cherry's fingers trailed over his muscular arms and she drew in a breath when they came around her waist and pulled her in tight. A moan escaped. His strength and virility made her feel safe and secure. Never once had she felt that with Brody.

"I want this pussy. It's mine. Will always be mine. Say you want me. Deep. Here and now."

"Yes. I can't wait a second more. Please, Dante!"

"Unzip me."

Cherry quickly obeyed. Her fingers fumbled over the button in his jeans. As she opened his fly and glimpsed his navy blue boxer-briefs, her desire increased tenfold. She licked her lips and gently drew him out. The head of his cock tempted her to taste.

As if reading her mind, Dante stroked her hair and murmured, "Later, we will take our time, baby. For now I need to feel your tight clutch."

It was the same for her. "Yes."

He grabbed a condom from his pocket and instructed, "Guide me in. Show me how much you like being my sweet little submissive. Take us both there, little one."

His erotic words had her heart pounding harder and her body quaking with need. "My pussy is dripping for you. It's been too long, Master."

He chuckled. "It's only been a few hours."

"Like I said, too long," she whispered. Then she took his heavy cock in her hand and slid him inside. Her inner muscles contracted around him, tight and hot. She shuddered, flung her head back and rode him.

"That's my girl. Fuck it good, Cherry. Show me how much you want me," Dante urged, then he clutched her hair in his fist and lowered over her, feasting on her breasts through the cotton of her shirt.

The heat of his mouth seeped through the thin material, stealing the breath from her lungs and driving her into another world. When his fingers found their way over her nub, expertly flicking it in just the way she liked, Cherry's body seized. Her muscles clenched as she rode him faster, harder, their bodies slapping together, melding until there was no separating them. Soon Cherry was there, spiraling out of control. Her hot pussy bathing him in wet satisfaction as he sank his mouth over hers and captured her shouts.

As the desire began to ebb, Dante clutched her hips and pushed into her once, twice, then he arched his neck and moaned her name as he climaxed.

Cherry's breath came in short pants, her body sweaty, the shirt clinging, Her legs shook from exertion as she collapsed against Dante's heaving chest. No way could she ever move again. Dante's arms came around her shoulders, holding her tight against him, as if unable to release her. She wiggled, gaining his attention. As his eyes came to hers, she saw raw hunger in their passionate depths. If he hadn't just spent himself inside her, she would have thought he was ready to go again.

"I think I'm going to be a bit sticky," Cherry teased, trying to inject some casualness into the intensity that now surrounded them. It didn't work.

"I could fuck you twenty-four hours a day, seven days a week and it still would not be enough."

She had no words for such a bald statement. Thankfully, he didn't seem to expect any, merely slipped out of her and stood her on her feet. "Come, let's shower."

Several minutes later, Cherry was once again sporting one of

Dante's T-shirts and watching him slip back into his jeans. Watching Dante dress was a fascinating show in masculine grace.

When he caught her staring, her face heated and she looked away. He strode across the room and slid both his palms up her thighs, then cupped her mound possessively. "You never cease to amaze me, Cherry. So volatile and shy at the same time. So much of you still mystifies me. It's a pleasure learning your secrets, baby." He leaned in and kissed her lightly on the forehead, then wrapped his strong hands around her middle. "Mmm, now you can have your coffee."

"I don't think I need it anymore."

"Then I'll cook you breakfast. Trust me, you're going to need your strength."

She shuddered.

"He hasn't lost interest, Cherry."

"How do you know? It's been a week and I've not heard a peep from him."

Wade looked away. "It's been five days, not exactly an eternity, and I just know that's all."

Cherry wasn't sure what was going on, but it was clear Wade knew something. She hadn't heard a word from Dante after he'd dropped her off Sunday night. All she'd gotten were flowers. Two dozen red roses. Who cared about roses? She wanted Dante!

"Wade?"

"Huh?" he mumbled as he stared at a spot on the carpet.

She crossed her arms over her chest. "What do you know that I don't? And don't you dare lie to me."

Wade shot out of the chair he'd been lounging in across from her desk and ran his fingers through his hair. "I was sworn to secrecy, damn it."

She glanced at the clock on the wall. Good, she had fifteen minutes before her next appointment showed up. Plenty of time to pummel an answer out of Wade. "I'm feeling very violent right now, Wade. Start talking."

Wade licked his lips and said, "Fine, but just remember, it's not my fault."

"What's not your fault?"

"Dante has spent the last week with his—"

"Mom."

Cherry and Wade both turned at the low baritone. Dante stood in the door to Serene Comfort, another large bouquet of flowers in his hand, this time pink tulips, and a scowl on his face. The tight, faded jeans and black T-shirt devastated her senses. "I thought you weren't going to say anything?"

Wade turned red. "Hell, she's tenacious; you should know that by now."

Dante grinned. "Yeah, I love that about her."

Cherry stood and came around the desk, not about to be swayed by flowers, even if the pink bouquet were her favorite. "Flowers won't make up for an entire week of no phone calls."

He frowned. "I called. Twice actually."

Her eyes narrowed. "There weren't any messages."

He stepped closer. "I left two."

"Well, I never received them," she stepped back and bumped into her desk. Crap.

Dante kept coming, when he was within inches of her, he bit out, "Then that means I called someone else and told them I missed them."

She ignored that and addressed the other issue. "What's all this about your mom?"

"She lives in Pittsburgh, it's almost a four hour drive from here, but I wanted to tell her in person that I'd met the woman I wanted to marry."

She wanted to believe him, she yearned to believe him, but fear of being hurt again kept her from leaping into his arms. Out of the corner of her eye, she noticed Wade slip out the front door. She'd deal with him later. "You drove to Pittsburgh?"

"Yes. I would've been back sooner, but Mom insisted on coming back with me. She wants to meet you, which meant making arrangements for someone to watch her house and her cats while she's here. Since Dad's heart attack, she's ended up with four cats. Probably to compensate for not having Dad around. At any rate, what should have been a two-day trip turned into almost a week." He paused, then brushed his fingers over her cheek. "I'm sorry, baby; I thought you got my messages."

"I was afraid you didn't want me. I thought..." she stopped, unable to form the words.

Dante pulled her into his strong arms and held her tight. "I should have told you in person where I was going, but I wanted to surprise you."

"Surprise me?"

Dante stepped back. When he reached into the front pocket of his jeans, brought out a small blue velvet box and lowered down on one knee her mouth fell open. "Cherry DuBois, would you do me the honor of becoming my wife?"

The elegant beauty of the princess-cut diamond stole her breath. "Oh, Dante," she murmured, as the tears she'd been holding back spilled over.

"Before you answer, I want you to know that I'm prepared to wait. I'm not trying to rush you, little one. I guess I just wanted to prove to you that I'm not going anywhere."

"We only just met," she hedged.

"I know, but it doesn't matter. Not to me. I knew. Before I asked you to dinner, I knew you were the one. I've never wanted a woman the way I want you and I've sure as hell never proposed to one before. This is the real deal for me."

How did a girl fight a statement like that? "I love you!" Cherry shouted, then flung herself into Dante's strong, sturdy arms.

Epilogue

The last eight months had been a whirlwind of activity for Cherry. Dante had found a new building for his expanding financial consulting firm. He'd snapped it up and it wasn't long after that he'd talked her into moving in with him. She'd caved right after he'd brought out the Ben Wa balls. They'd set a date for the wedding, too, though Dante wasn't thrilled that she'd insisted on waiting a year. He'd caved right after she'd squirted the cherry flavored oil onto his chest.

Serene Comfort kept her in the black and she'd even hired a receptionist. Gracie was working out great, even though she and Wade mixed as well as oil and water. Cherry secretly hoped the two would eventually realize they were attracted to each other and do something about it already.

"You're an amazing massage therapist."

She felt triumphant at Dante's praise. Finally, someone who understood her need to help people feel good. Working class people who deserved to pamper themselves every once in a while. She placed her palm against his chest and murmured, "Thank you, Dante."

"But," he interjected.

"I knew it was too good to be true," she grumbled.

"I don't like you massaging other men. Clinical or not. You're going to be my wife soon."

She understood, especially after he'd taunted her with the image of him touching another woman.

Dante had come a few minutes early for his appointment and inadvertently walked in on her and a male client. For the last hour, he'd been trying to get her to see his side. When he'd asked how she'd feel if he became an MT and massaged beautiful women all day, it'd hit a nerve.

"I do see what you mean, Dante. But I can't very well be gender specific."

"I know," he conceded softly. "It's my problem and I'll deal with it, little one."

"How come Wade doesn't bother you. You've never been jealous of him, not once."

"Wade is like a brother to you. It's so clear the way he feels toward you."

"That makes him safe?"

"Yep."

"I just don't understand men."

His gaze pierced her clear to her soul. "You only need to understand me. Other men don't matter."

She smacked him on the arm. "You're ridiculous."

"But you love me anyway."

"Don't push it."

He wrapped his hand around her nape and pulled her down for a kiss that curled her toes, then whispered, "I'll always push you to your limits, Cherry, and I'll make sure you enjoy every second of it too."

She wanted to say something snappy, but her mind just wasn't able to keep up with his. He was doing it again. Making her weak and wet. It drove her to her knees each time. When he lifted to a seated position and dropped the sheet to the floor, her mouth watered. He hadn't gotten aroused during the massage, but now he was huge and ready to party. Her eyes darted to his face and the grin said it all.

"How much time do you have until your next client?"

She looked at her watch and wanted to cry. "None." They both heard the front door chime, signaling her next appointment. "He's here and you need to get dressed and leave."

"*He?*"

She sighed. "Dante, don't start."

He stared at her another second, then nodded and left the table to dress. She watched, unable to pull her gaze away from his tight ass and mouth-watering biceps. He was such a picture of perfection. When he turned and caught her staring, his smile wasn't at all pleasant. In fact, it was a little scary.

He closed the distance between them and took her into his arms. "I want to fuck you so bad when you look at me like that, baby."

In an instant, she went breathless and dripping with arousal. "How am I looking at you?"

"Like you want to bend over and offer yourself to your Master. It drives me through the damn roof."

His darkly whispered words pushed her into another realm. She could easily drop everything and grant him his wish. If it weren't for her client, she would have caved. She shoved herself out of his arms. "Go. I'll see you at home later."

Dante stood there another second, then he kissed her. It was gentle and swift and so sweet she felt it to her toes. He drifted his lips away, opened the door to the massage room and peeked out. Apparently satisfied with the looks of her next client, Dante turned to her. "I cannot guarantee that I'll be civilized if I see you massaging a man," he warned. "So, next time I want to take you to lunch, I'll call first. Fair enough?"

He was trying. Meeting her halfway. Damn, he really was

the perfect fiancé. Helpless to her own emotions, Cherry went to him, raised up on her tiptoes and kissed his cheek. "Fair enough. I love you, Dante."

He smacked her ass. "You can thank me properly tonight, baby. I bought more of that cherry flavored oil."

"You really like that stuff, huh?"

He reached out and traced a path over her lips, then murmured, "I admit, I've got a real thing for cherries these days."

Her heart leaped. "Oh."

Dante leaned in and kissed her, then ordered, "Be a good girl today or I'll be forced to discipline you."

After issuing that outrageous warning, he winked and left. She forced her blood to stop rushing through her veins and went out to the front, ready to get on with her workday. The rest of the afternoon crept by. She could only think of Dante and what he might have planned for them. He was quite the inventive sort. It was anyone's guess what he had in mind for the night to come.

Damn, she was one lucky lady.

If you enjoyed *Some Like It Rough*,
turn the page for a special excerpt
from Anne Rainey's sizzling

BODY RUSH

An Aphrodisia trade paperback
coming in April 2013

Prologue

The loud music hit her the instant she stepped through the doors. Lydia loved it. Going to Charlie's, her favorite hangout, after work on Friday night always helped her forget about the lawyers she worked for. There were three of them and they were all exasperating. Working at a law firm sucked in ways that most people couldn't grasp. Her only escape from the stress came when she met up with her two best friends, Roni and Jeanette. They'd known each other since grade school. While everyone else had moved on and forgotten about their school pals, the three of them had stayed in touch. Sometimes she thought they were closer now than ever. Maturity maybe. Who knew the reason, all Lydia knew for sure was that she'd be lost without them.

As she moved through the crowded room, Lydia felt someone's hand on her ass. She turned and glared at the man sitting with a group of men, all grinning like idiots. The hateful look she tossed his way must have worked because he pulled his hand back and started to scope out his next victim. Lydia spotted her friends sitting at a high round table at the back of the bar. Roni waved her over. Lydia smiled and headed toward her.

As she reached them she noticed her favorite drink, a fuzzy navel, ready and waiting. Roni moved to another chair, giving her the one on the end. "Why is it men think it's cute to grab a woman's ass? Do they really think it's going to get them laid?" Lydia shouted in an attempt to be heard over the noise. She slid onto the chair and grabbed her drink, wondering if she'd look like an alcoholic if she downed half the glass in one gulp.

"I'll never understand why men do half the things they do," Roni tossed back with an angry edge to her voice. "Trying to figure them out is a waste of time."

Jeanette leaned close and said, "There is one particular guy I wouldn't mind grabbing my ass. The only problem is I don't think he even knows I exist."

Lydia and Roni both moved closer, their attention rapt. Lydia spoke up first. "Are you still hot for that motorcycle dude coming into your café?"

Jeanette's gaze filled with unbridled lust. "If you saw him, you'd be drooling too. I'm telling you, he's the yummiest thing I've seen yet."

"You've lusted after this guy for what, a year?" Roni asked.

Jeanette laughed. "It feels that way sometimes, but it's only been about six months."

Lydia took a sip of her drink. Already she could feel herself relaxing, as if the last several days were a distant blur. She looked across the table at Roni and shook her head. She still couldn't picture her sharp-tongued friend as a psychologist. On a good day she was hard to get along with. On the other hand, Jeanette's job seemed to fit her to a T. Owning a quant little coffee shop seemed the perfect choice for her introverted friend.

"If you don't ask him out, someone else will," Lydia taunted, hoping to push her friend into making a move.

Jeanette bit her lip. "I'm so damn shy around him. He comes in with this black leather jacket and tight, faded jeans and I just want to jump him. All that dark hair and those dark eyes." She sighed. "Every time I see him I think, this is it. I'm going to ask him out. Or at least find out if he has a damned girlfriend. But I just get all tongue-tied. Like I'm in high school again." She clenched her fist around the longneck bottle of light beer she'd ordered. "It's frustrating as hell."

Roni piped up with her usual bit of sensitive logic. "He rides a motorcycle, he's gorgeous as hell and he comes to your shop every morning. Get a clue, girl; he wants to fuck you!"

Jeanette rolled her eyes. "What makes you think he wants me at all? He comes for the coffee, not the owner."

"Bullshit. He comes because you're hot and he wants to lay you across the counter. He could get coffee anywhere. Hell, he probably doesn't even live near your shop."

Lydia could see her friend's spirits perking up. "You really think so?" Jeanette asked.

Roni laughed and swallowed the last of her sex on the beach before waving the waitress over and ordering another. After the waitress had hurried off to fill their order, Roni said, "He's just watching you squirm a little. Enjoying the way you blush and stammer. It's a game. He's wondering how long you can hold out."

Jeanette started to peel the label off the beer. "I've never asked a guy out before. Usually they ask me. I'm not shy exactly, but I am a little old fashioned, I guess."

Lydia spoke up this time. "I think Roni's right. It's a new world these days. Men like it when a woman is sure of herself. You should definitely ask him out."

Jeanette's eyes grew round. "This coming from the shyest one of all?"

Lydia shrugged. "I've been doing some thinking. It's time we livened up our lives a little, don't you think?"

Roni narrowed her gaze, as if suspicious all of a sudden. "In what way?"

"I don't know," Lydia admitted as she looked down at her

half-empty drink. "It's just that we come here every Friday and nothing is ever any different. We work all week, date boring men and then come here to bitch about it. I'm getting sick of it. I'm ready for a change."

"*You* might date boring men, but that doesn't mean we all do." Lydia knew that tone. Roni always got her back up when someone pointed out that she wasn't perfect. "Oh, really? What about that guy you went out with last weekend? You said he took you to the opera and you wanted to sleep through the whole thing it was so boring."

Roni slumped. "Men always think they're going to impress me by bringing me to some expensive restaurant or some fancy theater. Or they go the opposite route and attempt to please me by playing on my kinkier side. Just once I'd like to go out with a real man. Someone who isn't trying to impress."

"See? That's exactly what I mean. We all have these secret desires, but we don't act on them." Lydia looked at Jeanette, who'd remained silent throughout the exchange. "Just once wouldn't you like to toss caution to the wind and do something . . . wicked?"

Jeanette sat back in her chair and crossed her arms over her chest. "Yes, I would. I can't tell you how many times I've wanted to strip naked and just offer myself to Mr. Motorcycle Man. But how can I possibly do that when I don't know a thing about him? These days it pays to err on the side of caution."

Lydia nodded. "I agree we should be cautious, but that doesn't mean we can't, just this once, do something completely out of character." When Roni and Jeanette both started talking at once, Lydia held up her hand. "Hear me out. If you don't like my idea, then we'll forget I ever mentioned it. Agreed?" Both women looked at each other before giving her the floor. "Roni is ready to get down and dirty with an honest, blue-collar kind of guy. Jeanette, you're so hot for Motorcycle Man I can practically see steam coming off you. I have my own little fantasy in mind too. I say we make a bet to see who can make their fantasy come true first."

Roni snorted. "Are you serious? We're going to bet to see who can get laid faster?"

"Not just laid, dork. The bet is to see who can make their fantasy become reality."

Jeanette gasped. "I cannot believe you're suggesting this. I can see Roni suggesting something like this, she's half crazy, but you? I've never even seen you loosen the top button of your blouse, yet you're sitting there proposing we make our wildest fantasies come to life?"

Lydia's face heated. Jeanette was right. It was insane to think she could actually make her own fantasy a reality. If her friends had half a clue what she wanted to do, they'd commit her to a sanitarium. She was about to call the whole thing off when Roni spoke up

"What's the winner get?"

Jeanette's gaze swung to Roni. Lydia couldn't speak.

"You're actually considering this ludicrous bet?" Jeanette squeaked.

Roni grinned. "Why the hell not? It sounds like fun. And Lydia's right, our lives are boring as shit. While I admit I do have some pretty wild sex, there's still something missing. I want more, damn it."

Lydia wished she could be more like Roni. She took life by the horns. All Lydia could ever control was her cat, Socrates. "I haven't thought that far. What *should* the winner get? While we're at it, what does the loser have to do?"

Jeanette held up her hand. "Wait, I'm already confused. How does one lose?"

"By not making your fantasy real," Roni answered.

"So in order to win, I need to ask Mr. Motorcycle Man out?"

"Not just ask him out, but you have to do the very thing you've been dreaming of," Lydia said, already wondering what she'd gotten herself into.

"I've had a lot of dreams about that man."

"Make one of them happen and you're safe from losing," Roni said as she finished off her second sex on the beach.

Lydia took a deep breath and went for broke. "So, back to the question. What does the winner get and what does the loser have to do?"

"The winner gets to have her fantasy come to life, obviously," Roni chimed in. "The loser . . . buys the rest a round of drinks?"

"No, that's not incentive enough," Jeanette said, as if she were beginning to warm up to the idea. "The loser has to . . . strip naked and walk down main street."

Lydia shook her head. "Illegal. It can't be against the law."

"Then the loser has to clean my car," Roni tossed out.

Lydia and Jeanette both shuddered. "That's cruel and unusual punishment, Roni," Lydia said. "Damn."

Roni rubbed her hands together. "But it's legal and it's incentive enough to get you two busy."

"What makes you so sure you're going to win?" Jeanette shot right back, her back stiffening in pride.

Roni winked. "Because I never lose, honey."

Lydia sucked down the last of her fuzzy navel, then ordered another. "Okay, now for the next part of this wager. We each have to reveal our fantasy."

Jeanette shrugged. "Mine's already been revealed. I want to have wild and crazy sex with Mr. Motorcycle Man."

Roni frowned. "I want a man who wants me for me. A man who isn't out to impress."

Both women looked at Lydia. "I want to have sex with a stranger, no strings, no names, just sex." *Or maybe with two,* she thought, but she wasn't ready to admit that.

Jeanette's jaw dropped and Roni's eyes filled with awe. "Damn, I've never admired you more than I do right now," Roni mused.

Jeanette laughed and soon they were all cracking up. Deep down Lydia shook like a teenager on prom night. *What the hell did I just get myself into?*